PRAISE FOR

BRIT PARTY ANTHOLOGY

Outstanding Read ~ What do you have when you combine the talents of Lacey Thorn, Brynn Paulin, Ashley Ladd, Dakota Rebel, Desiree Holt and Lisabet Sarai? You have the incredibly sexy anthology called **Brit Party**… This is the hottest anthology I have ever read!... From the first story to the last, **Brit Party** is sure to turn you on! ~ *Simply Romance Reviews*

Reviewer Top Pick ~ This Brit Party Anthology is a celebration I couldn't wait to get started on and hated even more to let go. These tantalizing tales were entertaining and not afraid to explore our fantasies of alternate lifestyles with the ultimate realization of lasting love. If you're looking for an enticing and exhilarating read to keep on your bookshelf, this is the one.~ *Night Owl Romance*

Brit Party is a fabulously scorching collection of ménage that is certain to bring about the need to douse some flames. I absolutely adored this multiple partnered tale, and I am hard pressed to pick one story that was better than the others. ~ *NovelTalk*

BRIT PARTY ANTHOLOGY

MAGGIE'S MÉNAGE
LACEY THORN

BOY TOYS
BRYNN PAULIN

BEST MATES
ASHLEY LADD

THE WAGER
DAKOTA REBEL

FOUR PLAY
DESIREE HOLT

MONSOON FEVER
LISABET SARAI

BRIT PARTY ANTHOLOGY
ISBN # 978-1-906590-42-0
Maggie's Ménage ©Copyright Lacey Thorn 2008
Boy Toys ©Copyright Brynn Paulin 2008
Best Mates ©Copyright Ashley Ladd 2008
The Wager ©Copyright Dakota Rebel 2008
Four Play ©Copyright Desiree Holt 2008
Monsoon Fever ©Copyright Lisabet Sarai 2008
Cover Art by Anne Cain ©Copyright 2008
Interior text design by Claire Siemaszkiewicz
Total-E-Bound Publishing

Published in 2008 by Total-E-Bound Publishing 1 Faldingworth Road, Spridlington, Market Rasen, Lincolnshire, LN8 2DE, UK.

MAGGIE'S MENAGE

Lacey Thorn

Dedication

To family and friends both new and old for never
allowing me to stop believing in myself.
I am because of you! Thank you.

Chapter One

"You want me to play the whore for you? For the good of the company?"

"Watch your mouth Margaret Rose. Twenty five is not too old for a spanking young lady." She turned to look her father in the eye, saw the rising colour on his face and couldn't resist.

"Oh. You think that will make the men you have waiting hot for me. Show them a little kink to get them revved up?"

"Damn it Margaret. That is enough." That vein was really throbbing in his head now. And the colour was slowly going from red to purple.

"Does the business mean that much to you, Daddy? More than me?" She already knew the answer but some inner demon forced the question out of her mouth.

"I've spent my whole life building this company and I'll be damned if it dies out after I'm gone. The name Houston will count for something long after I'm gone."

That demon was still there whispering in her ear. "I could run it. I know the ins and outs of the business. I thought you were grooming me for just that."

He laughed. Her father threw his head back and laughed and that last bit of the needy girl searching for the crumbs of her father's love disappeared. In her place was a woman he would regret creating.

"Like I would ever leave my baby to a woman. Your mother proved to be one failure after another. Only one child and even that was second rate. The damn woman couldn't even stay healthy. It was a blessing when she died."

Yeah, it probably was. For her mother. But for the four year old girl left behind it had been hell. She had always known that her father only let her work for him because he didn't know what else to do with her. But that tiny spot had remained, unwilling to give up hope that she was wrong.

There was a knock at the door and her father Dom Alexander Houston turned from her. Dismissing her without a second thought. And the anger began to grow inside her.

"The gentlemen that you've been expecting are here Mr. Houston." Her father's personal assistant said from the doorway. The woman was young, blonde and built. And most certainly sleeping with the boss. Maggie felt sorry for her. She wouldn't last any longer than the rest and when her father was done that was it. The poor girl didn't have a chance.

"Send them in."

Maggie stayed her ground refusing to leave without him coming right out and telling her to. If he forgot she was still here long enough then she would stay. Appearances meant everything to him and he would do nothing to seem more than a doting father.

Two men stepped into the room. Both were tall with dark hair. One was maybe six feet even with broad shoulders and a stocky build. His body rippled with muscles beneath the suit that was obviously tailored just for him. His hair was clean cut, almost military short. What there was of it was a dark brown, almost a mocha shade. His eyes when he glanced her way were a dark chocolate brown with what looked like flecks of gold in them but she would have to get a closer look to be sure.

The other one was taller, maybe six-foot-two or so with a much slimmer build. His clothes were just as tapered but revealed longer, leaner muscles. His hair was longer touching the top of his collar in back and dark as night. His eyes were a startling shade of blue that made one think of a perfect sky.

Testosterone oozed from them and filled the room. A shiver went down Maggie's spine and she wondered which one her father wanted her to marry. She had to think that they must want it as much as the old man did or they wouldn't be here. Neither seemed like the type that would be easily manipulated. No these were definitely alpha males. What she was planning for them might be more fun than she anticipated. But best of all it would destroy her father's plans to marry her off to the man of his choice. She couldn't contain the grin of triumph that tugged at her lips. Let the fun begin.

Alex looked at Patrick and read his mind as if it was his own. It would take a dead man not to notice the woman standing behind Dom Houston and they were both very much alive. She was a cool drink of water in a calf length skirt that hugged her body from her lush hips down. Her shirt was a soft shade of pink that buttoned all the way up to her throat but was fitted to showcase the tantalising mounds of her breasts. Her hair was a multitude of different shades of blonde, at least from the bit that was showing where she had it piled on top of her head. The face was classic, one that would only grow better with age. Her eyes a delicate shade of hazel, more green than blue at the moment.

By the expression on Patrick's face, they were both thinking the same thing. Getting her naked and fucking her. One at a time, together. It wouldn't matter as long as she was naked and willing. Damn, Alex wondered who she was.

Mr. Houston followed their gazes and seemed startled that the woman was in the room.

"Margaret. You'll excuse us now," was all he said before turning back to them and dismissing the woman, Margaret once again. He missed the emotion that flashed through her eyes but Alex and Patrick saw it. She quickly contained it and giving a nod left the room pulling the door shut behind her. And releasing the two of them to get down to the business they had come here for.

"Those weren't the men I was expecting you little idiot!" Dom thundered at the twit who was good for nothing unless she was on her knees. "Next time you send someone into my office you better make damn sure of who they are and what their business is first! You could have just cost me a lot with your stupidity."

He watched as tears filled her eyes saw them tremble on her lashes for a moment before slipping down her cheeks. "I'm so sorry. So sorry. I promise that it won't happen again." Her eyes were pleading with him and her chest was starting to rise and fall with her effort to control her anxiety.

His eyes slipped to those beautiful breasts that he knew so well. "Lock the door." He never moved from his position behind the desk as he delivered his order. He knew without a doubt that she knew what was coming, and that she would do whatever he told her to. Money and power could buy a lot of obedience.

The lock clicked and she slowly turned back to him, her hands already on the hem of her shirt. He nodded and watched as she pulled it over her head revealing the low cut white lace bra underneath that he knew would match her panties exactly. He should know since he bought them. She reached back and released the catch letting the bra slide down her shoulders to land on top of the shirt at her feet. Her breasts were high and firm, the nipples a rosy pink that flushed darker as the cooler air hit them and caused them to tighten further. They would blush red before he was done with them.

She moved her hands to the waist of her skirt until he stopped her. "Leave it. You won't be receiving pleasure now. Only good girls get pleasured. Do you want to be a good girl?"

She nodded, her eyes still luminescent with tears.

"Then come over here and show me how sorry you are." He pushed his chair back from the desk spreading his knees and making room for her to kneel before him. He stopped her when she stood between his thighs and leaning forwards took a nipple into his mouth sucking fiercely and biting the tip several times before moving across to the other one. He loved breasts, always had. Nipples were made to be sucked hard, to be nipped and even bitten when the mood struck just right. And hers were perfection, the reason why he still had her around. Well that and the fact that she could suck a cock like no other woman he had ever had. And that was saying something since he had been with more than his fair share of women.

She moaned softly though he knew she wanted to cry out several times from what he was doing. But she was good, the best whore he had ever had and she only rested her hands lightly on his shoulders and moaned just the way he liked.

When he finally released her, her nipples were flushed bright red and swollen from his mouth. They were beautiful.

He reached his hands out and pinched them both between his fingers using them to tug her down to her knees. She reached for his pants, releasing his cock and pulling it out to bob in front of her mouth while he continued to tug and pinch at her over sensitised nipples. Yes, she was a very good whore. He groaned as she took him immediately to the back of her throat and began to milk him, her tongue reaching out to lave at his balls while she swallowed along his shaft. Almost good enough to make him forget about the two private investigators she had allowed into his office.

Maggie had followed the two men back to a hotel on the outskirts of the city. It wasn't where she had expected them to stay but still at least it seemed clean. It was one of those places where the doors to the rooms opened on the outside of the building with one floor of rooms stacked on top of the other. At least the two men were in the same room at the moment. That would make what she had in mind easier. She just had to work up her courage a bit.

She'd never been a seductress before. She'd had sex, plenty of sex. But even the most risqué acts came off feeling like vanilla sex. Perhaps it was because most of her partners were boring, mundane, vanilla men outside of the bedroom, and sometimes inside as well. But that was all going to end as soon as she stepped from the car and put her plan into action. Her father wanted her to marry one of the two men in the room she kept staring at. Expected her to do whatever it took to ensure that happened. Instead she was going to ensure that they thought of her as a wild promiscuous woman, definitely not the type a man would want to marry.

She took another deep breath and opened the car door, easing her frame out and shutting the door behind her. She stood there for a moment smoothing her hands down the grey pencil skirt she wore before reaching up to make sure her hair was still up. She tilted her chin up reminding herself just what was at stake. Everything.

Resolve filled her, giving her the courage to walk up to the door the two men had entered more than an hour before. An hour she had spent sitting in the car watching. It was now or never. Maggie took a deep breath and raised her hand to knock, but she didn't need to. The door opened and the taller, leaner of the two men stood before her in nothing but a pair of jeans which rode low on his hips. His chest was covered with a smattering of dark hair that encircled each nipple and trailed down over his abdomen disappearing into his waistband. He was sexy enough to have her mouth and more intimate places filling with fluid. But when he parted his lips and spoke in a husky British accent she could actually feel herself melting like butter.

"We were wondering how long it would take you to head this way love." His voice slipped down her spine leaving a fiery warmth coursing through her. She was more than ready for her plan, more than ready to do anything he asked of her.

"You knew I was here?" It was a whisper, all she could manage with her heart galloping in her chest.

"We've been watching you since you arrived." It was the other who spoke this time and he had the sweet southern tones of a Texas man. You could hear the "aw, shucks" in his voice and she knew beyond a shadow of a doubt that these two must work well together. What one couldn't get the other would definitely be able to. He was still dressed in the suit from earlier and looked just as heavenly now. Though he was a few inches shorter than the other man he was more muscular and filled the suit out like it was custom made for him. If he moved in the same circles as her father then it probably was.

Thinking about her father was enough of a jolt to snap her out of the lust induced haze and remember that she was there for a reason. A reason that would take care of her itch just fine. Maggie casually moved around the man in front of her entering the motel room as if they had invited her in. She focused on the more dressed of the two and said the first thing that popped into her mind, a habit that she really needed to work on.

"So you like to watch, do you?"

Husky laughter filled the room as both men found her comment amusing. Her own smile trembled on her lips when she heard the door snap shut behind her and the click of the lock being turned.

"Watching is fine," Mr. Brit said as he moved up close behind her. "But participating is even better." His hands cupped over her shoulders and as he moved closer into her, there was no mistaking the heavy length of his erection where it touched along her spine.

"Both of you?" It was a question, an invitation, a wish, uttered from her lips as she did all she could to keep from rubbing wantonly back against him.

"Both of us," South Texas said. He stepped in front of her and when all she did was blink at him he reached out and began to slowly unbutton the top buttons on her shirt. "You want both of us don't you? Isn't that why you came?"

"Yes," she murmured as he changed the angle of his head to place kisses along each inch of exposed flesh. "Oh, God, yes."

Husky male chuckles sounded again and they were like foreplay along her skin. Her cheeks grew flushed, her breasts tingled, the nipples puckering more, and her sex grew damp, her channel pulsing with a need to be filled. She had dreamed of this, two men at the same time. Two men focusing on her pleasure, her needs and desires.

"Oh, yes," she murmured again and allowed her body to relax into the man behind her, rubbing herself against his erection.

It was his turn to groan and his hands flexed once on her shoulders before moving down to cradle her hips and pull her even closer. He rubbed blatantly against her seeming to enjoy the sensation as much as she did.

"Do you want that Margaret? Do you want both of us at the same time?" Her shirt was tugged from her waist band and wide open to the lusty gazes of both men. Her full breasts were barely contained by the sheer lace of her bra, her nipples a proud display behind the white material. His voice was a warm breath of air on her skin and his knuckle was sheer fire as it brushed across her nipple.

"Just two things," she panted roughly, "then I'm all yours."

"What?" The British accent was thicker, his hands hard where they gripped her hips.

"Tell me your names." It was a whisper but in her mind it was a demand.

"Alex," Mr Brit spoke into her ear following it with a slow flick of his tongue along the lobe before nipping it softly with his teeth.

"Patrick," South Texas said before closing his lips around one turgid nipple and sucking gently on it.

The cry left her mouth at the sheer pleasure of their touches, the torture as it wasn't enough.

"And two?" Alex whispered.

"Maggie," she managed. "Call me Maggie."

Chapter Two

Alex knew he should be focusing on the investigation. The woman could be just the lead that he and Patrick had been looking for. And they both had a lot to prove. Patrick to his older brother Shawn O'Grady, who had left Pat in charge of the P. I. firm while he went off on some secret excursion with his best friend and business partner Tommy. Alex had something to prove to himself, mainly that he was still capable of doing the job he loved even if it was no longer for the MI6 unit that had once been like family to him. Yeah, they both had a lot to prove. Unfortunately neither of them seemed to be thinking with the right head at the moment.

He grabbed the material of her pink shirt at the shoulders and slid it slowly down her arms. Patrick was still rubbing his knuckle over her nipple but his other hand was already making its way down to the side closure on her calf length skirt. She helped him remove the shirt arching back into his chest and thrusting her breasts forwards with a rough sigh. Seconds later her skirt pooled around her feet and Alex groaned. She was wearing a garter belt under that skirt, an honest to God garter belt with real silk stockings attached to it. And they matched her white lace bra to perfection. He didn't know what part of her he wanted to touch first. But Patrick had no such hesitation.

Patrick buried his nose in the Promised Land and inhaled like it was bliss. Alex was pretty sure that it probably was. He slid his hands from her hips, up along her stomach and cupped those tempting breasts in his palms giving them both a full squeeze. Her cry filled the air around them leaving no doubts of her pleasure in their actions. When her head hit his shoulder and the smooth column of her neck was exposed to him, Alex couldn't resist. He bent down and buried his face there. He licked and sucked his way up to her earlobe and then worked his way back down along the tendon to the base of her neck. She tasted like the sweetest ambrosia. When he finally made the journey back up to her ear he gave it a sharp tug with his teeth before whispering to her.

"I want to fuck you. Can you feel how hard you make my dick?" Alex ground his erection against her only then realising how sheer the lace was on her ass. God, she was exquisite. His groan matched hers as he pushed forwards again, bending his knees so that his cock hit right between the cheeks of her lush ass. "I want to fuck your pussy, your ass, and that sweet little mouth of yours." Her gasp let him know that she wanted it just as much.

There was a ripping sound and Alex knew that Patrick had torn the gusset out of her panties. He glanced down the length of her body and met Patrick's eyes. Patrick's eyes were almost black with lust and Alex envied him his current position. Patrick lifted Maggie's right leg up and Alex hooked his elbow underneath it pulling it high and wide allowing Patrick the perfect access to the pussy they both wanted. Damn, Patrick looked like he was in heaven.

Damn, Patrick thought. *I've died and gone to heaven.* The seductress in front of him was a goddess built for sex. Her legs were long and lean, her breasts high and firm. And her pussy. It smelled sweet, looked divine and he couldn't wait to taste it on his tongue, suck it and if he lasted long enough fuck it. It had been too damn long since he had been with a woman. And he never shared but there was something erotic about seeing her braced back against Alex. Something carnal in knowing that Alex was going to take her the same as him, that maybe they would both enjoy her at the same time.

Her blonde hair looked good along side of Alex's black hue. Her skin a blanket of white next to Alex's tan. Patrick loved the way her thighs trembled, the way her sex puffed up and blushed from pink to a tantalising shade of soft red. Moisture was already coating her and without thought he leaned forwards and ran his tongue along her slit. Her cry covered his moan but just barely. If Alex wasn't holding her leg up she probably would have fallen the way that she was trembling. But none of that mattered as her taste coated his tongue, exploding on his taste buds and sending him delving for more.

He used one hand to separate the folds of her lips wider so that he could run his tongue all around, up one side and down the other glancing over the spots of interest in favour of collecting more of her unique nectar. On the second time around he stopped for barely a moment to play his tongue over and around her clit watching it swell tighter and seem to grow a little bigger at his touch. On the third pass he folded his tongue up seeking to make it smaller, firmer so that he could fuck her with it. And with the first two strokes of it inside her channel, she broke. Her lips puffed bigger, her clit seeming to pulse, and fluid flowed over his tongue and down his chin until he flattened his tongue out and tried to use it to lap up as much of her as he could. She was moving against him now pressing her sex harder to his face, her staccato cries filling the small room. He groaned and looked up, his eyes locking with Alex's.

Alex had his hands filled with her breasts, the cups tugged down to reveal her turgid nipples and his fingers were busily working them, pinching and tugging. His face was buried in her neck which was red from the combination of bites, sucks, and whisker burn. His eyes were so dark a blue they were almost black and his voice was guttural when he spoke.

"We need to move to the bed unless you're ready to fuck on the floor."

Patrick nodded and stood but before he could do more than reach for Maggie, Alex had her up in his arms and was already heading to one of the queen size beds in the room. He set her on her feet beside the bed and with quick work removed both her bra and the frayed remains of her panties. When her hands reached for the belt of one of her garters he shooed it away, muttering, "leave them on." Patrick stood back and started stripping, enjoying watching the byplay between Alex and Maggie.

"Get on the bed and lie back," Alex ordered her as he picked his duffel up and snatched an unopened box of condoms out of it. "I want your hands up above your head," he demanded and when she complied he added, "Higher." He tore the box open scattering condom wrappers everywhere as he haphazardly tossed a few onto the bed before placing one between his lips. He reached down and with one tug popped the buttons on his button fly jeans. His cock bounced out and he caught it in his palm running his hand from balls to tip before shrugging out of his jeans and letting them fall to the floor. He was prepared to take things slow. It would be hard after the long dry spell he'd had, but he could try. That was his intention, but all that went out the window when he heard her moan and looked up in time to see her eyes transfixed on his cock. And when her pink tongue flicked out and wet her lips his cock pulsed and bobbed and the only question left was whether he would get the condom on in time.

Pat moaned and Alex glanced over to see his best friend totally naked, his cock being worked by the slow glide of a hand. He looked like he was ready to combust from the lust rushing through his veins and Alex understood perfectly. He glanced back to where Maggie was writhing with anticipation on the bed.

"Feeling hungry, baby?" he murmured as he continued stroking his rock hard cock.

Maggie's eyes flew between Patrick's thick cock and Alex's longer length. She wanted them and she didn't care where. She was her father's daughter in more ways than one. She had dabbled in all kinds of sexual games and fantasies, some of which she was sure even her father would blanch at. Fact was that Maggie loved sex, loved the rock hard shaft that could deliver pleasure better than any toy on the market. In her pussy, her ass or down the back of her throat. She'd take it all and demand more. Hell yeah she was hungry.

"Yes," she nodded locking her eyes over on Patrick's cock. Yeah, she wanted that thick width stretching her mouth wide, wanted to feel it all along her tongue, nip it with her teeth. She lifted her eyes to his and asked as seductively as she could, "Want to feed me?"

Patrick groaned and once again it was Alex who gave the orders. "Get up on your hands and knees baby. Face toward the end of the bed. Hips right over here by me." He watched with hooded eyes as she complied and he couldn't help but think of how perfect she was for him. She was great with obeying his orders and not questioning. She'd let him fulfil his need to dominate and be the perfect foil for his dark side. Fuck! He wanted her so bad that he could spend the entire week locked in this room. Oh yeah, and he would take her every way imaginable and then some. He couldn't wait to bury his dick so deep inside her pussy that she could feel it in her womb. And he wanted that ass as well. Hell the more he looked at the flair of her hips, the perfect curve of her buttocks, the hungrier he got. She was made to be mounted this way, she was perfection on her hands and knees. He didn't even have to tell her to arch her back the way he liked. She was already doing it. He stood there for a moment just admiring the view, letting the anticipation build for both of them.

Patrick had other plans. He immediately headed closer to the bed, closer to the tongue slicked lips of the goddess on the bed. Damn his dick was dancing with the need to feel her tongue and teeth. As he approached she re-wet her lips, the slow glide of her pink tongue a torture all its own. He wanted to fuck her just as badly as Alex, but he wanted to feel that mouth all over his cock right now more than anything else.

He stopped before her and almost lost it when she leaned forward just enough to swipe her tongue over the head taking the drop of pre-cum with her. Her moan of pleasure at his taste was almost as loud as his was. He moved in closer and pressed the full head of his cock against her lips seeking entrance. But she surprised him by moving to the side and nuzzling it along her cheek while her lips spread kisses over his groin. Her tongue flicked out and stroked over his balls until they were so tight with need he wouldn't be surprised if they burst. She moved underneath and sucked one globe gently into her mouth working it with her tongue until he didn't know if he would feel her mouth before he came all over them both. But she seemed to read his body well and every time orgasm approached she backed off and moved to something else. He was ready to die when a sharp slap filled the air and her head jerked with a cry. He was ready to step back and knock Alex out until he focused on Maggie's face and saw the flush of desire high on her cheeks, the way her eyes were so dark a green that they almost glowed. Oh, she liked what Alex was doing. She liked it a lot.

"You want this pussy fucked," Alex said stroking his fingers along the flushed lips of her sex loving the red print left from the slap he'd given her there. She was dripping she was so excited and that jacked up the desire inside him as well. He dipped a finger inside and then two coating them in her juices before pulling out and slapping her flesh with them, right over the little bud that was blooming so beautifully for him. Yeah, he wanted to suck her clit between his lips 'till she filled his mouth with a fountain of sweet cream.

"Oh, yeah. You want my cock buried up this tight pussy, don't you baby?" Alex knew the answer even before her cries filled the room.

"Yes! God, yes! Please fuck me. Fuck me so good." Maggie pushed her hips out more, deepened the arch of her back so her sex was even more exposed to him.

"Want it hard baby?"

"Yes."

"Fast?"

"Yes."

"Deep?"

"Yes!" She screamed it this time looking over her shoulder at him and pinning him with her fiery green orbs. "Hard, fast and so deep that I can feel you everywhere. Just fuck me. Please, fuck me."

Alex brought the condom back up to his teeth and ripped the package open, tossing the wrapper to the floor then easily rolled it over his shaft. "I'm going to fuck you baby. And it will be harder, faster and deeper than you've ever had it before. I promise you that. But first you're going to face him and suck that fat dick of his down into your throat and you're going to keep doing it until he fills your mouth with his satisfaction. That okay with you?" He didn't always remember to ask that but then Patrick would if he forgot. The southern boy wouldn't cum anywhere without a woman's okay. Alex wouldn't either but he couldn't remember ever being this worked up over a woman. Hell, some foreign entity seemed to be inside him and it wanted to lose the condom and ride her skin to skin, something he had never done in his life. He never played without a slicker. Rule number one.

She nodded her head vigorously, undulating on the bed and her sex flushed darker even as he watched. "Yes, I love the taste of your cock," she told Patrick. She licked her lips and opened and closed them several times. "I want you to fuck my mouth. Give me all of that cock. Right here," she moaned and licked her lips again. "I want to taste your cum on my tongue."

"Fuck," Patrick cried and used his hand to guide the head back to her mouth. She opened wide this time and sucked him deep the first time. She was done playing and if he thought that she would kill him before he hadn't known what he was talking about. He was fixated on the way his thick girth stretched her lips wide, the slight scrape of her teeth along his shaft as she sucked him deep before easing off his length. And when only the mushroomed head remained in her mouth she worked her tongue in the groove just underneath and sucked hard on him. He wasn't going to last at all.

His gaze latched on to Alex's and he confessed just that. "I ain't going to last buddy. Fuck!" he cried as she sucked him deep once again. No he wasn't going to last at all.

Alex stepped up to the bed and moved to his knees on the mattress behind her. She was sheer perfection and he had yet to feel her slick walls tightening around him. She was flushed, her lips spread wide, the opening to her pussy wet and ready to be filled by him. He'd never been so happy before that a woman wanted hard and fast. Because that was all he could give her this first time. It might last three minutes depending on just how sweet she was. But somehow he knew it wouldn't last much longer than that.

He lined up and slammed home with one hard thrust of his hips against hers. She cried out around the cock in her mouth but didn't let it go. Alex pulled all the way out loving the feel of her pussy grasping him like it didn't want to lose him. With a harsh groan he plunged deep again and she took him moving back into his thrust with her body. And that one small movement shattered the remains of his control. He grabbed her hips firmly between his hands and rode her like a battering ram. He wanted to slow down, wanted to savour her, wanted to do so many other things both to and with her but now was not the time. Those things would have to wait until the next time. This time he took like an animal and she blew him away with the way she not only took what he gave but used her body to demand more. Her hips slapping against his as she strained closer to him, her back arching so high that her belly almost hit the mattress. And the entire time she never let go of the cock filling her mouth and from the glazed look on Patrick's face she wasn't slacking on the sucking action she was giving him either. Yeah, Alex had found the perfect woman, the one who would be able to satisfy his every desire and whim. Maggie would probably have some demands of her own as well and damned if he didn't relish the thought of being the man to fill them for her.

Patrick's bellow filled the room and his hips locked in a forward position and Alex could tell by the expression on his buddy's face that it was one hell of an orgasm. Alex's face would have a similar expression in just a few minutes. He watched as Patrick finally stepped back from Maggie, his cock releasing with a loud pop as if she was reluctant to let the spent flesh go. And with Patrick no longer in the picture Maggie turned into a wild cat beneath him, bucking and thrusting back at him. He tightened his grip hoping that he wouldn't leave bruises on her white skin but afraid that he would anyway. She dropped her arms down on the bed and buried her head on them and a keening cry filled the air telling him just how close she was to orgasm. She turned her head and looked back at him. Her eyes were glazed and there was a spot of white on her bottom lip that he figured was a remnant of Patrick's cum. "Fuck me," she demanded in a guttural voice slurred by the intensity of her desire.

Alex held tight and stroked faster between her thighs lifting her hips slightly off the mattress with every thrust. Three strokes, four strokes, and on the fifth she broke. The walls of her pussy closed over him gripping and working his dick, her cries of completion the headiest aphrodisiac he'd ever known. On the eighth stroke he was joining her with an orgasm so intense that he saw black dots that made him fear for his sight. The person who said masturbation could make you go blind had obviously never known a woman like his Maggie. He roared out as the thought filled his head. His Maggie. Fuck, he'd fallen in love with a woman that he didn't know. A woman whose very life he may shatter depending on how well she knew the man he and Patrick were here to investigate, Dom Alexander Houston.

Chapter Three

Maggie didn't think that she could move and prayed that they wouldn't ask her to. Alex was behind her on the bed lying crosswise with his hand firmly planted on her ass. It was as if he was afraid she was going to spring up and leave. Hell, the man had just given her the best sex of her life so he had nothing to worry about. As a matter of fact after this episode she was sad that she couldn't marry him and spend the rest of her life with him. He was everything that she had been searching for sexually in a man. But sex wasn't everything and she would never give her father the satisfaction of getting what he wanted from her. And the old man had been very clear on how he expected her to seduce one of the men into marriage. She had just played with his plan a little bit. She almost laughed out loud but, thankfully, caught herself. Instead of seducing one man, she had engaged in an amazing sex session with both of them. Hell, she could go a few more times if they were up to it. She stretched and groaned and did laugh when she heard Patrick moan from his reclined state beside her.

His feet were on the floor with only his hips and upper body lazing on the bed. He must have had one hell of a glance at her breasts when she arched up. Maggie glanced his way and smiled when she saw his cock full and hard again. His thick staff bobbed up against his stomach and Maggie reached out to cup him in her hand, to caress the soft skin that covered the steel length. Patrick groaned again and she felt more than saw Alex turn his head to see what they were doing. She stroked him from balls to tip spreading some of the pre-cum leaking from the head with her fingers.

The male penis had always fascinated Maggie. They all looked remarkably the same when in the flaccid state but when a man was aroused... Wow. That was when they became works of art. Each one different and unique. Hell the two men in the room with here were a perfect example of this. Patrick was so thick that her fingers couldn't encompass the width of him. The head was a mushroom shape, blooming over the top of the shaft, and amazingly was about a half an inch thicker than the rest of his cock. It was a true mushroom cock.

Alex on the other hand was long, so damn long but nowhere near the thickness of Patrick. The head of his cock barely tapered making the entire length the same width. Where Patrick only reached midway to his belly button, Alex was all the way up to his. And as she glanced back to see what he was doing at this moment she saw that he was also hard as stone and slowly guiding his hand along the beauty between his thighs. She desperately wanted to do that for him, wanted to taste him in the same way that she had Patrick. Felt a desperate urge to replace Patrick's taste with Alex's. What was it about this man that screamed at her and brought out emotions that she had never engaged in during sex before? It was much more than his pretty looks and that sexy British accent, though those were fantastic. No, it was something about the man himself that called out to the woman inside her, the one she tried to hide from everyone. She went to try and roll over to her hands and knees but both men stopped her.

"On your back this time baby," Patrick said. "I want to eat a little more of that sweet cream of yours before I slip my cock inside you." He glanced over at her as he stood up from the bed and reached for one of the condoms lying on the floor. "Are you okay with that? You want me to fuck you? Put my cock in that tight pussy until we both explode with pleasure?"

Damn he was good. A man who knew how to sway a woman to what he wanted. And that southern boy charm was as evident as the Texas drawl that left his lips. Hell yeah she wanted him inside her but some devil inside her made her glance at Alex as if seeking permission. What the hell was up with that? That just pissed her off. He was nothing to her but a casual lay that she might or might not see again. But then Alex smiled at her and reached out to stroke her hair. And his voice, his voice was like warm water trickling over her sensitised skin.

"I want to see him fuck you as much as you want him to. Almost as much as he wants to. I want to watch him pleasure you, watch you come with him inside you." His fingers came up and traced over her lips. "And I want to feel this incredible mouth sucking my dick while he's doing it."

Maggie couldn't help it, she moaned deep in her throat and it came out sounding like a purr. Like she was a damn cat being stroked by her master. But damn it all she wanted that more than anything. She did her best to give him a sultry smile, arching her back up off the bed, her breasts reaching towards the ceiling and her legs spreading wide.

Unfortunately she was facing the wrong way and her mouth was at Patrick and her thighs were spread by Alex. And the damn man grinned as if he knew she was trying to shake off the affect he was having on her. He reached his hand out and dipped it between her spread thighs, plunging two fingers into her sheath and spreading them to stroke along the walls as he thrust in and out with them. Maggie moaned and cried out realising just how sensitive she still was from sex with Alex. She closed her eyes and lost herself in his hands. She knew that it was Patrick at her breasts when a warm mouth wrapped one of her nipples and sucked greedily at it while fingers plucked at the other one. Then Alex's fingers disappeared and she did open them wide only to squeeze them tight when she felt his tongue taking over. His thumb played with her clit rubbing in lazy circles around the nub while his tongue plunged inside her pussy and undulated before he pulled it out and licked along her labia. God he was perfection there as well. Was there anything the man didn't know how to do? Then she just didn't care anymore as he brought her to the brink of orgasm and held her right there at the edge for what seemed an eternity before pushing her over.

She came in waves until her body felt like it was floating on the surface of a warm pool of water. She felt warm and secure, totally sated and damn it, happy. These were things she didn't associate with sex. Sex was sex. A need that the body required to expend certain energy. It was not about romance and heaven forbid she ever used the "L" word unless it was lust. What were they doing to her? What magic did one man have that he could even direct her pleasure at the hands of another? And why was she even now licking her lips with the anticipation of having him in her mouth? She flicked her eyes open but it wasn't the Cheshire grin on his face like she expected. No, his cheeks were flushed and his eyes were hooded. His face was still wet from her pussy and somehow she knew that he would not let her walk away until he was ready for her to. And that terrified her more than anything else in the world.

He walked slowly up to the foot of the bed where her head was and stopped far enough away that she could only look at him but not touch him yet. She licked her lips again and his eyes darkened from the sky blue to a deeper darker midnight shade. She heard the rip of a package and broke away from Alex's gaze to watch Patrick sheath his cock and move onto the bed between her legs. He lifted them high so that they were over his shoulders and bent over her, lining his cock up with her pussy. He ran the length up and down her labia coating his condom covered cock in her juices before tucking the head into her pussy and starting a slow in and out friction that had him sinking a little deeper inside her with every stroke. She closed her eyes and arched up further, wanting all of him buried in her now. She wanted him to fuck her to the point that she forgot about the other man in the room. But as if he read her mind, Alex's dark chuckle filled the room and she felt the liquid tip of his cock rubbing over her cheek. She kept still, kept her eyes squeezed shut and tried like mad to focus all her attention to what was happening between her thighs were Patrick was finally buried to the balls. Her sheath flexed around him trying to adjust to his width and his groan told her exactly how much he was enjoying that.

"Tight," Patrick rasped as he began a slow rhythm his hands planted firmly on the bed beside her hips. This was nothing like Alex's fast animalistic pace and damn it, where had that thought come from? "You're perfection Maggie. Sheer perfection. I could fuck you forever."

"Hmmmm..." Alex spoke, his husky accent sending shivers over her and her eyes sprang open and locked with his. "Yes, she is sheer perfection Patrick. A woman made to be pleasured and to give pleasure." He moved his cock along her cheek again and she couldn't stop her face from turning toward him and letting him coat her lips with the fluid already slipping from the head. "Open up Maggie. Open up and let me feel that wicked tongue caress me. Let me feel the back of your throat as you swallow me." He pushed gently against her lips and she knew that it was only a matter of seconds before she gave in, before she opened wide and took everything he had to give her. "Open up Maggie," Alex's eyes locked with hers and for a brief moment there was something there, some emotion that Maggie didn't think that either of them were ready to deal with. How the hell did you fall for someone in one moment of madness? Then the eyes changed and the plea became a demand as if he were afraid of the feelings charging the air between them as well. "Open up Maggie and suck my dick."

That was what she needed to hear, that thick British accent demanding to be pleasured, not the husky plea of earlier. She needed it to be just about sex, just sex and mutual pleasure and nothing more. Never anything more. She opened wide and with one thrust he was filling her mouth and then some. Even when he hit the back of her throat there was still a bit of him that wouldn't fit in her mouth and she reached up to use her hand on that last bit. But Alex stopped her grasping her hands and leaning over her to brace them above her head while he continued to stroke in and out of her mouth.

"This is for my pleasure Maggie. I'm going to fuck these beautiful lips of yours and you're going to let me. Aren't you Maggie?"

She nodded her head frantically afraid that he would take it away if she didn't, afraid that he would make Patrick stop that slow torture between her thighs. Yes, this was just sex, dirty raunchy, nasty sex. This was just what she wanted.

Patrick took one hand up and used it to move one of her legs up so that they were both over one shoulder and thrust hard inside her. She cried out around Alex's flesh and glanced at Patrick. He grinned at her and somehow she knew that he had done that to get her attention focussed on him for a bit. Hell, she had it bad if even Patrick knew that she was fixated on Alex. His smile softened and she knew that he must be reading some of the fear and anxiety in her. That slow southern boy charm hid a very sharp mind and she had best start remembering that. Now that he had her attention he increased his rhythm until he was moving like a piston each hard thrust dragging along her sheath and bringing her that much closer to orgasm. She closed her eyes and felt Alex wrap his long fingers in her hair using them to keep her face and mouth at just the angle he wanted them. But Patrick was finally giving her what she needed from him, a hard, deep fucking that helped her push Alex to the outskirts of her mind and had her focusing on her pussy and the pleasure it was receiving. Yes, this was just what she needed, what she wanted. She hummed her pleasure around Alex's dick and felt him jerk as the vibrations moved along his shaft and down into his balls. She could actually feel the globes tightening against her chin and that made her feel triumphant, like she was pushing him toward the same pleasure she was reaching, like she was stealing his control. So she continued her humming while she undulated under Patrick trying desperately to push her hips up against him to intensify the invasion of his every thrust. This was pleasure, the bone deep kind that left you completely dazed and sated at the end. This was what she needed from them and what she needed to give them before she walked away. And she would walk away, no matter what was beginning between her and Alex. She would never give her father the pleasure of doing what he wanted. And God alone knew that her hatred for that man would far outweigh her love... Oh hell no was she using that word. Her lust for any other man. Yeah, lust. That was all sex was ever about and all that it ever would be about as far as she was concerned. Men were a dime a dozen and there would be plenty of others in her life after she walked away from Alex. And Patrick.

Patrick slammed her back into the present with a stroke hard enough to make her tighten her teeth around Alex which had him crying out as well. Hell, he seemed to like her teeth if the flex of his shaft meant anything. So she nipped again allowing her natural instinct to take over while Patrick became an animal between her thighs. He was moving so fast now, his jaw tightened with the pleasure he was feeling. The drag of his cock burned her flesh and when he reached down and pushed against her clit with his thumb she exploded. Black dots danced at the edges of her vision and she screamed her pleasure. Alex pulled out of her mouth and she was almost ashamed of the teeth marks that showed on his length. But Patrick kept thrusting and each one sent her spiralling further into oblivion. She was on the edge of unconsciousness when she heard the roar and felt the shudder going through Patrick's body. His hips slammed into hers and held there with only small flexes as his cock thickened and burst inside her. His release triggered another one in her but it was only small waves and didn't have the intensity of the first one. He stayed there for a moment lost in his own pleasure and then his chocolate brown eyes opened and for just a moment they looked sad.

He eased her legs off of his shoulders and bent down over her until his face was in front of hers. "Thanks Maggie. You're incredible." With that he kissed her lightly on the lips, just a touch from his to hers and then he was pulling away, pulling out and leaving the bed. "I'm hitting the shower," he tossed over his shoulder to Alex and without a single look back he was gone.

"Maybe I should go to?" Maggie said and started to rise from the bed. But Alex was there and easily pushed her back to her back. He was strong but she knew that it was because she really didn't want to leave. She knew what was coming and she wanted it more than anything.

Then he was there, back between her legs only this time he was above her instead of behind her. This time there would be no hiding the emotions flitting across her face as he took her body and gave it everything that it had been longing for. This time there would be no pretending it was meaningless sex with a stranger although that was exactly what it should be.

Alex thrust into her and she gasped at the feel of him wondering at how great he felt. The second thrust made her eyes flash wide as she realised what the sensation was. Skin on skin. Naked flesh inside naked flesh. He wasn't wearing a condom and she had never had sex without protection in her life. She wanted to let him keep going, she was on the pill but that would only make it that much harder to walk away when the time came.

"You're...You're not wearing anything," she whispered and heard his harsh expletive split the air. So he hadn't realised it either. She heard the rip of a package and then he was back inside her the condom doing nothing to change the sensations of what he was doing but somehow managing to dull the emotions churning inside her. Her last coherent thought was that she would be okay as long as he didn't kiss her. Then she locked eyes with him again and as his head lowered toward hers she knew that after this her entire life would be changed. Nothing would ever be the same for her after Alex.

Chapter Four

The only thing Alex knew in that moment was that he had to kiss Maggie. He rarely did that somehow feeling that a kiss was too intimate in his casual sexual affairs. But he needed Maggie's kiss like he needed food, water, air. And then his lips were on hers and when she gasped against him he slipped his tongue inside the tender lips that had nursed his cock so well just moments before. He touched her teeth and remembered the feel of them nipping and biting at his shaft as he pumped between her plump lips. Then he was caressing her tongue with his and after a slight hesitation, almost as if she was as unused to kissing as he was, she was rubbing along his tongue as well. He held her close refusing to let her mouth go until they were both gasping for breath.

He moved his lips along her jaw and then down the arched column of her throat. He could taste the unique essence of her sweat on her skin, and the smell of their sex filled his nostrils. This was what it meant to make love to a woman. This was what it felt like when there was more than lust involved in the physical act. This was making love and it rocked him to his core. In all his life he had never made love to a woman. He'd had sex with numerous women, some who knew what he did and some who only guessed. It was the James Bond syndrome, or at least that's what his buddies and he used to refer to it as. When you worked for MI6 you were often surrounded by beautiful women and rarely did they say no. Some of their cases took them to great places and some buried them in places that no man would ever willingly go.

Hell it was a woman that had him playing private eye with his buddy in Texas and no longer a member of MI6. He'd left it all behind when one of his friends and colleagues had been shot and killed on one of their cases. Shot and killed when he should have been with him. Instead Alex had been wrapped between the legs of a woman who was doing her job a lot better than he was. She'd kept him long enough to make him exactly ten minutes late, ten minutes that had cost his buddy his life. When he had arrived his buddy was the only one there and he had been lying in a pool of blood. It was a vision that haunted Alex's dreams often. He had completed the case and made damn sure that those responsible had gotten just what the deserved. But he had crossed lines during the case and for him, there was no going back. And his superior had known it or at least considered it because he hadn't been surprised when Alex has tendered his resignation. He would never be completely free of MI6, that was the nature of the agency. But for now he was on his own doing his best to deal with what he had done.

He glanced at the woman beneath him, the sheer beauty of her face, the feel of her warm flesh against his and for the first time in a long time Alex felt alive. And somehow it was all due to this woman. He may have just met her. Hell, he may know absolutely nothing about her but one thing he did know. He would do whatever it took to keep her in his life, in his bed because she was the only woman that had ever managed to find a way into his heart.

He took her lips again and invaded her mouth like a marauder searching for treasure. And she was full of treasure. Her taste, the feel of her hands on his shoulders and stroking up and down his spine, the rake of her nails, the rasp of her nipples, and the clasp of her thighs on his hips was his entire world right now. He was completely enmeshed in this moment, in this woman. And more than anything he didn't want to let go.

It was more than sex between them this time and he wrapped himself in the moment. The slow glide of his dick deep inside her, so deep that he felt as if they were one person at times. The soft sighs that left her lips almost as if against her will. But mostly it was the warmth that filled him up and overflowed. The beat of his heart seemed to be in synch with hers and, God help him, but he didn't want this to end, didn't want them to find their pleasure and find release. He wanted to keep them right here, right now, for as long as possible. He pushed deep and held still enjoying the sheer feel of her capturing and holding him inside. Her gorgeous green eyes flicked open again and he locked on them as he took her mouth again. And when she responded immediately this time she sealed her own fate. That one unguarded moment let him know that she was feeling the same thing that he was.

This time when she tried to encourage him to move faster and harder he knew exactly what she was trying to do. She was trying to make him like every other un-emotional sexual encounter she had ever had. But this time he wasn't complying. This time he was demanding everything from her and the more she fought it the more he wanted it. In the aftermath he held her close, something he had never done before with any other woman and wasn't even surprised when he felt the wetness of her tears on his chest.

He glanced up as Patrick left the bathroom fully dressed and nodded as his friend headed to the door and left him alone with Maggie. His buddy knew that there was something more between him and Maggie and being the gentleman he was he left to give them some time alone. Oh, Patrick had enjoyed Maggie and if Alex and Maggie wanted, he was sure that Patrick would join them again. But for now he needed to make Maggie see that there had to be a next time. He had to make her believe that he was more than a casual encounter.

Her tears stopped and Maggie tried to pull away from him. Alex held her tight and refused to let her put physical distance between them when she was already doing a good job of putting emotional distance between them. He placed his fingers beneath her jaw and tilted her face so that he could see it. She refused to meet his eyes but the watery brilliance along with the tear tracks on her cheeks made him bend down to place kisses there. She was beauty in every way. The woman even looked gorgeous when she cried.

"Look at me Maggie," Alex coaxed and took the shudder that rolled through her body into his as she finally met his eyes. He was shocked by the look in her eyes. She looked so sad and for the life of him he couldn't figure out why. "What's wrong baby? What's bothering you?"

Maggie shook her head, her lips sealed.

"I know that you felt it too Maggie. I know that this was more than just sex for you and I'm not going to let you pretend otherwise." Her eyes flicked up to his again and he didn't check the impulse to bend down and take her mouth again. He could taste her tears and they humbled him as nothing else could. "I want to know you Maggie. I want to know everything about you. Your hopes and dreams. Your worries and fears. I want to know that you're not just a dream. I want you." He knew that he was revealing things that he shouldn't but this woman made him give what he never had before.

"I can't." Maggie shuddered against him and her chin wobbled as a lone tear made its way down her cheek. "Don't you see that I can't let him win? I can't let him get his way."

"Who?" Alex demanded and he didn't care that his voice was rough and hard at the moment. Some other man was causing Maggie's anxiety and he would take care of that immediately. Maggie was his woman now, whether she realised it yet or not. "Who is going to win? What are you talking about Maggie?"

"He wants me to seduce one of you and marry you. He demanded that I put the company first and do what my duty was." She looked as if her heart was breaking but she kept his gaze and didn't look away. "I've spent my whole life trying to please him, trying to make him proud. But it was never enough. I was never enough. Because I was a woman. And now I find myself wanting to do this, wanting to be with you. But once again he's the ghost in the room. And I can't. I just can't, Alex."

"What are you talking about Maggie? Who wants you to seduce one of us and marry us? You're not making any sense." Alex was totally lost in this conversation except for the fact that she said that she wanted to marry him. Instead of scaring the hell out of him it made his heart beat faster and opened a place in his heart that he hadn't been aware was empty.

"My father Alex. The man you met today. The man who ordered me from the room before he spoke with you and

Patrick. He wants me to seduce you and marry you so that he can have the man he wants take over his company. And no matter what I think I might be feeling for you, I can't do what he wants. I can't." Maggie was almost crying again and if the shaking of her body was any indication this was taking a lot out of her.

Alex lay there for a moment holding her close while he waded through what she was saying and where he had met her until everything clicked into place. Then he threw his head back and laughed and laughed. He felt Maggie stiffen up next to him and only squeezed her closer when she tried to pull away. This was sheer perfection.

"Your father is Dom Alexander Houston." It was a statement but he looked down at her waiting for the slight nod before he laughed again. "Oh sweetheart, I'm the last man your dad would want you to hook up with. And Patrick would be a close second." Maggie started to open her mouth, to argue with him probably but he took her mouth with a kiss again. Lord, he couldn't get enough of this woman. "Where did you go when you left the room?"

"I went to my office and packed my stuff up. I didn't plan to do what he wanted so I emptied my few personal items out of the office and took them out to my car. I'm not going back to the office, to the house, or to him. I'll find a job elsewhere and make a life for myself away from him and everything to do with him." She had fire in her green eyes and she was making his dick twitch again though he had already had her twice in the last hour and a half.

"Had you stuck around you would have met the two men that your father was waiting for. I'm sure that both of them were exactly what your dad was planning for you." He laughed again at the look of confusion on her face. "I don't know why I didn't put it together when I saw you in the office and he called you Margaret. I should have but I seem to have trouble thinking of much of anything around you. Except being inside you, your body, your mind, your very soul."

"What are you talking about Alex? What other men?" Maggie shook her head but there was no hiding the shining light of hope that shone from her eyes now.

"When your father found out why we were there he sent us away as soon as he could. On our way out there were two other men there that his secretary was telling that he wasn't seeing anyone else today. She must have confused us with them," Alex shrugged and grinned down at Maggie. "But then he surely didn't hire her for her secretarial skills."

Maggie giggled and buried her head in his shoulder sharing the joke with him. "He must have been very angry with her. Guess she won't be the flavour of the month too much longer." She giggled again and looked up at him then seemed to realise what else he had said. "What were you there for? Why would he send you away?"

"Have you ever wondered about your mother's family Maggie? Have you ever wanted to meet them and get to know them?"

Maggie's eyes went sad again as she shook her head. "Dom made sure that I knew that they didn't want anything to do with me. They never saw mom and didn't even come to her funeral." She stopped as Alex shook his head gently denying what she was saying.

"Lies, Maggie. All lies. Your Grandmother and the rest of your family had no idea that your mother was even dead until recently when one of your cousins started doing genealogy and came across her obituary. They had no idea about your mother's death or anything else. Your Grandmother said that it was like she disappeared when she married your dad." He leaned down and kissed her softly on the lips, just a gentle brush of his against hers. "She wasn't even sure that you existed."

"So you're a private investigator or something?" Maggie asked as emotions rolled through her. She had a family, a real family. A Grandmother and cousins and all that. She had more than her dad. "They hired you to find me?"

"Your grandmother hired us to find out about you and your mother. She wants to meet you but most importantly she wants to know that you are okay." Alex smiled down at her and she wondered how a British sex god got hooked up as a private investigator with a smooth southern boy. She sensed that there was a hell of a story behind it, one that he would eventually share with her. "So what do you say Maggie. Want to go meet your other family? Want to go with me and see what happens?"

"Yes," she breathed and she knew that he understood what she was saying yes to by the smile that took over his face. He was everything she'd been searching for alright and now she was going to grab on with both hands and see where this took her. She'd never really had a relationship that was more than a casual thing and would be lying if she tried to pretend that she wasn't afraid.

"So what was your plan Maggie? Were you going to sleep with both men and then walk away from both of them?"

"Something like that." She smiled up at him and laughed when he gave her a mock glare.

"Well you're lucky that you got the wrong two men baby. I'm not going to deny the shock of jealousy that goes through me at the thought of you with anyone else."

"Even Patrick?" She questioned and actually giggled again when he smacked her on the butt.

"Oh, I'm sure that we could persuade Patrick to join us again for the occasional ménage as long as you realise one thing."

"What?" Maggie asked.

"That Maggie's ménage is Alex's too," he murmured and rolled over pulling her atop him. His cock was long and full between her and she needed no encouragement to mount up. He reached blindly along the bed for a condom and ripped it open. She rose reluctantly off his flesh only long enough for him to roll the condom into place before she took him inside again. "Not without me baby. Not without me there to protect you and make sure that you are taken care of."

"Not without you," she agreed thinking that she would never need a ménage again as long as she had him in her life. "Never without you."

Epilogue

"Where the hell have you been young lady?" Dom demanded as Maggie entered the room. He was appalled that his daughter was in jeans and sandals with a casual shirt. She looked common.

"Why I've been busy daddy dearest," Maggie cooed and it was then that he noticed the rock on her finger.

"So you married one of them. Which one was it?" Dom demanded. He'd of course have to make them redo the wedding vows, a big society splash filled with all the right people but at least the girl had finally shown some common sense and done what he'd ordered.

"I didn't marry either of those men."

"Well, who then? Who did you marry Margaret?" Dom could feel the vein pounding in his temple and knew that his face was turning red with anger.

"Do you remember the two men that came into the office the last time I was here? The two that were sent to discuss things with you?" Maggie smiled up at him when he snarled at her.

"What the hell have you done you stupid little girl? Those weren't the ones you were supposed to entice. Can't you do anything right? Do I have to do everything for you?" He turned away and moved behind the desk. "I'll take care of the dissolution. Just tell me where the ceremony took place and I'll get you out of this mess."

"San Antonio," she murmured and waited for the bomb to drop in the room as her father processed that bit of information. When understanding lit his eyes she just grinned and nodded her head at him. "That's right. I've met the family you tried to keep from me. I've met them and they're wonderful."

"You don't know what you're talking about. Your mother couldn't wait to get away from them," he declared.

"Because she thought your money would buy her happiness. She learned a different lesson though, didn't she?" Maggie's eyes went cold now as she took in the man in front of her. It was amazing what a little bit of knowledge and distance could make you see. He was nothing. And she had spent too much of her life trying to please nothing.

"You're just as stupid as your mother," her father thundered as he stood from behind the desk planting his meaty fists on the surface and leaning towards her. She was almost afraid that Alex would enter the room and hoped that Patrick would keep him out there waiting for her instead of helping him into the room. And just the thought of Alex made her smile and release the rest of the pain at having a father who didn't love her, who saw her as nothing more than a possession.

"No, I'm nothing like my mother, not anymore, and never again. It took me long enough but I've finally realised something that she never did." Maggie looked again at her father and felt a deep sadness for him. As much as he surrounded himself by people and things when he died he would be all alone. And he had no one to blame except himself.

"What is it that you think you've learned little girl?" he demanded but the bluster had dimmed and she realised that he knew she was leaving.

"That money means nothing if you don't have someone to enjoy it with. That life is more than wearing the right thing and going to the right places, being seen with the right people. But more importantly, I've learned that I don't have to spend my life trying to please a man who will never be happy."

"You'll regret this little outburst Margaret and you'll come crawling back to me begging for my help."

Maggie just smiled and shook her head. "No. I'm doing the one thing that my mother never could. I'm walking away and I'm not looking back." With that she turned to leave the room barely hearing her father bellowing her name. All she could think of was that just outside that door was the man she loved, the man she'd married after two weeks. As she pushed the door open and saw Alex's face a smile lit her face from the inside out and she ran to him. This was the life she'd always dreamed of. And to think she found it all in the heat of a ménage.

BOY TOYS

Brynn Paulin

Dedication

To my boy toy. Kisses, baby!

Chapter One

Dana Matthews stared out the car window at the passing English countryside and tried to tamp down her resentment over this assignment. Okay, perhaps it wasn't resentment. It was more frustration than anything else.

Since her research scientist position in the United States had been eliminated, she'd been dancing on a taut wire — taking the same job within a different branch of the company, transferring to a new country, leaving behind her husband. Ex-husband now, she reminded herself. He'd been set to join her until she'd discovered a few months abstinence had been too much for him. He'd screwed their next door neighbour, Miss skeezy pants — Miss I'm-twenty-two-and-you're-not skeezy pants — and tried to claim it was a mid-life crisis.

"You okay, Dana?"

Dana glanced over at the brown-haired man beside her and nodded. Jason Kerzi and the other passenger of the car, Christopher Brown, were part of her problem. Also research scientists, but working different projects, the two were headed to London to meet with the Powers-That-Be and explain the findings on their latest work...something about frog DNA and a cancer gene. She hadn't worked on their experiments so other than witnessing excited whispers from the other side of the lab while they ran computer models, she didn't pretend to know what they'd discovered.

Their work had little bearing on her own experiments. Which made her question her presence on this trip.

There was no doubt in her mind, she'd been sent to chaperone the dynamic duo while they met with the big wigs who were flying over from the Former British Territories AKA the United States. It galled her. Why should she play mother-hen to the boys? Thirty-seven wasn't old, damn it. Certainly not eighty. Surely the twenty-somethings could keep themselves in line for a few days.

This assignment put her last frayed nerve on edge. Not because the meeting would suck up her weekend. Not even because she had to chaperone. She took a deep breath and inhaled the intoxicating scents of her companions' colognes.

Her tension stemmed from the fact that she found both men unsettlingly attractive. Attractive? That was an understatement. She wanted them both with a lust befitting a nubile co-ed. And she'd done her best to hide it for the last eight months. That didn't stop her from alternately fantasising about one or the other of them in her bed each night.

She sighed, hoping neither of them caught her mooning over them this weekend. How embarrassing would that be? Hopefully, they'd get to their hotel and she could closet herself in her room until morning. After several hours closed in this car with them, she could use a break from their magnetism.

Maybe she was going through some sort of mid-life crisis. She stifled a snort. She'd always told her husband she'd trade him in for two half his age. At twenty-seven each, Christopher and Jason almost qualified.

Christopher turned in his seat to look back at her, the late-afternoon sun catching his golden-blond hair. "Are you sure you're not feeling a bit off? We should be there soon and you can nick a bit of sleep before tonight."

She raised her eyebrows. "Tonight?" she repeated slowly, looking between the two of them.

Jason's blue eyes sparkled with mischief. "Yes, we've been talking —"

"Plotting, you mean," she interrupted.

He laughed and her pussy immediately clenched. Her fingers fisted on the seat beside her. *Please, God, don't let them be able to smell how aroused I am.* Aroused? Pathetic. What would they think if they knew their co-worker, a woman ten years older, wanted to fuck them? They'd probably be horrified...especially when they discovered she harboured thoughts of having both of them at once.

Jason patted her hand, sending a tremor to her core. "You've never visited London except for a brief trip from Heathrow. We want to show you the sights."

"I don't think so," she replied, her voice a bit shaky. "It's been a long day. You two go party — or whatever you've got planned — and I'll hang out in my room."

The men exchanged a glance, then each resumed a face-forward position. She suddenly suspected there had been a plethora of silent communication in their small exchange. Great. Now she was paranoid, too? She took a deep breath and tried to remember she was a respected scientist in her field. This lack of self confidence wasn't necessary.

She smoothed her hand over her skirt, conscious of the few pounds she'd gained since her early twenties. She wouldn't stand a chance with a guy if she stood side by side with Miss Skeezy Pants.

Stop it! her brain yelled. Her nails dug into the car's armrest. Good lord! She needed to get out of this car. Shutting down her thoughts, she mentally recited the chemical periodic table by rote. A sense of calm came over her, and she temporarily relaxed as the letters and numbers floated through her head like sheep lining up to be counted on the way to sleep.

She almost forgot Jason and Christopher were with her. Almost, but not quite. Their presence was so thoroughly imbedded into her subconscious that they were never completely removed.

Damn. She was too old for a crush. Or would it be crushes? Whatever. She'd apparently lost her mind.

Forty minutes later, the vehicle rolled to a stop before the Blakesbury Hotel. A uniformed doorman rushed towards them while Dana gawked at the five-story building like a gauche bumpkin. Her company, Cranston Enterprises, hadn't scrimped on their accommodations. The Blakesbury was top notch.

To her surprise, Christopher jumped out of the car and opened her door. She glanced at his outstretched hand then tentatively placed hers in it. A strange spark rocketed up her arm. What the hell? Her eyes went wide and she swallowed looking away from his deep brown eyes.

Was that interest in his gaze?

You're crazy, Dana. She glanced again and whatever she'd seen was gone. She chided herself that it had probably never been there. Desperate... Was that what she was? Not good. Perhaps she should visit the bar tonight and find a nice older gentleman to spend the evening with. Yeah, someone more suited to her age might fuck away this idiotic craving over her colleagues.

Sudden confidence filled her and she grinned as she straightened and smoothed her clothing. Excitement trilled through her as her heels clicked on the walkway. Getting laid might just do the trick.

Jason watched the sway of Dana's hips and wondered how the hell he would survive this weekend if she refused to spend any time with them. Christopher's arm slung around his shoulder as his friend tilted his head and watched their colleague's progress into the building.

He released a dramatic sigh.

"Buck up, Mate," Christopher said. "The weekend's young. She'll come around."

Christopher always knew what he was thinking. Not surprising since they'd been research partners since college.

"Young might just be the problem," he replied. "I don't want to fuck this up. Our research—"

"Don't worry about our funding. We've worked too hard to mess up now...besides, no one's as close to the leukaemia cure as we are. They need our brains."

They both knew being close was still a million miles away, but Jason nodded anyway. "And Dana's. They need Dana's brain. Maybe we shouldn't go through with this... If she gets pissed and runs, we'll be on the carpet."

She didn't know it, but her research might just be the key needed to break the code he and Christopher had been deciphering for so long.

He grabbed his suitcase from the boot of the car and turned to find Christopher staring at him.

"What?"

His friend shook his head. "I'm just wondering who the hell you are. What have you done with Jason? Who planned this trip and underhandedly got Dana hooked in? Who practically writes sonnets about her legs? Who growls when another man talks to her?"

"All of those things apply to you too. Look, I'm not wussing out...I'm just being cautious."

The growl Christopher had mentioned rose in Jason's throat as he glanced towards the electronic doors in the front hotel. Dana stood there, flirting with the doorman—a bloke who appeared ten years her senior. Christopher grabbed the back of his shirt as he started forward.

"Easy, mate. She's not really interested in him. Look at the way she's got her arms crossed in front of her."

Jason took a deep breath.

He knew the plan...there was a plan. Before tonight ended, Dana would know exactly how they felt. And where they wanted her.

His arms fairly trembled with the need to hold her. Be patient, Christopher had advised—damn his minor in psychology. And he'd been right, but it hadn't been easy. The first moment he'd seen her, he'd wanted her. It had been like a knife to the chest to discover she was married. Bollocks! Then he'd felt like a wretch when he'd wanted to cheer over her divorce. Of course at the same time, he'd wanted to strangle that idiot in America for causing her pain.

Dana seemed to come through it okay, though some of her vibrancy had faded. He wanted to return the glimmer to her eyes. He knew he could. He saw traces of it whenever they spoke...or touched...or he caught her looking his way.

It was that spark which had precipitated this plan. The big wigs from Cranston Industries headquarters, the company for which they worked, were flying in tomorrow for a day, which was why the group was meeting in London rather than the small town which housed the subsidiary offices. There wasn't time for the cross-country drive north.

Seeing an opportunity, he'd outlined the reasons why Dana needed to be involved in the trip and why her research should meld with his and Christopher's...not an untruth which made the plan all the more viable.

The thing was...the project was dear to him, but truth be told, his need for Dana overrode all but the most deep-seated of his concerns over the project.

He swallowed as she peeked over her shoulder now. "Are you coming?"

Not yet.

Christopher paused as Jason started after Dana into the building. As much as he chided his friend, he too had reservations about this weekend. Jason wanted to find the cure because his mother had died from leukaemia. He on the other hand had something to prove.

It didn't escape his attention that Jason was treated as the brains of their operation, while he was viewed as the tagalong companion. What else should a bad boy expect? Despite his attempts at respectability, he couldn't shake that tag...

Bu Dana didn't view him like that. He loved her easy, teasing grin. His cock twitched at the grin she'd shot over her shoulder. She was up to something. He studied her sexy walk while he wondered what was going on in that head of hers.

If you'd get your eyes off her ass, you might figure it out, ignorant git.

The car pulled from the kerb and Christopher hurried to meet his colleagues in reception. "We have one room listed," the man at the desk said to Jason and Dana as Christopher joined them. He placed his hand casually on Dana's back, the silk of her shirt smooth beneath his palm. He smothered the urge to trace the ridge from her bra with his fingertips.

"Oh for God's sake," Dana muttered. "How cliché is that? You're kidding me right."

Her breathing accelerated beneath his hand and there was no mistaking the rapid beat of her heart. A quick glance showed she wasn't particularly angry. Excitement, then?

"There should be two rooms," Christopher said. "I have the confirmation if you need it. Two rooms, already paid in full by our company."

The clerk blinked at him, then started tapping away at his computer again. A few minutes later—unfortunately—he supplied the keys for *two* rooms on two different floors. It wasn't what he wanted but it was the right thing. Dumb though, because if he and Jason had their way, they'd only be using one room anyway.

Dana turned to them at the lift. "See you tomorrow morning. Shall we meet in the lobby?"

"You sure you don't want to see the sights?" Jason replied. "It's not so late that we couldn't get tickets for a show."

She laughed and shook her head. "No, you two go ahead. Have fun. The old lady of the group is gonna rest."

Christopher scowled. Dana was anything but old. She might have a few years on him and Jason, but good lord, she didn't look a day older. He'd never known a woman to pull off sexy and classy with the flare with which Dana did. Everywhere she went she garnered glances from men, and they weren't just benders admiring her glossy brown hair in its bouncy cut nor the brand of her killer high-heel shoes. Christopher couldn't have guessed at the brand, all he knew was that they were hard-on specials. Just a glance at her long legs, accentuated by the spiky shoes, and his cock went to instant attention…like now.

He adjusted his garment bag to hang partially over his crotch. What was it about her that made him want to bang all day—and night—long? He wasn't some randy teenager. He'd outgrown this sort of nearly uncontrollable need years ago.

"You're going to stay in your room all night, then?" he asked in disbelief.

A faint pink tinge spilled up her cheeks. "Uh…" She looked away and he knew she had a plan that didn't include her two co-workers or staying all night in her room. "Mostly. If I feel like it later, I'll come down and get something…to eat."

Eat? Right.

Jason glanced at him over her head. *Now what?* his gaze seemed to say.

"All right, luv," Christopher agreed, though it was the last thing he wanted. "We'll catch you later. Ring us up if you're not so knackered later."

Jason turned on him as soon as the lift's doors closed, shutting Dana away from them. "Bloody hell! What was that? I could have convinced her."

"Did you really want to drag her out to show her Buckingham Palace, Big Ben and the Thames?" Christopher laughed. Jason had it bad. He'd never seen him this overwrought. Not Mr. Charming. No, normally he could seduce a woman out of her knickers in five point two seconds—unless her name was Dana Matthews.

"No but I don't want to spend the night playing naughts and crosses, either."

Good lord, neither did he.

Chapter Two

A hot bath, some hot thoughts, perhaps a quick but hot finger-fuck and maybe she'd relax. She needed to forget the idea of sex with Christopher and Jason. They were her co-workers, for God's sake. She might need affirmation that she was still a sensual woman, but not with them. Trouble was, she didn't really want anyone else, even if it was career suicide.

She just needed to keep this obsession to herself. They didn't need to know.

Four hours in a car with them was about three hours fifty-five minutes too long. Their presence had seemed to fill the vehicle while their scents...

Their colognes were different yet similar with woodsy under-notes which mixed with their natural aromas to knock her off balance. It was such an intoxicating blend of...man. Her sex throbbed as she recalled it. He ex's scent had never spurred such arousal. It was namby pamby at best and didn't inspire thoughts of being dragged up against a warm, hard chest. Or two.

She grinned. She was so bad, imagining both Christopher and Jason at once. Fucking the two of them had been the theme of her fantasies for months and she didn't reckon that would change any time soon. There was something decidedly naughty about the idea of taking her pleasure with two men...but the fact that they were both ten years her junior titillated her senses beyond reason. She chuckled. In her dreams they could be her boy toys.

Mmm...yeah. Her own personal boy toys ripe for her bidding. She liked that.

Slowly, she unbuttoned her shirt. Her eyes drifted shut as she thought of Jason, his intent chocolate brown eyes filled with passion as he reached for her while Christopher reached for his fly. Jason would be the unbuttoning type. Christopher would be a ripper. Since she didn't want to ruin her blouse, she went with the least destructive.

His fingers would graze her breasts as he slowly pushed one pearlised button after another through the holes. Her breath caught as knuckles brushed her skin. Her nipples tightened without being touched and suddenly her lacy, underwire bra seemed too tight. A sigh trembled from between her lips as her top slipped down her arms and floated to the bathroom's tiled floor to land beside the skirt she'd discarded earlier.

Moisture flooded her pussy, lubricating the folds she'd soon caress. Moaning, she cupped her breasts enclosed in Victoria's Secret's finest. Sexy lingerie was her secret indulgence and one she'd never fed when she'd been with her ex. He didn't care what she wore...she did. Now she bought what she wanted and what she wanted was naughty panties and bras. No one else saw them but they made her feel good.

Her cream seeped into the silk over her sex as she imagined her boy toys seeing what she wore beneath her suits. One hand drifted down over her slightly rounded belly. She ran her palm over the garter holding up her stocking. Christopher would kneel in front of her and run his hands over her silk encased legs. Of the two, he was the more tactile. She'd nearly gone through the roof when he'd put his hand on her back earlier. Only a bite to the inside of her lip had stopped a moan and the urge to beg him to slide his hand south.

She did moan now as she tormented her nipple with one hand and pushed the fingers of the other beneath her satin and lace panties. Sensations shot between her breasts and pussy, making her thighs tremble. The muscled in her abdomen tightened as heat coiled in her womb and her body readied for an impending explosion.

Not yet. She wanted this to last. She wanted to be so sated that she wouldn't think of Jason and Christopher for a few hours. Like that would happen...but she happily deluded herself while she slipped her fingers through her nether curls. Her folds were slippery as she leisurely stroked through them turned on by how *turned on* she was. She flicked over her clit, shuddering as lightning surged through her.

She jumped as a knock rattled on her door. She struggled from the sexual haze which had enveloped her. Spinning, she spied the white courtesy robe left out by the hotel's housekeeping. Slipping into the voluminous garment, she tied the belt tightly around her waist and kicked off her heels. The knock came again accompanied by a deep, "Room service."

She sighed. Christopher. What timing. What would he think if he knew she'd been fantasising about him touching her just moments before? After flipping open the deadbolt, she swung open the door. Her eyes went wide at the sight of not one but both of her companions outside the door. They'd changed and were now dressed in faded, low slung jeans and T-shirts which clung to their muscled curves. Damn, these men didn't look like scientists...they looked like models. Hot, well-developed models.

They crowded into her room before she could stop them, and Jason pushed shut the door. He held a champagne glass in his hand. She realised that Christopher did as well— actually, he had two glasses and a bottle of bubbly. Where the hell had they gotten that? She'd wager it was even chilled.

"We thought maybe you'd like a drink," he said, reaching to set the glasses and bottle on the counter just beyond her. Jason's followed.

She shook her head, her heart starting an erratic pounding rhythm. "Guys, this isn't a good idea—"

"It's a perfect idea," Christopher responded, stepping close so that the space between them disappeared. So did her air. She couldn't breathe. She couldn't think. The sexual haze returned, clouding her vision.

"And a long time coming..." Jason added, taking her trembling hand. His lips closed over her fingers as Christopher's mouth covered hers. All thoughts of saying no, all reasons to deny this, disappeared. She wrapped her free arm around Christopher's neck. Lifting on her toes, she opened for his thrusting tongue while she pressed her breasts to his chest. The thick terrycloth stymied feeling him fully, but it couldn't disguise the hard planes pushing at her nipples.

"Mmm, what's this I taste?" Jason growled. "Naughty, naughty girl. Having a bit of fun were we?"

Dana's eyes went wide as she realised which fingers he'd sucked into his mouth. Oh man...her drenched folds trembled. This was really happening. They were really here, together, taking what they wanted and what she'd wanted to give them for so long. She moaned into Christopher's mouth as her eyes closed again.

"Thinking of us?" Christopher asked against her lips.

"Yes," she replied without thinking. Embarrassment shot through her and she tried to pull from them, but Christopher's grip around her waist was like iron as was Jason's hold on her wrist.

"Don't be embarrassed, luv," Christopher said. "We've wanted you too. Late at night, alone in my bed, I've thought of your lush thighs embracing me. Your sweet body pressed to mine while I lose myself in you."

She felt hands at the robe's belt then cool air as the garment fell open. A hand splayed over her belly.

"We've tried to be subtle. That hasn't worked," Jason said, his fingers inched lower. "Now it's time for hard and fast. Say no. If you don't want this, say no now." His breath riffled the fine tendrils of hair at her temple while his fingertips probed just below her waistband. "Say it now, before it's too late."

Christopher pulled back a fraction of an inch. She gasped for breath, feeling his heat and Jason's hand ever so close to where she wanted to feel them both.

"I can't," she replied. "Don't...stop..."

This was insanity. She should make them leave her room. They should forget any of this happened. What happens in London, stays in London and all that...

It could. They could have this weekend then go home and forget it ever happened. She'd wanted a fling. Here was one readymade.

"I need to see you," Christopher announced. He took a step back and she fought the urge to cover herself. They wanted her, she guessed they should see what they were getting. She bit her lip...would they think she was too fat? Guys like them could have skinny Miss Skeezy Pants types instead of a more rounded, older type like her.

Or would they think she was too wanton? A horny Mrs. Robinson type? She could only imagine what they'd see as they looked at her in her sexy lingerie with the robe draped on her arms where it had caught on the crooks of her elbows. She straightened her arms and let it fall to the floor.

"Bloody hell..." Jason murmured, his words sounding more like a prayer than a curse.

"Yeah..." Christopher enjoined. "Dana, I've never...you're so...Christ..."

Her lips turned up at the corners, but the grin faded as Jason closed in on her. She couldn't smile in the face of the lust lurching through her. She could barely do anything but feel.

Jason swung her into his arms. "I want to taste more of you — directly from the source."

"Oh God," she breathed.

"What are your thoughts on bondage?" Christopher asked behind them.

"Uh..." Thoughts? She was supposed to have thoughts?

"Being tied up. Ravaged by the two randy men you've tormented for six months."

"I didn't—"

"Oh yes you have," Jason interrupted. "Your fuck me shoes, your sexy walk, the disapproving glances when we cut up...not giving us the time of day even when we try to woo you with candy bars and daisies."

"I didn't realise—"

"And to think you've been hiding these lovely lacy things beneath your clothes. Definitely a naughty naughty woman."

Flashes of their now obvious courting bombarded her. How on earth had she missed that?

"Very naughty," Christopher added. "I think she'll most definitely need to be tied up."

"Christopher is into a little bondage," Jason whispered. He winked. "I guess I am too."

"Okay?" she squeaked, her answer more of a question. They wanted to tie her up? And do what? If she was restrained, they'd be able to do whatever the hell they wanted.

Her heat level knocked upward several notches. She'd never fantasised about that...

Jason set her on her feet facing the bed, while Christopher sat on the edge, his legs bracketing hers. Moving behind her, Jason skimmed his hands lightly over her back. "So smooth," he told her as his fingers went to the clasp of her bra. Tingles raced through her like an uncontrolled shiver, vibrating from the epicentre in her core. She loved to be touched and if anything, it had been what she'd missed most since coming to England. The touching. The closeness.

The two men crowded close, pushing aside the aloneness which had plagued her. Warmth from their presence flooded over her. "Cup your breasts, baby," Jason said behind her. Show Christopher what you do when you're all alone and thinking of us."

Staring into Christopher's eyes, she lifted her hands and did as Jason instructed. The full globes weighed heavily in her palms. She hoped they didn't sag too much, that they found them attractive, that at least one of them would fuck her soon...

Jason's hands came up beneath hers and tightened on her hands. "Squeeze those pretty pink nipples." She pulled on the tips, whimpering as another wave of arousal flooded to her pussy. Each time she rolled the hard peaks, her body responded until her legs trembled beneath her.

Christopher leaned back on his elbows and watched her. His hand drifted to his fly, running over the hard arousal there. His eyes seemed completely black, his breathing ragged. "God, I want to fuck you."

Good. Because she wanted nothing more. She stared at him, never breaking her gaze as she danced her fingers over her nipples.

Suddenly, Jason tipped her forward and she landed on Christopher's chest, pushing them both into the mattress. He chuckled and hooked his hands beneath her arms, sliding downward towards her hands. Grasping her wrists, he pulled her arms wide until she was trapped and couldn't push upward from her position. Every hard ridge of his youthful body pressed into her.

"Bondage," he murmured into her hair, his fingers tightening slightly on her wrists. "At our mercy."

A tremor went through her.

"You like that, don't you?" he asked.

Did she? Her cream was about to escape her panties and trickle down her legs. She nodded, pressing her burning face in his neck.

"Dana, look at me."

Slowly, she lifted her head and gazed into his dark eyes.

"I want to see every reaction. I want to see your pleasure."

Jason splayed his hand on her back. The pressure urged her sex against Christopher's pelvis. She imagined riding the obviously large cock hidden inside his pants, the wanton images pushing her arousal to new heights. She'd never felt like this!

"Relax," Jason said as he smoothed his hands along her legs. He toyed with the top of her stocking. "I like these. Hot. You know what will be hotter?"

"No," she choked as his fingers hooked in her panties, dragging them down.

Christopher stared directly at her. Was it possible to fuck someone with a gaze…? Because he was doing it. He nipped her bottom lip never breaking the eye contact. She trembled, trying not to look away.

"When they're coated with your release…and ours," Christopher rasped. An involuntary whimper escaped her and he captured it with his lips, hungrily taking her mouth and feasting as if he'd never tasted a woman before.

"Spread your legs farther apart," Jason gently ordered, his voice distant as Christopher ravaged her mouth and sent her senses spinning. She automatically complied, gasping when Christopher slipped his knees beneath her legs and pushed them apart, spreading her wide.

This was bondage as she'd never imagined. Restrained and spread wide not by ropes or steel, but by flesh.

Held wide, she couldn't flinch away when Jason licked the inside of her thigh, starting at the silk and working his way to her pussy. Parting her with his thumbs, he slashed his tongue along her folds. A near orgasm tumbled over her as she cried out, her hips jerking beneath the pleasure.

"Yes, luv," Christopher whispered. "Give over to him. Let him taste your sweet cream. I love the sounds you make as you cry more. The way you tremble in our arms. We want everything you have."

What the hell had happened here? The boy toys she'd fantasised about were now here in the flesh and giving her orders. She hadn't considered this scenario. In her thoughts, she'd always been the one in charge even though in reality, that was the last thing she'd wanted.

Jason's wide shoulders brushed her upper thighs. "So wet," he murmured as he dragged his thumbs along her dewy folds. "And hot." He pushed two fingers into her sheath, stretching the tight muscles. It had been so long. Even before she and her husband had parted, it had been months since they'd slept together.

"Baby, I can't wait to feel you squeeze my cock and milk every bit of my cum from me."

Her eyes went wide and Christopher chuckled, the movement of his chest causing his shirt to chafe her nipples. "Didn't your ex talk dirty?"

"I don't think he knew how," she managed, though right now she couldn't remember his name. She barely remembered hers. Jason's fingers pushed in and out of her. Her back arched as she reached for more pleasure. He pressed his mouth to her, drawing her clit between his lips, and she couldn't contain her shriek. Release pulsed over her and shot dagger-like pleasure through her limbs.

Relentlessly, he continued to fuck her with his fingers while he lapped her escaping fluid. "Mmm, so good," he said.

Pulling his fingers from her, he reached up until they touched her lips. She froze. She'd never…

But this was all new. Tentatively, she parted her lips and sucked her juices from his fingers, surprised by the tangy, not unpleasant taste. Her tongue darted along his knuckles, cleaning every bit away and caressing the flesh as if it was his cock. He groaned when she flicked his fingertips. He jerked away his hand. "You'll make me lose it."

"My turn," Christopher said before she could respond with a cheeky comment. She thought he'd tumble her onto the mattress and dive between her legs, instead, his hand knotted in her hair and he dragged her down for another kiss, sweeping his tongue inside to gather the taste of her cream.

Then he did tumble her over beneath him. Her arms went around his shoulders and she realised he'd released her. Pressing her heels onto the edge of the mattress, she moved towards the middle of the bed. Christopher followed. His hands were everywhere.

To her surprise, she felt Jason's hands too as he unbuttoned Christopher's pants and pulled down the zipper. She pulled her mouth away from Christopher as his pants were tugged down.

"You two are…" *Gay? They couldn't be.*

"Not bloody likely," Jason muttered.

"No, not exactly," Christopher panted, using the break to yank off his shirt.

"Then how exactly?"

He stroked his fingers down her cheek. He continued to her shoulder and then to her breasts. His thumbs stroked over the taut peaks, sending shards of delight through her. She pressed upward into his touch, wanting more. Her breath caught as he pinched one tip.

"Luv, neither us is into men. My hands were busy, and Jason is impatient. He wants me to get on with it, so he can…get on with it."

He knelt between her knees, his impressive erection rising from a thatch of wiry, dark blond curls, his jeans bunched around his knees.

Jesus, he was hot.

Her lips twitched and she tried for the disapproving school marm look she gave them when they were horsing around at work. "I'm not fucking you with your pants shoved to your knees like a teenager sneaking his first sex."

"No?"

Okay. Maybe she would. She lifted her knees and braced her feet apart to welcome him inside. It smacked of illicit sex, quick and hot…not that she really wanted it quick.

Christopher grinned that wicked smiled that always made her crazy with need. "I think you'd like it."

She thought he was probably right. Her garters and stockings, his worn jeans and muscles, reminded her of the old fantasy of the socialite and the handyman. She had a few things she'd like him to fix and she knew just where he could put his tool. She reached for Christopher, even more turned on than she'd been before.

"I want you to fuck me. Hard."

"I want you to wear these," Jason said and she suddenly realised he'd disappeared and returned. Now, he sauntered from the bathroom, her shoes dangling from his fingers. "I want to fuck you in your 'fuck-me' shoes."

She bit her lip, lifting a foot up beside Christopher's side. He grasped her ankle, holding it up. Jason slowly slipped on the first heel, stroking his fingers up her calf. He gently placed her foot back on the bed. They repeated the process with the other foot.

Amazement duelled with her arousal. No one had ever treated her with such care. And she'd certainly never thought anyone would be turned on by her footwear. She pressed her heels into the blankets feeling sexy and naughty and well…wanted. In marriage she'd felt like a commodity, like electricity or running water. Christopher and Jason made her feel like a rare delicacy.

Looking into Christopher's eyes, she lifted her hips and traced her pussy with her fingers. "I want you here. Please…" she whispered.

He leaned forward, the tip of his cock parting her folds. "Oh balls," he swore.

"What?"

"Condom... Luv, you have me so worked up, I almost forgot. I never forget."

She smiled smugly as he pulled a square of plastic from his pocket and ripped it open with his teeth. So she'd made him forget? A worthy, if dangerous, goal to repeat.

Reaching between them, he parted her. He surged forward. She cried out in unison with him as he seated himself to the hilt, filling her with one forceful stroke. Even as her body adjusted to his wide cock, she loved the feel of every inch. Filling her. Stretching her. Claiming her.

He began a driving rhythm, pushing deeply with each thrust. Beside her, Jason shoved down his pants and climbed onto the bed. She drew him closer with an arm around his waist. The head of his cock bobbed before her face and she took him between her lips. Her tongue swirled along the underside, pressing the ridge there as she worked up and down the shaft with the same momentum as Christopher's shoved in and out of her pussy.

"Blood hell, Chris. I can feel you pounding her," Jason gasped.

And if feels so good, she thought, never slowing. Her awareness split as she met Christopher's thrusts, yet paid equal attention to Jason. His hands buried in her hair, pulling slightly as she moved. And she loved it. She wanted more and more of their possession. More and more of their youthful abandon.

She moaned around the cock in her mouth as the one below stroked across her sensitised tissues. Tension balled in her womb, small tendrils reaching for release. The strands continually tried to break free and explode through her body only to be reined in at her edge. Her orgasm trembled there. Almost...almost...

Her lips clamped around Jason as he fucked her mouth, the head of his cock sliding along the roof of her mouth on one push and pressing against her tongue on another.

"Oh baby. Oh my God..." he cried as she increased her suction, lightly scraping him with her teeth then soothing the hard length with flicks from her tongue. He stiffened as he shoved deep, one last time. Cum sprayed down her throat and she swallowed convulsively, struggling to swallow his salty tribute.

She licked her lips and smiled as he pulled free. Breathing heavily, he lay down beside her and kissed her. His hand pressed over her belly and she almost screamed as the sensation of Christopher's pummelling intensified. Her breaths gasped from her as Jason abandoned her mouth and moved to her ear.

"Do you know how hot you are? Letting both of us fuck you? I can feel your belly quivering beneath my hand. You're about to lose it, aren't you?"

She whimpered, his words focusing her being on her pussy and Christopher's cock.

"It's coming isn't it?" Jason continued. "You're going to squeeze him until he can barely move. Those tight little muscles I felt are going to suck him dry."

She panted, her hand unconsciously going to her breast, squeezing the mount, and sliding up to pinch her nipple.

Jason nipped her earlobe. "I can't wait to be inside you, too. I'll fuck you until you writhe for release but I won't stop...not until you're screaming out your second...or third orgasm. Then I'll fuck your ass, but I won't wear a condom. I'm gonna fill you with my cum."

She screeched, his words shoving her over the edge as she lurched upward onto Christopher's cock, her pussy slamming into his groin. A wildfire of sensation raced through her as her whole body convulsed in rapid-fire explosions.

"Yes, you like that. Squeeze him. End him. So I can have my turn."

Her head shook from side to side as Christopher continued to piston in and out of her fisting cunt. She couldn't take more. How could Jason talk about more? A second orgasm followed on the heels of the first. Her body gushed around him, soaking his pelvis and her thighs.

"Oh yeah, luv," he groaned. "Feels so good." His fingers tightened on her hips. He kept going.

"Baby, he's almost there," Jason rasped. "His teeth are gritted. The tendons in his neck are tight. Look at the muscles in his arms."

She could barely see for the sexual haze over her. When she looked up, Christopher's dark eyes stared down at her, his chest heaving. Captured in his gaze, another release took her. Her fingers fisted in the pillows as she cried out. Wave after wave of pleasure washing over her.

He groaned, deep from his chest, and slammed forward one last time. Drained he fell to the side. Jason immediately took his place.

"No," Dana gasped, her head rocking on the pillows. She couldn't take more.

"Yes," Jason hissed his wide cock sliding into her still convulsing passage. New pleasure shot through her as he slowly eased in and out of her.

"Yes..." she sighed. Her body calmed slightly.

"Baby, you feel so good." He turned so she was over him. She gasped as he slid deeper. He grasped her ass urging her to move. Cautiously, she moved feeling exposed in this position. There was no hiding anything that bounced or jiggled or sagged. She was distantly aware of Christopher moving from the bed.

"Harder," Jason muttered. "God you're beautiful. Ride my cock. Fuck me." She did, but he met her stroke for stroke, surging his hips upward and grasping her hips to pull her down on him. Her thighs burned, the sensation travelling up in to her ass then her pussy, heating her and driving her wild.

The bed depressed behind her and she felt Christopher against her back. His hands worked over her body, caressing her, cupping her breasts and rolling her nipples. One hand drifted down to rub her clit. She cried out wildly and reached her arms behind her to hug his body close. She closed her eyes, feeling the sensation of Christopher's pubic and thigh hair abrading her ass as she bounced up and down Jason's cock, ever mindful not to get too wild or she'd stab her thigh with the heels she still wore. Reaching down, she pulled them off, flinging them aside, then embraced Christopher again.

She felt his hand working between them, stroking the crack of her ass and slowly working between the globes. She stiffened as his fingertip circled her anus.

"Relax, luv. I won't hurt you," he said. He kissed her shoulder. He tossed a small packet on the bed beside them about the same time she realised his fingertip was slippery and he was working it past her ring of untried muscles. She went rigid and his teeth sank into her shoulder. She jerked at the pain, even as she was aroused by his primal move.

And his finger was all the way in her.

He'd bitten her as a distraction. Bad bad man. Sliding her hand down, she pinched his ass in retribution. Wild ribbons of illicit pleasure wove through her as she journeyed a path she'd never taken...riding one man...another's fingers—at least two now—in her ass. Christopher mimicked her rhythm over Jason, plunging and withdrawing in time to each stroke.

Who was this wanton woman?

Invigorated, she leaned forward on all fours over Jason, slamming down on his cock and grinding her pelvis to his with each downward drive.

"Faster," Christopher urged.

Jason's lips clamped over one nipple, pulling and tugging as she rocked. His teeth grazed the sensitive peak and he soothed it with his tongue the way she had with his cock.

Thought slipped away and she became a ball of sensation. Bodies, hands and mouths became like one. All she knew was the pleasure arcing over her like electric surges dancing over her skin and through her blood. Orgasm after orgasm wrung from her as she cried out hoarsely. She may have screamed. She didn't know. She was vaguely aware of Jason stiffening beneath her, his cum spraying inside her. Their hot fluid coated his cock and dripped from them as he continued to move.

The pungent aroma of sex filled the air. Dana wanted it to fill her, further arouse her senses. Behind her, Christopher withdrew his fingers and left her to complete her ride with only Jason's cock filling her. Another mild release riffled through her before she collapsed on Jason's chest.

She slid sideways onto the mattress, exhausted, her fluid and Jason's cum running onto her thighs.

"Oh my God," she mumbled.

"Yeah," Christopher replied.

"You didn't wear a condom," she said, vaguely indifferent to the knowledge. Shouldn't she care? Too much effort right now. She'd care in the morning.

"Mumps," Jason murmured. "Sterile...and clean."

"Sorry."

"It's cool. Christopher's fine...when we decide to be parents. Makes sex easier for me."

"Mmm...we'll have to do that again." But not now...she couldn't move.

"At your command," Jason panted.

"Whenever you want," Christopher said at the same time.

Together, the men pulled her up the bed to lay properly on the bed instead of sprawled across the middle.

She smiled, burrowing her head into the pillows as Christopher snuggled into her front, his thigh between hers, and Jason spooned her back. Her boy toys...

Her brow furrowed. But how long could she keep up with them?

Didn't matter. This was a weekend fling. Before she knew it, they'd be on to whatever young thing caught their eye and she'd have some great memories.

She squeezed shut her eyes as overwhelming pain hollowed her middle. How would she bear it?

"How long before you're ready again?" she asked. Tonight was about sex...tomorrow about business and Sunday about going home. Until then, she didn't want to think.

Chapter Three

Dana slowly came awake. It took her a moment to remember she wasn't at home in her own bed. It took her a few seconds longer to remember why two heavy weights crossed her middle, holding her securely.

Jason and Christopher. Last night had been...

She had no words for it and for once in her life she wasn't going to do the scientist thing and analyze it to death. They'd fucked her like crazy and she was still tingling.

And she needed a shower. She shifted, feeling her legs stick slightly from their secretions. Um, yeah. She needed a shower bad.

She carefully scooted from between the two men who instantly snuggled together like puppies. She couldn't suppress a grin. If they were into ménage, then they had to be used to touching each other once in a while in non-sexual ways. The two of them were so adorable she wanted to take a picture. They wouldn't appreciate that.

Tucking the sight away in her head, she padded into the bathroom and quietly shut the door. Carefully, she peeled away her stockings, thinking they weren't so hot now that they were sticking to her skin. After tossing them on the counter, she turned on the water in the shower. While the temperature adjusted, she set out her towel and put her toiletries in the enclosure then stepped inside.

Stinging needles of water pummelled her already sensitised skin. She sighed and relaxed beneath the spray, though she hurried so she could return to her lovers. In just a few minutes, she switched off the faucet and reached for her towel. And found bare porcelain.

Shoving the hair from her eyes, she scanned the floor. No towel. And the door was open.

"Who took my towel?" she yelled. She reached for one off the rack over the toilet and found empty metal. "Hey! Who took all the towels?"

Jason appeared in the doorway, naked, his arms crossed over his chest. "Come on out, baby. We'll dry you off."

Christopher stepped beside him, taking the same stance. The two of them blocked the doorway, two muscle-bound gods with erect penises. "I woke up hugging Jason," Christopher groused. "Not cool."

"I didn't mind you kissing my shoulder."

Christopher shoved him. "Shut up."

Jason made a face, clearly having won the match and turned back to Dana. "You left the bed without permission. Seems like grounds for punishment."

Permission?

"Come along," Christopher said, crooking his finger. "We'll get you dry, luv. Then wet."

Dana stared at them from the shower. Her skin was getting a trifle chilled while her insides were heating up and melting, ready for more fun with her men. And they were...men...regardless of what she called them in self defence. And that's what it was when she called them boy toys. It was her way to make sleeping with two men ten years her junior acceptable in her eyes—as a fling, but nothing more.

"I'm going to need another shower," she said dryly.

"Hopefully." Christopher tilted his head. "Are you going to come along, or shall I come and get you?"

Oh the choices. She'd be happy with either.

Pushing her hair from her eyes again, she lifted her head and straightened her shoulders, then stepped regally from the shower. They parted as she reached them. Grabbing their cocks, she continued walking and pulled them into the sleeping area.

She let go of them and crossed her arms beneath her breasts.

Christopher reached for a towel. There were several others wadded up nearby, leading her to believe the guys had done a little clean-up of their own while she'd been showering. She expected him to dry her but instead Jason guided her towards an overstuffed chair on the far side of the room. Gently, he bent her over the padded arm. When she moved to plant her arms in front of her, he pulled them behind her and tied her wrists with something that dangled over her buttocks. A glance revealed one of her stockings. It trailed over her rapidly drying skin, tickling her as she squirmed.

They were serious about the bondage.

Before she could contemplate the implications and what might come next, the other stocking covered her eyes, but instead of immediately tying it behind her head, Jason looped it around and ran the two ends between her parted lips before he tied the ends behind her. Dampness having nothing to do with her shower flooded to her cleft. Dana whimpered behind her gag, wondering what the hell she'd gotten into.

Trepidation and excitement merged as she waited for Christopher and Jason's next move.

She was surprised when fluffy, soft fabric rubbed over her body. One of the men guided her back to standing and whoever wielded the towel, worked it over her torso and then her legs, avoiding her pussy. The process was repeated on her back.

A moment later, she heard the thump of the damp fabric hitting the floor. Large hands bent over the chair again. No, over knees. One of them sat in the chair now and she was lying over his thighs.

"Legs apart," one of them said, his voice rough and unrecognisable. She complied knowing her cunt must glisten with her arousal.

She had no way of knowing which man was where. Neither spoke again nor gave any indication.

A hand stroked her ass and she shuddered. She hadn't been spanked since she'd been a small child but she'd read things...titillating things about it. She moaned hoping it would happen quickly. Surely that was what they intended.

The draping tails from the stocking tied around her wrists were lifted and dropped onto her back. Suddenly the hand was gone only to return a moment later with a resounding smack against her buttocks. Despite the sound, the spank wasn't particularly hard. Still, needles of pain prickled from the spot. She cried out but the sound had barely escaped her when the hand landed again and again.

The pain mutated quickly, transforming to heat which flooded through her. She rose up, offering her behind for more as pleasure began to fill her. Again she wondered who this wanton woman was who gave herself with such abandon to these men. Whoever she was, Dana liked her. She wanted to remain as this woman who was far removed from the prude she'd been as a married woman.

The blows continued, hard enough that she could feel them but light enough that she had no doubt she'd be able to sit through their meeting this afternoon. She wanted more.

All at once, the spanking came from the other direction and she knew the other man had taken over. His hand fell more heavily and seemed to cover more of her bottom. She moaned and squirmed as heat from it travelled upward into her back and downward to her pussy. She longed to press her legs together and relieve the tension and need in her sex.

Two legs braced hers apart when she started to move and she groaned in frustration. She needed... She needed to be fucked.

Again? After all the times they had last night? Yes. Hard and fast, thankfully, just like Christopher and Jason seemed to like it.

Instead, she received another stroke against her ass.

She shrieked when sudden cold replaced the heat. Slowly, an ice cube was dragged over her burning flesh. When it was gone, another replaced it. Her torturer made lazy trails over each buttock, tracing the underside before travelling down to her thighs. She tried to squirm away as another cube travelled up her thigh. An arm held her in place.

Cool tendrils of water ran down her as the ice continued to melt. She flinched when cube traced the centre of her sex. The cold seemed at first unbearable. As it pressed inward, the sensation turned to pleasure. The deft fingers pressed a new piece of ice over her clit, then worked it into her throbbing channel. The fingers remained, pushing in and out of her.

She squirmed, her passage flooding with the melting water and her cream. What would it feel like to have Christopher or

Jason's fiery cock ploughing into her chilled passage? How long before she found out?

Two more fingers probed her ass and she felt a chill unrelated to the ice as lubricant was worked in and out of her tight passage. Slowly, something unfamiliar probed that area, slowly sliding in until it popped into place, the base pressing her buttocks.

A butt plug? No way!

Again she was shifted, until she lay across the arm of the chair again. Her shoulders rested against the seat and she turned her head, waiting. Excitement pulsed through her, and despite the ice, her body was heated. She sighed in pleasure as a cock pressed to her entrance. Slowly it slipped inside.

God how she wished they'd talk. Still their anonymous, silent actions turned her on more than she would have ever thought. Why had she ever thought of them as boy toys or thought she could take control of this liaison? She never had been. They were. And they were showing her now in their slow, seduction of her senses and possession of her body.

She trembled as she submitted to whatever they wanted. Her thighs quivered and she wanted to beg them to fuck her hard just the way she liked it. She whimpered, pushing against the wide head of the arousal parting the slippery folds at her entrance.

Jason she decided as he surged forward. She hadn't heard the rattle of a condom being opened. His shaft speared though her sensitive tissues. It was so full. She hadn't imagined how the butt plug would press against her passage and double her sensations. Mindlessly, she tried to get more of him as he pulled back just as rapidly, but she couldn't control anything in this position. Perhaps that was the point. He thrust once, twice more, then suddenly withdrew.

No! He couldn't do this! Tears of frustration filled her eyes as she felt him move to the side.

But then a second cock was there, pushing inside, claiming every centimetre of her tender passage. Again there were two more strokes, and he was gone. No wonder she hadn't heard a condom, Christopher didn't intend to come. Neither of them did.

Over and over they fucked her, neither taking more than a few hard strokes. Nonetheless, the pressure built inside her until she knew her release was imminent. It loomed before her, a gaping door, promising fulfilment.

She wobbled as she was pulled to standing. Two sets of fingers probed her pussy.

"So hot and wet, baby. You want to come?"

They rubbed her clit as she nodded. She had to come. She needed to. This wasn't just about want. One of them pinched the small bud and lightning shot through her. She lurched, a cry trapped in her throat. Her knees gave out and she would have fallen, if not for strong arms holding her upright.

Relentlessly, they tormented the nub, bringing her orgasm after orgasm until she hung weakly in their arms helpless from the pleasure and the need clutching her. On each release, her body called to be filled, but they denied her, giving her what she now recognised as a half-life. Release without true fulfilment. She needed them in her. She needed them over her.

She could never go back to the fantasies she'd used to sustain her.

How had they known her thoughts? How had they known she'd planned to go back to that and try to forget this after the weekend?

But they had known and she couldn't go back.

Finally, they laid her on the bed. Her legs bent over the edge. Her bound arms beneath her lifted her pelvis towards them. She heard a condom wrapper. Christopher. Thank goodness. He lifted her legs, drawing them up so her feet rested on the mattress and she was spread wide for him. With anyone else, she might have tried to squirm away from being displayed. But not with Christopher. Not with Jason.

Christopher ploughed into her so quick and so deep, she didn't have time to breathe. Her release came so quickly, it took her by surprise. Her body clenched around the plug, clenched around Christopher.

The bed sank beside her and she felt Jason lean over her. His mouth fastened on her breast. He pulled at the peak, drawing it deep as she continued to squeeze Christopher's cock — not that it stopped the relentless pistoning or the unbelievable tremors quaking through her. Christopher groaned, driving deep one last time. His fingers dug into her thighs.

Jason's mouth brushed her ear. "You scared us this morning…"

But she was just in the shower.

"You've brushed us off so many times. We thought maybe —"

She shook her head, denying his words.

"Don't push us away anymore, Dana," Christopher enjoined.

"You need to see us for the men we are… We're not kids playing at adulthood."

"We're grown men with grown-up responsibilities, commitments and desires. And we know what we want."

Jason traced a finger between her breasts before splaying his hand over her breastbone. "We want you, Dana. All of you. Your companionship, your body."

"Tell us you want us too, luv."

"We need you, baby."

She nodded her head, shocked, but so full of love for them, she could barely bear it.

They pulled her to her feet again. Wonderment filled her and she speculated on what would come next. God knew. These two surprised her at every turn.

And they did again.

They started dressing her. She tried to shy away. She couldn't dress. She needed to shower again.

Christopher pulled her against his chest and breathed deeply. "I love the smell of your arousal. Just knowing it's because you've fucked us... By tonight I'll be so randy, I might fuck you all night again."

Well who needed sleep anyway?

"And I haven't come yet," Jason added. "Who knows when it might overcome me? I might have to drag you off to a dark corner of the Tube and have my way with you while the trains speed past."

She made a small aroused sound in her throat. Right about now, she probably would let him fuck her in public if he wanted to. She couldn't wait to spend the day with them before rushing back here to meet with the executives flying in from the Cranston Industries headquarters.

The sooner she was dressed, the sooner they could go. She didn't fight as they fastened her garter belt around her waist and helped her into fresh stockings. A skirt followed. Her wrists were released, and a silk blouse slid up her arms and was buttoned. No bra. No panties. Did they expect her to traipse around like this today?

"Don't remove the blindfold, yet," Christopher ordered when she lifted her hands. Obediently, she dropped her arms to her sides. This was the game they were playing and she'd abide by the rules.

A hand patted her ass, running over the end of the plug. "Do you like our present?" Jason asked.

She couldn't respond with her mouth gagged so she lifted a shoulder.

The sound of dressing came to her then the door opening. "After we go, you can take off the blindfold," he said. "Meet us in the lobby in twenty minutes. As you are."

The door closed. Leaving her alone in silence. She stood there for a moment, listening to the sounds of the building. She heard nothing but the tick of the clock on the bedside table.

Lifting her hands, she removed the stocking. She blinked at the sunlight streaming through the far windows. Her room was in shambles and it looked like an orgy had taken place there. She ignored the mess and went directly to the mirror to check her appearance.

Walking was...interesting. Her legs still wobbled—God that had been amazing sex. Each step accentuated the plug in her ass and drew her attention to the play of muscles there. Experimenting, she sat on the edge of the bed. The plug pulled slightly and pressed deeper inside her. A moan tore from her at the wicked pleasure. Was it supposed to feel this way? She'd been wrong about the spanking too. Her buttocks had reminded her of what had happened as soon as she'd sat. Already, she needed to come again, and the pleasure-pain only reminded her of that.

Need or not, she had no desire to bring herself to release. Not after this morning.

She stood and returned to the mirror, gazing at her unfettered breasts behind the white silk blouse. The tips of her nipples poked against the soft fabric. She straightened and the aroused peaks became more evident. If she looked hard enough, she could see the faint shadow of her areola, too. The muscles in her cunt flexed in reaction.

She panted, trying to breathe away her arousal and only succeeded in inhaling the scent of sex. Oh lord! Could she actually leave the room like this? She was a walking bundle of 'fuck me now' energy.

What would her superiors think? She bit her lip and noticed how her eyes sparkled. At the moment, she didn't care what they thought. She was already hired. Her work was valued. They wouldn't fire or demote her for not wearing a bra and only three people in the room would know she wasn't wearing panties.

Thankfully, the plug wasn't visible through her clothes. She couldn't have gone along with that.

This weekend might have started out purely as a business trip, but now it was about Christopher and Jason. For someone who'd always been business minded, it was as if she'd lost her mind.

About time, too.

* * * *

Jason paced the lobby. "How long should we give her?"

Christopher leaned against one of the posts facing the lifts. He glanced at his watch. "It's only been fifteen minutes."

Jason leaned his shoulder against the post for a moment then took off pacing again.

"Uh, mate..." Christopher said, trying hard not to laugh. "You should have just fucked her. Why didn't you?"

His lips quirked. "Truthfully? I figured once I started—once I *really* started—I wouldn't be able to leave the bed. I would have wanted to stay there with her all day. And now...I'm terrified that we scared her to death and she'd not gonna show. And if she doesn't, I'll bet my cock she won't let us past her bedroom door again. I don't even care about that part either. Well I care, yeah. But really, I just want to be with her."

"Yeah. Me, as well."

"How can you be so bloody cool about it then?"

Cool? His insides were a huge jumble right now. Sleeping with a co-worker wasn't exactly the way to be taken seriously at the job. Or in life. Unless things worked out, which he hoped they would. Still, if things worked in his and Jason's favour and Dana indeed wanted them, they'd still have issues. Their little home town was about as straight-laced and uptight as a place could get. One man married one woman. End of story. No one was gay. No one had a ménage fling let alone a relationship. Couples didn't live together unless they were married.

Two men and a woman in love would stand out.

He glanced at Jason. Perhaps they'd have to discuss moving.

The bell over the lift rang and he grabbed Jason mid-pace and turned him towards the opening doors. Dana stood there, more gorgeous than ever, a beauteous smile on her face. This wasn't the pinched smile she used at work nor the playful or naughty grin. This was a full out toothy smile.

She headed for them, her happiness never fading. "Yes," she said. "I want you. Both of you."

"Even though we're younger?" Jason asked. Christopher knew the root of that question. Jason had put up with being treated as an inferior youth for his entire life. The youngest of five children, he'd been babied. When his mother had died, that coddling had only intensified. Even now, his older sisters were sure he couldn't function on his own. He didn't want anyone thinking of him like that…especially Dana.

"Even though."

"And even though our taste in relationships is considered…ah…deviant by some," Christopher asked.

"Even though."

"For how long?" he pressed on.

"Christopher!" Jason admonished.

He shook it off. "Dana, I don't want you to do this because it's taboo and exciting. We're not a walk on the wild side."

"Christopher," she whispered. Gently, she pulled his head towards her and reached up to kiss him. Her mouth slowly opened, caressing his, worshiping. His hands loosely bracketed her waist as her soft lips feathered against his. "I said I wanted *you*," she repeated. "Not your image."

"What about me baby?" Jason laughed. "I have a complex too."

Leaving his embrace, she pressed into Jason's arms. Christopher bit his lip as she pressed her pelvis to his friend's. Lucky bloke…but then, he had one coming.

"You're perfect for me," she told Jason and kissed him in much the same manner.

"Hot damn, English chicks are hot!" exclaimed an American youth who happened to be sitting in the lobby nearby. "Didja see that?" he asked his friend. "She's with *both* guys."

Dana giggled and pressed close to Jason, pulling Christopher into their embrace as she peaked over Jason's shoulder at the boy.

"You got a sister who lives near here?" the other American asked.

"Sorry boys," she laughed. "No sisters and I'm not British."

"Holy crap! You're American, too. Let us know if you wanna come play with the hometown boys."

Christopher growled under his breath, turning his deadly gaze on the pair.

"Or not," they both said, cringing back into their chairs. "Jeez, touchy people."

Yeah, he was touchy. Dana belonged to him and Jason. No one else had better...touch.

* * * *

Dana was still laughing when they returned to the hotel hours later. Christopher and Jason had dragged her all over London. As soon as they'd learned she'd always wanted to see London Bridge, they'd taken her, showing her the Thames and introducing her to the Tube along the way. She'd seen Big Ben, a famous cathedral whose name she couldn't recall and the inside of a very questionable pub. But the food had been good.

A silly grin curved her lips at the memory. Hands had wandered underneath their table in a dark back corner, stealing beneath her skirt, while she'd caressed both their cocks. And every time one of them was close to coming, the waiter would appear. She'd been ready to scream with frustration, until Christopher had squeezed her clit while Jason's fingers darted in and out of her. She'd pressed her mouth into Jason's shoulder to suppress her howl as she'd climaxed right there in the middle of pub.

She'd insisted they leave the waiter a really big tip.

And poor Jason...

Still hard with no relief in sight.

Afterwards, they'd strolled through Hyde Park enjoying the sun and the chilly spring breeze. Dana had been enchanted by the greenery in the middle of the thriving city. Surrendering to her wanton side, she'd considered suggesting the guys find a secluded place...but even her wanton side didn't want a run in with the police — or the bobbies, as Jason had called them at one point during their jaunt.

All too soon it was time to return to the hotel and attend the meeting.

* * * *

Jason followed Christopher and Dana down the hallway to Dana's room anticipating what would surely follow when they entered. They had an hour and thirty before they needed to appear downstairs and all of them were vibrating with barely restrained sexual energy.

Christopher dropped back to talk to him when the neared the door and Dana went on. "I think I'm going to go to our room and go over the presentation."

Jason looked at him as if he was high. What the hell...? He glanced at Dana, then back at Christopher questioning him. "We know it backwards and forwards."

"You know it backwards and forwards. I could use a little refreshing. And you could use a little — well, I appreciate what you did this morning."

Suddenly, he understood. Damn for a brilliant scientist, he was thick sometimes. For some reason, Christopher was clearing out so he could be with Dana. "Are you sure? You don't owe me anything. It was just the way things happened."

"I'm very sure. Look, we both have to face it. Most of the time it will be all three of us, but occasionally we'll each have some alone time with Dana. I'm not jealous or resentful of that and I know you don't work that way either."

Jason looked at him, feeling the fuzzy kind of feeling one only found with family. "Love you, mate."

Christopher made a sound in his throat, laughing as he looked away. "Plonker." He shook his head. "Always knew you'd say it first."

"Always knew you'd avoid it."

Christopher punched him in the shoulder and he punched back.

Dana cleared her throat. "Should I just go read a novel?"

Jason dashed to her side, dragging her into the room. "Absolutely not!"

As soon as they entered the room and the door shut, Dana dropped to her knees and opened his fly. "You've been so patient," she said, shoving his pants and boxers to his knees. She immediately took him into the warm cavern of her mouth. He reached for the wall for support.

Her hands stroked up the back of his thighs until she cupped his ass. Gently, she squeezed, pulling him towards her as she took him deep in her mouth. Her wicked tongue flicked along his length, before she pulled back and flattened it over the head.

The whole while she gazed up at him, her eyes worshipful as she loved his cock. His balls drew up as she worked him, his mind focused on her mouth and the way her lips stretched around him.

Circling his base with her hand, she began a rapid forward and back motion and his fingers curled against the wall. "No, Dana. Baby, you've got to stop."

He pulled back, popping free of her lips. As cool air touched his skin, he almost regretted stopping her. Quickly, he tugged off his shirt and stepped from his pants.

Dana came willingly as he pulled her to her feet. Even through her shirt, her breasts felt so good against him. He pulled out her shirttail and worked his hand up beneath her shirt until he found her exquisitely shaped breast. He knew some women complained that they were too small at this size, but he found her perfect.

She shuddered as he brushed his thumb over her nipple. Corresponding satisfaction filled him. He liked bringing her pleasure. He loved watching her face as each sensation took her.

"I've been dying to fuck you again," he told her. "Today was agony."

"I've been thinking of little else since this morning. Seeing Big Ben was great, but I couldn't get my mind off Big Jason and his promise."

"Promise?"

She leaned up on her tip toes until her lips were at his ear. Her minty breath brushed across his cheek. "That he was going to fuck me in the ass and fill me with his cum. I haven't before, you know. Never had a man...or a dildo there. Just this plug. Today."

"Bloody hell, baby! You're gonna make me lose it!"

She laughed and turned, bending over the bed and pulling her skirt up around her waist. "Please Jason. I need you."

He bit his bottom lip, gazing at her rounded ass, highlighted by her dark garters and stockings, as well as, the dark skirt bunched around her. She was a school boy's fantasy, and now as a grown up, he finally got to have the dream come true. He licked his lips. The pink base of the plug peeked from between her cheeks. Slowly, he pulled it from her, her low cried wrapping around him as he worked it free.

"Now," she panted. "Please now."

He knew he should woo her to a higher level of arousal, but he chose not to. The entire day had been foreplay. Neither of them could move much farther along the sexual plane.

Quickly, he found one of the condoms he and Christopher had left out when they'd gotten ready for Dana that morning. Despite his earlier promise, he wanted to fuck both her ass and her pussy. This was the only way.

He slid on the rubber, then generously lubed the length of his cock with the lubricant which had been with the pile of condoms.

"Be careful," she begged, as he placed his tip at her crinkled rosette. "First time."

"I will, baby. I will." Bit by bit, he worked inside her measuring his progress by her whimpers and rasped entreaties. The tight hole clamped around him, squeezing him as he went. *So fucking tight.*

"Please, all the way. More."

Satisfied that she could handle it, he shoved forward the last inch until his groin mashed against her ass.

"Dana," he groaned.

"Oh God, I can feel you so deep." She took several choked breaths. "It's so...I never thought it would be like..." She pushed onto him. "More," she demanded in a guttural voice.

Carefully he moved, mindful of her untried passage, but before long, the segued into a deep thrusting rhythm. His fingers dug into her hips and he pulled her up into his drives. She shuddered, her already tight muscles fisting around her. He'd lose it quick at this rate and he wanted so much more.

"No!" she cried as he pulled free.

"Shh... It's all right, baby. Climb up on the bed."

He discarded the condom and followed her. Dana turned into his arms, her legs twining with his. "When I come, I want to be inside your pussy with you squeezing around me while I look at you," he told her. Shoving her legs apart, her surged inside her, his only thought that of uniting with his woman and finding release at long last. His hands buried in her silky shirt and he realised, he'd been so caught up with her ass that he'd forgotten her clothes. Damn, this was different without Christopher. Together, they would have had Dana naked by now, one pleasuring her while the other took care of business, both making her writhe.

He pulled free the top button of her blouse, kissing the skin in between as he powered into her cunt, stretching the passage and drawing hoarse chants of pleasure from her.

"Yes," she cried. "Yes, Jason!"

With a yank, he tore free the rest of her buttons, at least three going flying. He didn't care. He needed her skin. He needed to taste her and smell the floral scent she'd dabbed between her breasts.

There was no way to easily remove her skirt so he left it, along with her stockings. Her pussy was bare and hot as it enveloped him and he was in heaven...clothes or not. Dana writhed and he knew he wasn't alone. Her glossy brown hair spread out over the pillows, getting caught in her fingers as she fisted the pillows.

"You like that? Quick and hot?" he rasped.

She nodded, making a non-verbal sound as her mouth dropped open and she arched beneath him. Her body tightened with release and he struggled to keep from coming. He pushed her legs up towards her chest, holding her wide as he continued to thrust.

Bollocks! It had been too long today—holding off since this morning. He couldn't stop. As Dana's second climax washed over her, it grabbed him and dragged him along as well. A great surge started in his balls shooting forward and his cum exploded forth into her, marking her as his.

"Better?" Dana asked.

"God, yes."

She yawned. "You guys wipe me out. I wish we had time for a nap." She stretched and closed her eyes. "Mmm...can't. S'posed to keep you out of trouble."

"What?" he demanded.

She opened an eye. "That's why I'm here, isn't it? I'm doing a really bad job of it."

"No, baby. Not even close."

Reaching for the phone, he called Christopher and told him to come upstairs. They all needed to talk. He didn't want to move, but he forced himself out of the bed and went to retrieve his pants. Afterward, he waited near the door for his mate's knock.

Christopher rolled his eyes when he saw Dana half clothed and asleep in the middle of the bed. "Botched it up, did you?"

"Did not."

"Huh. Okay. She didn't want her clothes off?"

"Shut up. I didn't call you to critique my performance, though judging by her deep sleep, it didn't suck."

"I never thought it did."

"She thinks she's here to babysit us."

Christopher frowned, obviously displeased by that. "That doesn't bode well... Dana, luv," he said, sitting beside her and jostling her shoulder. "We need to talk to you."

Murmuring, she turned over and buried her nose in his hip. He looked up at Jason. "It really *didn't* suck."

"Not even close," Dana muttered. She stretched, her adorable face scrunching as she did. "Please tell me someone is making coffee."

"In a minute, baby. We need to talk to you."

"What?" she asked. Her eyes were suddenly alert as she pulled a pillow over her front and sat up, looking warily at them. Pain pierced through Jason as he recognised hurt and panic in her stare. Lord, she thought they were gonna dump her in the bin with the rubbish.

Christopher took her limp hand. "There's no easy way to say this and I want to get it out before we go downstairs—"

She pulled away. "It's okay. I get it."

She obviously didn't get it at all.

Her fingers shoved through her hair. "If you two could leave. I'll get dressed and—"

"Dana! Listen," Jason demanded. "We love you for God's sake. Will you stop trying to run away or shove us out?"

"Wh—love?" She looked from him to Christopher. They both nodded. Christopher opened his arms. For a moment, she gazed at him then she dove into his embrace. Jason climbed up behind her and hugged her from behind.

"Tell me," she said.

"I love you," he said, kissing her shoulder. Christopher murmured the same.

It wasn't what they'd intended to say, but it worked just the same. They'd hash out the rest later.

"Hey, you didn't tell us," Jason teased.

She rolled her eyes. "Of course I do."

Christopher leaned towards him, chucking him on the shoulder. "At least she didn't call you a plonker."

"Shut up."

"A what?" Dana asked. "What's a plonker?"

* * * *

"And that's our project in a nutshell. You've already reviewed the data we sent, but we could go over the numbers

100

or any questions you might have." Jason closed the folder in front of him which outlined the research he and Christopher had done, as well as the proposed direction of the project. He took a sip from one of the bottled waters the hotel had provided as a courtesy then looked back and forth between the men he and Christopher had addressed.

Dana stared at her lovers in amazement, the reality of their intelligence settling in once again. How had she ever thought of them as boy toys? They were destined for great things. In a few years their names would be famous in the medical science community.

Kyle and Marcus, the executives visiting from Cranston, glanced at each other then nodded. Marcus cleared his throat. "As you've mentioned, we've reviewed the data. The progress you've made is impressive and we feel it's just the start of what you'll do. We want to move this project back to the Cranston site in the United States. As soon as possible. Within the month at the latest. You'll find facilities there to better accommodate this particular research. Our lawyers have already started the process for testing permissions."

No! They were supposed to support the project, not move it. The reality of what they were saying punched Dana in the stomach and she thought she might be sick. This couldn't be happening. Jason and Christopher were leaving, going to America while she stayed in England.

All good things must come to an end...

"Excuse me," she said, getting up from the table. She had to get out of there before she threw up.

"Dana..." Christopher said as she passed. She shook her head and kept moving. They'd only had one weekend together. She shouldn't be so attached. Why then did it feel like someone had sucked the air from the room?

Spots speckled her vision as she headed for the restroom a couple of doors down from the conference room. She stumbled through the outer 'ladies' lounge' portion and headed to the sinks in the actual restroom. She closed her eyes, gripping the marble counter. The cool stone did little to alleviate the heat prickling across her skin.

She should have paid more attention to her yoga breathing… *Calm down Dana.*

She would be fine. So she'd had a weekend of bliss. It was the kind of fantasy most women her age only dreamed of — unbridled sex with two younger men. Two men who had treated her as if the sun and moon rose from her pussy. They'd made her their sustenance and the air that they breathed.

She felt the same.

But she couldn't deny them this opportunity to fulfil the dream they'd shared for so many years. They'd find a cure. She knew they would. Both men were brilliant beyond their years. She couldn't selfishly deny the world of what they offered…just to keep them in her bed.

Taking a deep breath, she turned on the water and splashed her face then dried it with paper towelling. The spots continued to pepper her vision. *Accelerated blood flow, rapid breathing,* she told herself. *Get a grip. So you go home and dream about them some more while you touch yourself. How will it be different?*

Now she knew what the real thing was, and it was a mere shadow of reality. She knew how the two men interacted, how they loved her…how she loved them.

Backing against the wall beside the sinks, she slid down the marble until she crouched. Leaning forward she pressed her head to her knees.

Get a grip, Dana. Get a grip. Breathe.

"Dana?" came Jason's frantic voice. "Are you okay?"

He was in the ladies' lounge? A guy?

"Dana?" Christopher. Equally distressed.

"I'm okay," she called. She slid back up the wall until she stood unsteadily on her feet again. Fuzzy lines now blocked half her vision. A migraine. Great. Nice timing. In about twenty minutes she'd be able to see again but the pain would be blinding.

Her hip bounced against the counter, and she stumbled as she slowly headed towards the door. She heard a whoosh as it was pushed open.

"What's wrong?" Christopher demanded. His voice seemed to thunder off the walls.

"Migraine. Please don't yell."

"Oh luv." She found herself lifted and carried back into the dimmer lounge area. He sat down with her across his lap and she pressed her face into his shoulder.

"Do you have pills in your purse?" Jason asked.

"Yeah, but—" She realised she had no idea where her purse was located. In the conference room? Or had she dropped it in the bathroom? Or on the way to the bathroom...? Oh crap.

She heard rattling, then a few tablets were pressed into her hand. "You left it by your chair when you walked out. Here. You looked ill, so I brought you one of the bottled waters, as well."

Muttering a grateful thank you, she downed the medication. With luck, the meds might take effect before the pain began.

Jason slipped onto the couch beside Christopher and pulled her so that she sat on his lap while she was stretched across his friend's chest. Slowly, he stroked her back and hip while Christopher sheltered her head with his own, cradling her against him.

"We're not going without you," Christopher murmured.

"You have to," she insisted weakly. "You've made such progress. You can do so much."

"So can you. We want you to work with us. We'll make that clear."

"Your genetics research coincides with our cancer work," Jason added. "Together they appear to take us one step closer to the cure. We think your research may hold a key."

They'd been scoping out her research without her knowledge? It should tick her off, but she didn't have the energy for it. She chuckled weakly. "So you want the old lady for her brain."

Christopher's arms tightened around her. "Call yourself old again and I swear I'll spank you."

Again? Didn't he realise that wasn't much of a threat? After this morning, she knew she liked it.

"You have a couple of years on us. So what?" he continued. "You're gorgeous. I feel you rolling your eyes. Stop it. You're perfect for us. No twig-like girl stands a chance beside you. You're a woman with curves and depth. Besides…between your years of uninspired marriage and our wild bachelor years, I think our ages are evened out."

"Now you're digging."

Jason caught her chin, making her look at him and she was pleased to see her vision was starting to clear. "The age thing doesn't matter. Say it."

"It does sort of."

He groaned, tipping his head back on the seat. "Dana!"

"Well…come on. At my age, we'll have to have the kids you mentioned right away."

Both men stared at her and embarrassment flooded through her.

"I mean—"

"Don't you dare take it back Dana Matthews! You're ours forever," Jason interrupted.

Well, that wasn't exactly what she'd said. It's what she wanted though.

Christopher kissed her, then Jason did, neither stopping until they were a jumble of limbs tangled on the couch. And then they started again.

A discreet cough eventually broke them apart. "Excuse me."

Wide eyed, Dana looked up at the two men standing over them. Heat flooded to her cheeks. Wait! This *was* the freaking ladies' lounge, wasn't it? What the hell were all these men doing in here? And now she was out-numbered four to one. Weird.

"I take it you three are together," Marcus said. "A threesome?"

"Yes," her lovers both said emphatically, hugging her tight.

Marcus looked at his partner, Kyle. "That solves the housing problem. Um…we hate to interrupt you three, but the staff in the hallway pointed us to you. We have to rush for our plane. Our wife is expecting any time and we want to be home, but before we go, we just wanted to tell you, Dana, we're sorry to uproot you again. This should be the last time, we hope. We hope all of you will love Cranston."

Kyle smiled. "You'll find the town very accepting of our lifestyle."

The pair shook hands with Jason and Christopher, nodding respectfully to Dana. "Congratulations, may this be the start of something huge."

Dana looked at Jason and Christopher as the men left, her heart full of her love for them. The start of something huge? She had a feeling it certainly would be.

BEST MATES

Ashley Ladd

Dedication

To my Borders crew: Stephi, Monica, Elizabeth, and Jala.
Thanks for watching my 'puter and running errands
while I'm caught up writing my stories. You're the best.

Chapter One

Alec Russert snuggled deeper into the crook of Kevin Crosby's arms and laid his ear against his lover's heart. Enamoured by the sexy swirl of dark blonde hair on Kevin's chest, he traced his lover's flat nipple. Despite his nearness to the sexiest man on earth, he couldn't get his mind off his best mate and her predicament. "That bloody sucks for Jennica. She believed Thad was 'the one'."

A low growl rose from Kevin's throat as he feathered a kiss across Alec's lips. "Bugger that. If he's 'the one', I'm a talking horse. She's far better off without that wanker."

Alec's heart ached for Jennica. "Yeah, I know. But she has her heart set on having a baby and her biological clock is ticking." Alec twisted in his lover's arms. When his cock grazed Kevin's, shudders of delight rippled through him and his cock flexed.

Kevin moaned and he wrapped his fingers around Alec's cock. "Righto. She's such a dinosaur. What is she? All of thirty-five?"

It was hard to think straight as his blood began rushing into his dick. It was an effort to stay coherent when Kevin's played with his cock, while his strong arm held him. Breathlessly, he murmured, "Thirty-six."

"Blimey, she's older than the dinosaurs."

His own desires surfaced. "We're not getting any younger, either. I know how she feels."

A frown pinched Kevin's brows, and he drew back. "We don't have biological clocks."

Missing his partner's warmth, Alec screwed up his face. "Not in the same way. But do you really fancy a kid when you're too old to enjoy it? I want one now, when I'm still able to get down on the floor and play with it."

Kevin stared at him cross-eyed. "You're serious about this, aren't you? Do you know how hard it is to adopt? Even for a married heterosexual couple? How expensive? It's a real ball-breaker."

Alec's mind clicked away at mach speed as a smile tugged his lips. "Who said anything about adoption?"

Kevin released his cock and jerked away from him, disbelief shadowing his soulful eyes. "Don't even kid about a thing like that. It's not funny."

Hurt, Alec pulled away, losing his erection. He poured a glass of sparkling wine from the bottle he'd left on the nightstand and took a sip. When the bubbles tickled his nose, he screwed up his face. "Who's joking? I want to be a dad. I thought you did, too."

Kevin swore and swung his legs over the side of their bed. The muscles in his back bunched as he hunched over and massaged his forehead. Wrenching around, he looked at Alec. "Well, yeah. Some day. Are you thinking what I think you're thinking?"

Alec did his best to keep a straight face as he downed the rest of his poison in one large gulp. Then he shoved his unruly hair away from his narrowed eyes. "What do you think I'm thinking?"

Kevin blew out a long sigh, his eyes blazing blue wildfire. "That you want to put the bun in Jennica's oven?" Wariness and a million more questions flooded Kevin's eyes. "Have you thought this through? Or is this another of your hare-brained schemes?"

Alec's heart twisted almost as wryly as his lips. He'd been doing little else but thinking about it. He walked on his knees across the bed and hugged the love of his life. He rested his cheek against Kevin's as his heart turned over. "I love kids. I love you. I want us to be a family. We have a lot to offer a child."

Kevin turned his head so that his breath warmed Alec's face. "With Jennica? Or would she raise the kid and we just get occasional visitation? Would he know we're the dads?"

Alec tried not to frown as he pulled back to study his partner's expression. Jitters ran down his spine. This was not how he should have proposed this suggestion, he realised. Instead of his post coital suggestion, he wished he'd prepared a romantic dinner, lit the room with dozens of flickering candles and played Kevin's beloved soft jazz CD. After plying his lover with his favourite chardonnay, then he should have brought up the subject. Alec wanted to kick his own bloody arse.

Before he could reply, Kevin continued, "Do you think she'd go for it?"

Alec took in a deep lungful of air and almost fell over in relief. "We're her favourite men in the world, aren't we? And we're a lot more bleeding reliable than any of those wankers she's been hooking up with."

A grin feathered Kevin's lips, and a rainbow of wonder dawned in his eyes. "You and I are going to be daddies."

Without warning, Kevin wrapped his arms around Alec and bent him back onto the mattress with a deep, heartfelt kiss. "So…which of us will donate the DNA?"

The thought of having a baby with Alec filled Kevin with a warm glow. God, but he loved the man so very much. Against his lover's lips, he murmured huskily, "I never thought I'd love anyone this much again."

Alec hugged him as he always did when any mention of Duncan, his former lover, came up. Kevin wished the words hadn't slipped out, that the memories would stop haunting him. Alec didn't deserve to feel like he was only second best or have to tip toe around his wounded spirit, especially not after this many years and all they meant to each other.

And yet, Duncan's dying words wouldn't stop reverberating in his head. "I love you. Don't blame yourself. Promise me you'll be happy."

Tears stung the backs of Kevin's eyes even though he was completely in love with Alec, completely happy. It was one of those mysteries of the universe he couldn't answer. It was as if he had two hearts, one for Alec and one for Duncan. One was whole and the other eternally broken.

With great difficulty, he tried to rein in his thoughts and control his rampaging emotions. He dragged his thoughts back to the subject at hand. "Are you sure Jennica should be the mother to our child? I mean this could complicate our friendship…" He swirled the amber liquid in his glass and stared into it, wishing it could provide a glimpse into the future. Maybe that was the key to submerging the past. But as much as he loved Jennica, she wasn't the easiest person in the world to be around. Sometimes he was a little jealous at how close she and Alec were, and although he'd never dream of burdening Alec with that knowledge, he felt left out.

He muffled the cynical laugh that tried to choke him. Who was he to be jealous?

Alec scooted forward and linked his hands in front of him. Staring into the distance as if he could see into the future, he said on a ponderous note, "There's nobody else I would want to mother our child. She's beautiful inside and out. She loves kids. Yeah, I'm one-hundred-thousand percent sure."

There was nothing in this world or the next that Kevin wouldn't do for or give Alec. However, he prayed friendship wasn't clouding his lover's perception. He downed the rest of his bubbly and gave Alec's hand a squeeze. Leaning forward he said, "If that's what you want."

A frown marred Alec's beautiful eyes and tugged at his lips. Hypnotically, he ran the pad of his thumb across Kevin's knuckles. He stared deeply into his eyes, willing him to bare his heart. "Isn't that what you want, too? Talk to me. This has to work for both of us, or it's a no go. We both have to be sure."

Kevin's heart jumped. Scared they could get sucked into a deadly quagmire of future regrets and hard feelings if he expressed his doubt, he shook his head. "Of course, that's what I want."

A beautiful smile dawned over Alec's handsome face and Kevin caught his breath. Alec's smile never failed to make his heart flip over in his chest and knock him off his feet. "I would never do anything to hurt you or to jeopardise us. You know that, right?"

As Alec poured another glass of the warming liquid and handed it to him, Kevin asked, "Do you want a girl or a boy?"

The touch of Alec's warm flesh, no matter how innocent, sent shivers through Kevin. Not even Duncan had had this incredible effect on him. Getting a little fuzzy between the liquor and Alec's intoxicating nearness, he set the glass down on the glass table beside him. With a snarky grin, he tried to keep the mood light. "It doesn't matter, so long as it doesn't get your big schnoz."

Alec punched his shoulder then towered over him with his fists affixed to his hips. With a flip of his sexy hair over his shoulder, he asked, "Oh, and you'd rather it inherit your huge Dumbo ears?"

"Who's got Dumbo ears?" Kevin felt his ears and walked to the nearest mirror to check out the situation. They were burning a bright red and standing out more than he liked. With his fingers, he pinned them to his head and then murmured, "They aren't that big."

"Hopefully, the kid will inherit Jen's beauty, all golden blonde like a Greek God. I could be father to a kid like that."

"So long as it's healthy and has all its limbs in the right places, I'll be happy," Kevin said, hoping Alec wasn't jinxing them. Just in case, he crossed his fingers.

Alec scowled at him. "You know I'll love our kid no matter what, even if it turns out lime green."

Continuing in a dreamy voice, he added, "I like the names Regan and Connor. What about you?"

He'd not given it any thought and shrugged. He'd never been a fancy kind of guy. "John or Mary." A more important thought occurred to him. "Whose last name will he have?"

Alec nuzzled his neck and snaked his arms around his chest. "We could take a paternity test and it will get the biological dad's name."

It was getting hard to breathe with Alec's nearness and soft lips seducing him. He did his best to keep his mind on topic. "Do we want to know which one of us is the biological father? Does it matter?"

Love swelled in his heart, for Alec and for the proposed addition to their family. The thought of a little one following around at his heels, looking up at him with unconditional love, needing protection and nurturing, made him melt. He wondered if the child would look up at him with Alec's beautiful eyes and his to-die-for smile or if he'd see features from his own family tree. Either way, the child would be theirs, and he would love it. He knew without a doubt they were doing the right thing.

"What if we have more than one baby?"

Kevin's heart almost catapulted through his chest and he whirled around. "You mean like multiples? Twins? Triplets?" He could barely suck in air. His father had triplet brothers. They ran in the family.

Alec shook his head and ran his fingers through his silky hair. "What I mean is what if we decide to have another baby and the second one is fathered by the other one of us? Will we be able to, and should we, give the kids different last names? That doesn't sound like a close knit family."

He didn't like the sound of that, either, and so he shook his head. He needed another drink and so he returned to his favourite chair and plunked into it. Before he continued, he downed a big gulp. "This parenting stuff is hard even before the kid's born. What will it be like after the kid's running around getting into everything and keeping us up all night?"

Alec's lips twisted and he continued in a grave tone as he ambled to the kitchen to check on the dinner he was preparing. "Maybe it should have Jennica's last name. Let's not borrow trouble. There's plenty of time to decide that. The tyke's not even conceived yet."

Wonderful scents wrapped around Kevin, and his stomach growled. Alec was the best cook this side of London. That was a good thing because if the kid had to rely on its mother or other father for a decent meal, it would starve. Kevin glanced down at his stomach and grimaced. Maybe Alec was too good of a chef. He'd have to start monitoring his intake, just not tonight. It smelled too delicious and his willpower was nil.

Alec hooted from the kitchen, his voice mingled with the sizzling dish. "Yeah, we are pre-ejaculating about this, aren't we?"

Kevin spluttered his drink all over himself. "I can't believe you just said that. You'll have to watch that dirty mouth of yours in front of the kid."

Alec stuck his head around the kitchen door and gave him a shit-eating grin. "Not yet, I don't. I still have time to be bad. You know you love it."

Kevin picked up a couch pillow and hurled it at the man who ducked in the nick of time. "Yeah, you know I do, but we'll have to watch ourselves in front of the kid. Things are going to change a whole hell of a lot around here."

"My mouth is the least of our worries, daddio." Alec's brows did a little jig as he shook a spatula at him and his gaze pinpointed Kevin's dick.

Kevin wasn't too worried about 'that' as he followed his lover's naughty gaze. "No parents invite the kids into the bedroom. That's why there's a nifty little invention called a 'lock and key'."

"Oh, yeah. We'll definitely have to invest in those one of these days, but I think we have a couple years before that'll top our priority list. Before we buy anything, we have to convince the mama-to-be to be the mama-to-be."

Kevin rubbed his forehead trying to follow that. Alec's wordiness sometimes drove him bonkers. "Huh? Simplify."

Alec leaned against the wall and crossed one ankle over the other. "I'm not one of your authors. You got me."

Kevin just stared at him, refusing to give in.

Finally, Alec clarified. "We have to persuade Jennica to mother our baby."

"I'm sure with your charming ways and my handsome mug, we won't have any problems. What red-blooded female wouldn't want two sexy blokes in her bed, worshipping her, making her feel like two mil?"

Alec frowned. "Get real. She might not go for this. You know, uh, some women, don't get who we are…" He spread his hands wide as if he'd lost command of his tongue.

The hurt in Alec's soulful eyes almost did Kevin in, and he hoped Alec was wrong. Knowing how cool and modern Jennica was, however, he suspected she'd warm up to the arrangement, especially when Alec's extraordinary culinary skills were thrown into the bargain. And once she learned just how expertly he could wield his tongue and his cock…whew! Still, one never knew for sure until the subject was broached. Obviously Alec hadn't forgotten the time they'd tried to have a ménage after the Christmas party with that cute little dish, Delilah, from his publishing house, and how she'd run out of their apartment screaming and hurling gypsy curses.

Wondering if Alec would change his mind, Kevin nursed the rest of his drink. "So, do you need more time to think this over? I'll go with whatever you say."

When Alec disappeared for a few minutes Kevin wondered why his lover was taking so long to reply, if he was having second thoughts. Then he heard plates clinking in the kitchen. Although Alec tried hard to conceal it, only those who knew him exceptionally well realised just how very sensitive he could be. Jennica being such a good friend would be attuned to this and tread carefully, but she still might back away with finesse.

Finally, Alec emerged wearing a floppy chef's hat and brandishing two beautifully made up plates. "Ta da!" He set down the china dishes on plastic placemats besides two tall goblets of sparkling spring water.

Alec said something in French that Kevin couldn't begin to understand as the man's pronunciation left a lot to be desired.

"So, do you want to go through with this, with Jennica?" Kevin repeated.

Chewing a mouthful of food, his cheeks puffed out, Alec nodded. After he swallowed and licked his lips he said, "We have to give it a shot. My gut tells me this is right."

"Then we'll go for it." Alec's excitement was infectious and he couldn't wait to experience the feelings of seeing their child grow inside Jennica, of witnessing the birth, and of cradling their little bundle of joy for the first time in his arms, against his heart. At least he hoped they'd be allowed to.

Full and sated, warmed from the earlier liquor and from the thought of "their" child, Kevin was more than ready for some affection. Alec was just too cute and too sexy to resist a moment longer. Primitive growls rose from the pit of his stomach and he pulled Alec up and into his arms. He unbuttoned Alec's shirt and pushed away the offending material. Nuzzling Alec's warm shoulder, he murmured against his flesh, "God, I love you so much."

Alec moaned and tilted his head to give Kevin better access to his neck. He unbuttoned his pants and worked his hand inside Kevin's pants and curled his fingers around his burgeoning cock. "I love you more."

Kevin doubted that, but he was too hot, too needy to argue the point. He caressed Alec's burning flesh, kneading his nipples, then moved lower following the trail of hair that grew broader as it dipped beneath his underwear.

Feverish, their lips met and their tongues tangoed. Before Kevin knew what was happening, they stripped each other and threw their clothing helter-skelter across the room. Kissing, nipping, and caressing each other, they somehow made their way to the bedroom.

Kevin pushed Alec deep into the mattress as he stuck his tongue down his lover's throat. Their cocks rubbed against each other, growing hotter by the second. He lifted his body enough to slide his hand between them and once again curl his fingers around Alec's throbbing cock.

His head spinning, he nibbled on Alec's ear and murmured, "Get on top. I want to feel your hot dick inside me."

Alec nodded with an eagerness that made Kevin's heart pound so hard it almost ripped through his chest. "If you'll do the honours."

"I'd be delighted." Kevin nodded, and his hands trembling with desire, he reached for the lube. He squeezed a dab onto his palms and it over Alec's velvety cock, massaging the scrim and head. It was so hot, so hard and yet so satiny in his hands he was in awe of God's handiwork. Bending, he kissed the tip, becoming thoroughly intoxicated by his lover's scent.

"I think you're more than ready, lover. Don't make me wait." In invitation, he got up on his hands and knees and pushed out his rear. "Whenever you're ready."

"God, I've been so ready..." Lovingly, Alec worked his cock in deep and then like a tease, pulled it out almost to the tip. Meanwhile, his hands slapped Kevin's rear.

Shudders shimmered through Kevin and his cock hung full and heavy, awaiting its turn to fuck Alec. His pulse hammered heavily as little drops of warm liquid slid out to coat the head of his penis.

His lover drove into him again, working his way deeper, spreading him wider. He gyrated his hips and massaged Kevin's buttocks.

Whispers of desire were fanned into a raging inferno and coherent thought fled. Wanting to feel his lover deep inside, to be united as one heart and soul, he thrust his hips back. "Ooh, that feels awesome. Oh, oh! You're so big...so wonderfully hard..."

He was coming, and it was the most wonderful feeling in the world. He bent his head and watched his cum squirt onto the bed. The thick, creamy puddle of white grew large, and he could imagine his seed seeking to plant itself deep into Jennica to make their baby. Or would it be Alec's seed that did the honours?

Alec became a wild man, and with the ultimate, powerful thrust, he tossed back his head and howled. His secretion was thick and musky as it coated Kevin's arse.

Sated, Kevin fell to the bed with Alec still holding him, his now flaccid cock caressing his arse. When Alec rolled to the side, he turned and wrapped his arms around his lover, cuddling close.

"I love you. You're the man of my dreams." Alec ran his flat palms across his chest as he possessively threw his leg over him.

Kevin still couldn't believe he'd been so blessed to have found Alec and that Alec could love him. After Duncan had died, he'd thought he'd never love anyone ever again. But he did, and more than he'd ever loved anyone. Could he love Jennica as much? For her sake, he hoped so. He certainly found her attractive and the thought of planting his cock into her blonde pussy made his cock flex back to life.

Chapter Two

Jennica Chapman felt so low she didn't think she could sink any further. Hurt and angry, she ripped up all the pictures she had of her ex, Thad, threw them in the sink and lit a match to them. As she watched the flames devour Thad's handsome but sleazy face, she gritted out between her teeth, "Up in flames with you. Kev and Alec had you pegged. Why didn't I listen?"

Afraid the smoke was getting too thick and would set off the fire alarm, she turned on the tap and doused the flames. Catching her blurry reflection in the tap's chrome, she stared at her distorted reflection. "Because you're a blithering idiot. Because you wanted a baby so badly, you would've settled for the wanker."

Mad at herself for letting the last two years tick away as her eggs grew stale, she scoured the sink and threw Thad's ashes into the rubbish.

Unfortunately that didn't make her feel much better. Neither did cranking up her music, soaking in the tub, or digging into a quart of Ben and Jerry's.

Her door shook with a sudden pounding and she rolled her eyes. Not in the mood to fend off a door-to-door salesman, and in particular hoping never to lay eyes on Thad again, she ignored it.

The hammering increased and Alec called out, "I'm not going away. I know you're in there, Chapman."

A rush of affection for her best chum washed out some of her raging anger. She raced for the door and flung it wide. Ecstatic to see friendly faces, she threw herself first into Alec's arms and then Kevin's.

She didn't know which was more handsome. They were both heartthrobs. Alec was the ultimate bad boy rocker with unruly hair that grazed his shoulders and a perpetual roguish smile that would melt her heart if he were straight — sometimes it did anyway. Bohemian, he always wore ragged jeans, a shirt that lay half-unbuttoned exposing a matt of very sexy chest hair, and gold earrings. Also like usual, he wore a sexy five o'clock shadow on his lean cheeks. She thought it the sexiest thing on earth. Well, maybe the second sexiest…
She had a hard time suppressing a naughty grin and keeping her gaze from drifting south to the sexiest thing between his legs.

Kevin on the other hand was the clean-cut, London book editor who always wore preppy clothes. His blond good looks and clear blue eyes had broken more than a few hearts, male and female. He kept his hair tapered short and well-groomed. Often she wondered how the two had hooked up, but she'd shrugged it off as opposites attracting.

Alec whipped out a big bouquet of her favourite flowers, purple daisies, and thrust them into her arms. "For you, sweetie. Moping time's up. We're taking you out for a night on the town."

Conscious that she was clad in a funky old robe and little else, she dragged them inside her flat. She looked pointedly down at her scruffy attire. "Do I look like I'm dressed for a night out?"

Alec winked and his eyes twinkled. Contagious mischief curved his cheeks. "You look gorgeous to me as always, beautiful."

Kevin, the more conservative of the two, tutted. "Run along and get fancied up. You've got ten minutes before I let Alec raid your icebox."

Her eyes grew wide at the ghastly threat, and she fingered the rings piercing her right brow. "You wouldn't! I'll have to go on the dole."

"Then you'd best move your cute little bum." Kevin pointedly checked his Rolex and tapped his foot. "Nine minutes left and counting."

She stuck up her middle finger. "Wanker." Then she fled to her room and threw on the first pair of clean jeans and top she could put her hands on. She tied on a pair of tennis shoes and sprinted out the door with a minute to spare.

Alec was already spooning her second quart of Ben & Jerry's into his mouth. He petrified at the sight of her. Guilt flashed across his eyes.

Murderous, intent on saving her goodies, she chased him. "Give that back!"

He yelped and leapt over the coffee table and dropped the spoon. "You can't kill your best mate."

"Best mates don't steal my ice cream! Surrender the goods or die!"

Alec darted back and forth. "Only if I get my best chum status back."

Calculating how best to catch the tosser, she gave him the evil eye. "No promises. Now hand over the food if you want to live."

Alec's gaze ping ponged between her and the ice cream he cradled in his arms. Finally, with a big pout, he turned it over. "I love you more. Here."

"Ahh." Her heart melted almost as much as her poor liquefied Ben & Jerry's. "That's so sweet."

Kevin rolled his eyes and snapped his fingers. With a raised brow, he looked at her feet. "Flip flops, darling. Chop chop."

Her brow arched and then happy enlightenment dawned. So that's why he was dressed down in Dockers and a Polo shirt. "Midnight pedicures? My absolute fav!"

Her feet danced all the way through the pedicure, the real dancing, and then a fancy meal. She was surprised when they took her to a romantic candlelit restaurant where a mariachi band serenaded her. She wished they'd warned her to bring more appropriate shoes.

Heat rising to her cheeks, she rested her elbows on the table and her face on her hands. "You're the best chums in the world. I love you two."

Kevin and Alec exchanged a knowing, suspicious glance.

A knot formed in the pit of her stomach and the formerly luscious manicotti lost its flavour. She had to force herself to swallow the now cardboard-tasting swill. "Spill. What are you two up to? What's this big set up all about?"

Kevin's expression became inscrutable but Alec broke into a big grin. He shook with excitement until Kevin elbowed him in the ribs. "What 'set up'?"

"Moi, your best mate, set you up? Perish the thought," Alec said very innocently.

Not believing either liar for a second, she let her fork clatter to the plate and she nudged Alec's leg with her knee and said, "Well?"

Alec sent a questioning glance to Kevin who nodded. Then he snuck his hand into Kevin's and the other one into hers. As Alec's fingers curled around hers, Kevin claimed her other hand.

She quaked with fear and she was glad she was sitting for she sensed their news would be monumental. Several scenarios ran through her mind, each so much more ghastly than the next that she was scared to voice them so she waited with trepidation.

She closed her eyes and whispered so that only she could hear, "Please don't tell me one of you is going to die. Please don't say that." She'd die without either of them.

Alec leaned closer. "What?"

Her eyes flew open. "Uh, nothing. The suspense is killing me. What's going on?"

Again, the two men exchanged meaningful looks. Kevin finally opened his mouth. "We want you to be the mother of our child."

The words reverberated in her ears. As if from a distance and through a thick fog, she watched the men regard her with concern. Relief freed her and then laughter, riotous and loud, bubbled off her lips. Soon tears streamed from her eyes, and she doubled over, unable to stop laughing.

Alec released her hand and jutted out his chin. With an offended glint in his eyes, he said, "We're dead serious. We want to father your baby."

Kevin just watched, remaining mum and crossed his arms over his chest as if he was deciding how to edit her words and reactions.

Sobering, she dabbed at her eyes with a napkin. To her chagrin, her mascara and makeup covered the thing when she pulled it back. "This is for real? Like how? Why?"

She felt like an idiot and couldn't quite spit out what she meant. "I mean, who gets the baby? Am I helping you or are you helping me?" The thought of being a surrogate and giving up a child she'd so longed for, ripped her apart.

Kevin said, his voice very businesslike, "We rather hoped and thought we'd help each other, that this would be 'our' baby, as in all three of ours."

"We'll raise the little tyke together," Alec said softly.

New pictures painted themselves in her mind, the four of them playing at the park, the three of them sitting at the firing squad of teacher conferences, the four of them curled up in front of the telly on cold, rainy nights. "You mean, we'd all live together like a family?"

It sounded both wonderful and scary, boggling her mind. So many implications, so many what ifs, plagued her. Her mouth felt as if it was stuffed with cotton so she took a sip of water.

"That's the plan," Kevin said as if it was so very simple.

She blinked. It wasn't simple at all! As much as she yearned for a child, as much as she craved a family, and as deeply as she loved Alec and Kevin, could she live without romantic love? Moreover, would they be upset if they found out about her secret life?

Jennica shot them a troubled look which Kevin feared didn't bode well. He prayed it wouldn't break Alec's tender heart if she turned them down. He wouldn't be surprised if Alec wanted a child even more than Jennica.

He noticed the waitress hovering behind them and didn't feel like airing their private life for public consumption. "Bill please." He handed over his credit card, wadded up his napkin and dropped it on his plate.

To his dinner companions he said, "We'll finish this back at our place."

He wondered if the look in Jennica's eyes was panic or mere caution? Her eyes weren't their normal tone of sky blue with specks of sunny yellow. Instead, they were the dark roiling hue of a turbulent ocean with dangerous murky green undercurrents. Her muscles were taut and the pulse at the base of her throat fluttered alarmingly.

She was a real beauty though a bit wild. Half of her hair was dyed an electric hot pink while the other was her own silvery-blonde. Several piercings lined both her ears, her right brow, and there was a stud in the right side of her nose. Tonight, she had combed the pink to the side so that it blended over the blonde and was quite stunning. He hadn't missed several appreciative male glances stealing her way.

Jennica yawned and patted her mouth. She kept her eyes averted. "I'm exhausted and I'd really like to sleep on this."

Alec frowned. "Tomorrow's Saturday. You can sleep in. Our place is just around the block and you sleep over all the time."

Kevin kept a close watch on her from his peripheral vision. Warring emotions obviously troubled her. It worried him. Delilah hadn't been the only would-be third who had run away from them. His gut clenched and he dug his hands deep into his pockets. Under his breath he muttered to Alec. "Pushing."

When Jennica rested her head on his shoulder as they left the restaurant, hope flared anew. "Have you guys really thought this through?"

He gave her shoulder a squeeze. His heart fluttered so fast it felt like a hummingbird's. Until now, he hadn't realised how much he too longed for a child. Moreover, he didn't want his child to have just any mother. He only wanted it to be Jennica and yet, he was afraid to examine his feelings too closely in case she shot them down.

"Yeah," he finally admitted after taking a deep, cleansing breath. "We've thought about this a whole lot, actually. We want a child and so do you. We want you to be the mother of our child."

She started to chuckle then cut herself short. She shuffled her feet, dragging behind.

Alec touched her elbow. "We know how much you want a baby."

She stopped under the circle of a streetlamp, so petite and delicate she looked like an ethereal nymph. However, she ruined the effect when she anchored a hand on her hip and screwed up her lips. "Someone's gotta bring it up so I guess it'll be me. Do you plan to donate sperm and implant the egg in vitro? And which one of you will do so?"

He tried not to show how humorous he found her very clinically asked question, but it was difficult. Jen was usually anything but politically correct.

Alec shot him a loud, plodding look. He nodded, his brow raised.

He put out a calming hand to Alec and cleared his throat.

"That would be so cold..." Alec splayed his hands as a cool breeze whipped his loose, shoulder-length locks about his face. With a grimace, he tucked his hair behind his ears.

Jennica looked from Alec to him and back to Alec as realisation pooled in her eyes. She touched her stomach and looked down at it. "You mean...?"

Before he could reply, she asked, "Which one of you?"

Chapter Three

Alec grasped Jennica's elbow and propelled her forward before pigeons decided she'd make a good perch.

"We thought," he said keeping his voice low even though foot traffic was minimal on the London streets at this late hour. "We'd like to make the baby the natural, old-fashioned way, except, it doesn't matter whose sperm actually fathers the child as we'll both be the fathers…"

Jennica laughed lightly and nonchalantly waved her hand. "Oh, so you want to have a ménage? With me?"

"Are you shocked?" Alec feared they were too-forward thinking, too erotic for an innocent, heterosexual woman. He prepared to catch her if she swooned.

To his amazement, she slapped her thigh and howled with laughter.

He watched in horrified fascination as she transformed into an alien. "Should we be offended that you find this so hilarious? I thought you were cool with us."

She calmed and clutched her throat. "I'm cool with you but the question is, will you be cool with me?"

Perplexed, he shook his head. "Huh?"

She rounded on them and walked backwards. "There's something I've never told you about me, something you might find quite odd."

"I can't imagine what," Kevin said without skipping a beat.

"You used to be a horse?" Alec asked, wiggling his brows.

Kevin unlocked the door, and they stumbled inside. "So what's this big secret that's so grisly we won't like you anymore?"

Alec couldn't imagine and he held his breath, his gaze riveted on her lips.

Not just any lips, not perfect lips, but intriguing lips with a ton of personality. They could change expression so fast it made his head spin. Usually they smiled with a mischief he found charming. Recently, they'd been frowning, pouty, seductive, and flirty.

He wondered what it would be like to kiss those lips, to delve his tongue deep into her mouth. The eroticism of her lips made him feel so sexy.

"I'm afraid you boys are too tame for me."

Huh?

Alec looked to Kevin who shrugged. "How so?" He leaned against the wall and folded his arms over his chest.

"I'm a sub."

So? "As in a teacher's replacement? What's so horrid about that?"

She playfully swatted him. "No, you daft cow. 'Submissive'. As in I like to be spanked and punished and have pain with my pleasure. You know — BDSM."

His ears rang, and the din grew louder as he stared open-mouthed.

Gently, Kevin slid a finger under his chin and pushed it shut. "Who are we to judge another's lifestyle?"

Alec heard him, yet he couldn't stop staring, wondering about his chum wearing all those leather straps...and nothing else. He wondered what it would be like to wear them, or to be spanked, or to do the spanking... His cock grew warm and flexed. He wanted to plunge it deep into her pussy, to feel its silky warmth, to shoot his seed deep inside her. He wanted to feel her tremble beneath him, to hear her intake of breath as she came.

Jennica tugged his hair. "See? I told you I'm too wild and crazy for you two."

Almost in unison, they both asked, "Who says?"

It was Jennica's turn to be surprised, but she kept a tight rein on her expression so as not to reveal it. "Fantastic. Which one of you is the Dom?" She watched closely, eyeing their body language. Her guess on Kevin.

Alec's frame shook and his eyes glowed. She was surprised to see the bulge in his slacks.

An answering shiver ran down her spine. *Maybe this could work.*

She couldn't help herself. "I don't know... You mean the baby might look like one of you two?"

Kevin guffawed as he stretched out on the lounger and crossed his ankles. "Poor kid."

Alec glared at him. "You're the one with the gigantic ears."

Kevin hurled a pillow at Alec's big schnoz.

Alec ducked and the projectile smashed into a vase, knocking it to the floor.

Jennica rolled her eyes. "You two are still kids, and you want to have one?"

"All the better to play with them, my dear." Alec hiked the pillow and threw it back to Kevin.

Kevin caught it then threw it down and jumped in the air, whooping. "Touch down! Yeah!"

Jennica helped herself to a bottle of water and took a swig. She wiped her mouth with her sleeve and said, "Grow up."

Kevin tweaked her chin. "You're the one into the really hard core games, sweetie."

She made a moue of her lips. Although she didn't miss Thad, she missed the "games". Claiming the duvet, she stretched out her feet and stifled a yawn.

Alec perched on the arm by her head. "The mother of our child should not have to sleep on the couch."

Kevin wrinkled his nose. "I'm not giving up my nice, comfy bed. You take the couch and she can sleep with me."

She plumped a pillow and stuck it under her head. "Got any blankets?"

"The three of us can share the bed. It's plenty big."

"Ooh, kinky," she said in the midst of another yawn.

"You're the kinky one. I'm just offering to share our Posturepedic mattress, not that we'd mind really 'sleeping together'. If you'd actually prefer to sleep out here, however, ..." Alec unceremoniously dumped a comforter on her head.

Considering the couch felt like a bed of nails, the Posturepedic sounded a whole lot better. Not sure about the "sleeping with" her two best mates part, however, she didn't comment. She bundled up the blanket and carried it to the bed. God, it looked like an oasis of comfort and she dove onto it. Knackered, she murmured almost incoherently, "No one wake me up till Sunday."

Chapter Four

Warm lips caressed Jennica's neck and she moaned. Her pulse hammered and she turned into the warm body, seeking the heavenly heat.

Hands kneaded her bum then her bare breasts. Suddenly, she realised that four hands roamed her. By now she was such a live wire of need, she didn't care if eight hands explored her as long as they didn't stop.

Still drowsy, she opened one eye a slit, and Kevin's handsome face swam before her eyes. A sexy five o'clock shadow lined his cheeks and a naughty grin curved his lips.

Groggily, she murmured, "Is it Sunday already?"

Alec nuzzled her neck and murmured huskily against it. "Who cares?"

Kevin plundered her lips, and his naked body rubbed against hers.

Embers sparking deep inside, she purred as she wrapped her arms around his neck. She played with the hair on his nape as she moulded herself to him.

Behind her, Alec sidled closer. His cock, erect and hot, seared into her back. His hands slid off her knickers then snaked about her, in a quest for her sex. Finding her clit, he massaged the hardening nub.

Out of breath, her blood simmering, she quaked against the two hard bodies.

Kevin twisted around and reached for something on his nightstand. She expected to see him snap up a couple condoms so she trembled with anticipation.

To her astonishment Alec drew her arms behind her and wrapped her fingers around his throbbing cock. "Your hands feel so good, baby. Caress me."

Surprise filled her as she tightened her clasp. "You're so long, and ooh, you're so incredibly hot."

Cold metal grazed her wrists as the lock clicked into place. Alec spanked her — hard — and she yelped. "What the hell?"

"Do you have permission to make noise, slave?" Kevin asked. He dangled a necklace looking thing with a large red ball before her eyes and then gagged her.

Her eyes widened and she squirmed as he tied the gag behind her head.

Alec drew a long peacock feather over her aching arse then tickled her nipples. He smiled down at her from his superior position as his beautifully sexy cock bobbed above her stomach.

Kevin pointed to the corner of the bed. "Tie her leg to the post," as he strapped the other with a fur-lined leather thong.

Alec teased the sole of her foot with the feather as strangled screams erupted from her throat and her hips thrust off the bed. Then he walked up the bed on his knees. Ravenous hunger etching his features, he dove and buried his face in her pussy and lapped at her clit.

"We're going to have ourselves a real ménage, BDSM style, baby. Hope you like it." Kevin picked up a tube of lube, propelled himself off the bed and rounded to Alec's back. He squirted a large blob of the gel onto his cock and then worked it on, shiny and glistening.

"Ooh, I like it," Alec murmured, his voice muffled against her sex.

A wildfire out of control, Jennica writhed against Alec's mouth, pushing her pussy into his face, hungry for more. She'd never expected anyone could turn her on so fast, so hard, but in particular, not her best mate Alec. She wanted to kick herself for not jumping into their bed eons ago.

Alec lifted his head and his lips shimmered with her juices. "What a wanton little slut you are. I never dreamed…"

Being called dirty names almost made her come. How she loved feeling like a whore in the bedroom, to be manhandled and appreciated by a man—by *two* hot, impossibly sexy men. Her gaze was riveted on Kevin's red, throbbing cock. She couldn't wait to watch him fuck Alec, but to her surprise, he handed an electric prod to his partner. "Zap her a couple times. Get her juices really flowing."

With a broad grin, Alec took it and held it up. "You asked for it, babe. Here it comes. Are we wild enough for you now? Are you getting super sensitised?"

She dreaded the jolt. She longed for it. She gave as much of a nod as her restraints allowed.

When Alec rolled the prod over her pussy lips, sharp jabs of pain seared through her and she spasmed as screams rammed up her throat. He electrified her again and again until she wanted to beg for mercy, until she was so raw, so highly sensitised the merest touch would send her into orgasm.

Blessedly, he ceased and tossed the toy aside. He administered a cool gel and then with long sweeps of his tongue, proceeded to soothe her.

Still raw, everything magnified at least ten fold, she was wracked with uncontrollable quivers. It was all she could do not to come all over his face, but she was holding out for something far better.

When Kevin worked his cock into Alec, who bucked and moaned against her, she craned her head to better see Kevin's beautiful cock sliding in and out, a rainbow of light reflecting off his slick flesh. Then she watched Alec's face, buried deep between her legs, rapture lighting his eyes, and she knew Heaven couldn't top this.

When Kevin's rhythm increased, Alec squirmed against her. He thrust his arse further back and his turgid cock swung heavy between his legs, drops of cum clinging to the red velvety bulb.

Exquisite pressure stoked between her legs then unleashed with the fury of an atom bomb.

Shock waves battered her as she pulled at her bonds with all her might. Screams of ecstasy were muted by her gag.

Greedily, Alec lapped her juices. His eyes squeezed shut, and he drank deeply of her as his hands massaged her breasts.

Finally, he stopped sucking and lifted his head, his chin dripping with her cum, his lips coated, and passion glazing his eyes. Propping himself on his elbows, he impaled himself on his other lover. "This is the most incredible night of my life."

Jennica's salty taste coated Alec's lips, his tongue, and slid down his throat. He hadn't lied just now. He couldn't wait to pump her full of his seed, to see her belly swell with their child.

On fire, his cock was ready to burst. His love for her expanded and morphed from friendship to a romantic, all-encompassing passion equal to what he felt for Kevin. In the throes of ecstasy, he could only bathe in the glorious feelings. No woman had ever before affected him this deeply even though he'd fucked several. He loved women, their naked breasts, their budding nipples, their slick fuckable pussies, but it seemed that men had better understood his needs, had been more in synch. But Jennica knew him as well as Kevin and was in tune with his needs. If asked, he'd be hard put to say which turned him on more.

Behind him, Kevin bumped and ground, moaned and then with one final thrust, he dug his fingers into Alec's arse and shot him full of his cum.

In paradise, Alec ground his arse against Kevin's cock, struggling to hold back his own orgasm. He wanted this special time to stretch into forever.

Slowly, Kevin pulled out, hugged Alec, and dropped a kiss on his back. "Your turn, lover."

Alec was dying to ask, "Have we passed the audition? Are we dominating enough?"

Muffled words tried to escape around the gag so he untied it. "You may speak, slave." He felt like an actor getting into his role.

With a smile that told him she was holding back, she murmured, "Not half bad."

He didn't like the sound of that and he towered over her. "Not half bad 'what'?"

"Not half bad, Master."

He couldn't let her get away with this. He'd have to keep fucking her until she shouted to the world that they'd given her the best fuck of her life, that she couldn't live without being fucked by them day in, day out. "Not half good, though?"

Kevin threw him a dark glance and shook his head. He picked up the lash and gave it a few flicks in the air. He regarded her soberly. "Re-gag the slutty bitch. We'll teach her."

She quivered and her expressive eyes spoke volumes.

"Take off the hand cuffs," Kevin instructed as he stood on the bed.

Alec did as bid, wondering if he was also the submissive for following instructions. The idea sent shivers down his spine. He did as bade and looked to his lover. "They're off. What next?"

Kevin cracked the whip across his arse and Alec yelped, reeling in surprise.

"What next, 'Master'."

The sting went bone deep, and he jumped to do Kevin's bidding. "What next, 'Master'?" Alec averted his gaze, instinctively knowing looking straight into the Master's eyes would be forbidden.

Kevin tossed leather straps to him. "Tie this around her breasts and legs. She wants to be bound and gagged, we'll grant her fondest wishes."

Jennica's eyes grew wide as her gaze flickered to her two Masters.

"What are you waiting for, slave? Tie her!" Kevin cracked the whip again.

The lash stung on Alec's arse and he jolted. Conversely, his cock flexed and his nerves sang. "Yes, Master." Hurriedly, he tied up Jennica, and her breasts jutted beautifully out of the straps. The sight was so erotic, so debased, he almost came. How had he lived so long missing out on this?

Kevin tossed a pair of clamps on the bed beside the submissive woman. "Attach the nipple clamps."

"Next time, use the clamps on me." Alec wasn't aware that Kevin had any of this equipment and wondered if he'd, too, been living a secret life.

The lash spanked him again. "Did I give you permission to speak, slave?"

Alec gritted his teeth and bent his head so close to Jennica's nipple her scent intoxicated him.

With a softer tone, Kevin added, "While the two of you slept, I took the liberty of visiting Jen's apartment and bringing back some of her 'equipment'."

Alec felt easier and let out a sigh of relief that his lover wasn't keeping secrets.

"Tie her hands in front of her this time."

"Yes, Master." Alec used the fur-lined leather straps. Then he attached the nipple clamps.

"Very good."

Kevin commanded, "Fuck her pussy."

That was one command Alec couldn't wait to fulfil. Holding her arse he drove into her moist depths. Her wet, warm folds felt so wonderful, he almost came. With great effort, he slowed his strokes and held back. He wanted to stoke her fire, too, before he had his pleasure.

To his surprise, Kevin grabbed his rear and ran the tip of his penis down the crack of his arse. Then, he gently worked his cock into Alec's arse hole.

Moans rose in Alec's chest and escaped his lips. His every nerve ending was on fire, in particular where Kevin's hips ground against his extra-sensitised flesh. No wonder Jennica was addicted to this.

He plundered her pussy as Kevin plumbed his arse. They fell into a steady rhythm, the back and forth rocking motion pushing him to the brink of the precipice.

Jennica's vaginal walls gloved his cock, milking the seed that was so ready to explode deep inside her. Her thighs squeezed him tightly, refusing to release him. His hands slapped her beautiful arse, and he massaged the hard nub of her clit to hurry her.

Shudders wracked her, setting off a chain reaction in him. His hands clenched and his seed spewed through his cock and erupted into her pussy. Envisioning it gushing like lava, seeking her eggs, creating their child, he'd never been so turned on. With Kevin shooting his seed into Alec simultaneously, it was as if their sperm was shooting into Jennica simultaneously, impregnating her with 'their' child. This baby would truly be a product of the three of them, created in the mutual act of making love. Had any child ever been thus created?

Kevin's fingers bit into his flesh as he ground his cock into his arse. "Oh, God. Why haven't we made love to Jennica before?"

Alec wondered the same thing. Why had they waited so long? Why didn't everyone form a sacred triad? They'd had other ménages, with women and men. Shanna had been his favourite woman to fuck, but their times with her paled in comparison to Jennica. He'd never had the desire to plant his seed in Shanna and join their lives forever with hers.

Pounding hammered the door. "Where's Jennica? You hiding her in there, you gay bastards?" Thad yelled.

Chapter Five

Jennica felt as if she'd died and gone to heaven. Sex with Thad had never been so amazing. This was a whole lot more than just sex. Love swelled her heart as never before, not just for one man, but for two. She couldn't begin to untangle her feelings for her two lovers. Both were special, both so very precious.

She willed Thad to disappear and sod off forever. Of all times to show up, the bleeding wanker had to pick now. She wanted to tell her lovers to be quiet and wait for him to go away, but of course, she was gagged so her words were muffled.

"Bollocks!" Kevin held her gently as Alec unlocked her handcuffs. Her lovers quickly unleashed her, their fingers fumbling in their haste.

As soon as Alec ungagged her, she licked her dry lips and tried to work them. Swollen and stretched, she found it hard to formulate coherent words. "Ignore him and he'll go away," she mumbled as if she spoke around a mouthful of marbles.

But the pounding grew louder.

Alec swore under his breath. "He's going to wake the neighbours, and they'll call out the constable."

"Let them." She didn't want to see the wanker, especially not here, not now. She didn't want anything to ruin this special night. Of course, Thad was already doing that. But maybe if he'd go away, they could get back into their rhythm and reclaim what was left of the night.

Kevin tugged on his pyjama bottoms and ground out through gritted teeth, "Get dressed. I'm going to tell that no good tosser where to get off."

In unison, she and Alec said, "Yes, Master."

They both burst out giggling.

Kevin rolled his eyes. "This isn't funny. Stay in here. I'll tell him to sod off." He marched to the door and closed it behind him.

She winced at the swelling on Alec's arse. Gently, she touched it, commiserating with his pain. "Does it hurt much?"

Alec twisted around, trying to look at it over his shoulder. He finally positioned his arse in front of the mirror. He whistled long and low. "Stings a bit. But I can see why you like it so much. Mad, isn't it?"

She couldn't help but smile. "Seems opposite, doesn't it?"

Alec shrugged into a robe as she found her jeans and pulled them up. Just as she closed her fingers around her bra, the door burst open, and Thad slammed in with Kevin in close tow.

Kevin stationed himself between them and the intruder.

"What in the bloody hell is going on here?" Thad's furious gaze bounced from Alec to her to Kevin and back to her, his gaze fixated on her naked breasts. "You...them? You can't be serious..."

She faced off against him, glaring. Standing at parade rest, she clamped her fists on her hips. "Why not?"

"They're sissy boys. You're a sub. I'm your Dom. You can't possibly prefer them over me."

Thad jerked his thumb at her bra. "Put something on. For Heaven's sake, you're starkers."

Laughter bubbled up in her. No way in hell would she get dressed now. She only regretted that Thad had another look at her naked breasts. But she refused to be submissive to him another moment and give him the satisfaction. She grabbed her bra, thrust out her boobs, and threw the scrap of lace to the other side of the room. "My days of listening to you are over. You're no longer my Master."

Thad's jaw dropped and his expression was comical. "You don't know what you're saying. You're just brassed off at me. You'll come to your senses. They drugged you, didn't they?"

Kevin stepped between them and towered over Thad. "I think the lady said she wants you to go, that she wants nothing more to do with you."

Thad tried to push past Kevin. "You have nothing to do with this. Get out of the way." He growled and grabbed Jennica's wrist, trying to propel her out of the room.

Jennica wrestled away her wrist and dragged her feet. "Let go of me. I'm not going with you now or ever. I'm through with you."

Alec grabbed Thad's shoulder and spun him around. His fist connected with Thad's jaw as he muttered, "Pathetic bastard. Get it into your thick skull. She doesn't want you. She wants you to leave and never bother her again. She's with us now."

Thad stumbled back several paces but then recovered. He fisted his hands, his expression murderous, his handsome features ugly with hatred. Like a bull, he bent his head, roared, and ran at Alec, butting him in the abs and pushing him into the wall.

Alec's head rammed into the wall with a thud and his eyes grew dazed. The walls shook and pictures fell.

Panic assailed her, and she ran to see if Alec was okay. Sitting on her haunches, she attended to her lover and cradled his head in her lap. She stared at his closed eyes, hoping they weren't dilated and he wasn't concussed.

Alec moaned and snuggled closer against her bare breasts.

"Open your eyes. You have to be all right." She stroked Alec's beloved face, his beard soft, yet rough against her palm. "If anything happens to you..." She started to choke up and twisted around to stare at the monster. "If you hurt him your sorry arse is mine. You won't recognise your little sub. You'll have to watch over your shoulder."

Kevin knelt down and took Alec's pulse. He put his ear to Alec's lips. "His heart beat is strong. His breathing's okay, lucky for you."

Thad paced, shoving his fingers through his hair. "He's fine. It's his fault for punching me first. I was just defending myself." He thrust out his hand to Jennica. "Let's blow these losers' place. I forgive you."

She blinked in disbelief. Slowly, she repeated, "You...forgive...me?"

"Yes, now let's go. This place freaks me out."

Kevin met her gaze and shook his head as if to say, "How did you ever hook up with that tosser?"

"'You give me the creeps. I'm not going with you now or ever. I'm home."

"'Home'? They've given you wacky weed or something. You can't mean it." Thad's hand dropped limply to his side. His shoulders drooped.

"I can and do mean it. I don't love you. I don't even like you. I'm in love with them."

Thad swore under his breath and kicked the bed. "You can't be 'in love' them...they're gay. They like fucking assholes."

It didn't take but a second to search her heart before the answer resounded in her soul. "Yes! I love them. Both of them. With all my heart and soul. We're a family. This is my home. I'm happy here."

Thad spat. "You're a delusional bitch. Who would want you anyway?" He pivoted on his heel and spun to leave.

Kevin jumped up and stopped him. "We love Jennica and she loves us. If you ever insult her or any of us ever again, you'll have to watch your back for me. That's not a threat. It's a promise."

Thad's blood drained from his face and even his fingernails went ghostly pale. Without another word, he gulped and scurried around Kevin. "You'll be sorry! I'll get you for this."

"Good riddance!" Kevin slammed the door shut behind him.

Jennica admired Kevin's strength and appreciated his power and protection, but she was more worried about Alec. Her heart weeping, she stroked his gaunt face. If anything happened to him, she'd perish. "Speak to me, lover. Be okay. This is all my fault."

Alec's lashes fluttered and he coughed. His body shook and his face brushed her breasts. His eyes opened a slit and a slow, steady smile dawned on his face. "Mama, I'm home." He kissed the tip of her breast and then began to suckle it.

Kevin chuckled and rose to his full height. "No worries. Looks like he's going to be just fine."

God, Alec's lips felt so good, so right on her, she forgot she'd been worried about him just moments before. Closing her eyes in ecstasy, she cradled his head closer, pushing her breast deeper into his mouth. Her pussy clenched and her knickers became soaked. Squirming against him, she wanted to be one with him again, to show him how very much he meant to her.

She ran her fingers through his beautiful, silky hair, mesmerised by his beauty. A child that looked like him, male or female, would be gorgeous. She'd be proud to have his children. And Kevin's.

Troubling thoughts gripped her. Would they still want her after all the trouble she'd been? She tried not to frown, but her lips trembled nevertheless.

Alec released her breast and his soulful eyes gazed into hers. "Is something wrong?"

She didn't want to burden them, to show lack of strength or indecision, but did she have a choice? The cool air whooshing against her wet breasts made her shiver against her will, but she was sure it was more than just the air that caused that reaction.

Alec struggled to sitting and placed his hands on her shoulders. He gazed deeply into her eyes, his long lashes sexier than eyes had a right to be, sexier than anything she had ever dreamed. His lips were soft, yet firm. He slid a warm finger under her chin and forced her to gaze into those eyes. "I've known you too long. Something's wrong. What is it, baby?"

She tried to slide her gaze away, to veil her eyes, but he tutted. "Look at me. I know you're not telling the truth."

Kevin joined them and lowered himself to the floor. He slid his arm around her shoulders and gave her a squeeze. "Whatever it is, we'll understand. You can always talk to us about anything. We'll always be here for you."

"No matter what," Alec finished. He scooted closer, his knees kissing hers. "We're a family, remember? The three Musketeers."

That made her laugh. She'd never heard that that the three Musketeers was a lover's triangle.

"That's much better. You have the most gorgeous smile in the world." Alec tucked the pink side of her hair behind her ear and cupped her cheek in his hand. "Are you going to tell us or do I have to tickle it out of you?"

She thought about that and her pussy grew hot again. "With the feather?"

Kevin grinned. "With anything you like." He cupped her breast and kneaded her nipple.

She closed her eyes and moaned as she leaned into him.

Kevin helped Alec to pull off the clothing that dared cover her lower half then helped Alec undress. Soon, they were all gloriously naked again.

Alec slid his hand between her legs and massaged her thighs, moving slowly, tortuously closer to her hot sex. "Do I have to get that feather?"

"Promises. Promises," she drawled. She hoped they would. She yearned for them to prove without the shadow of a doubt that they still wanted her despite the trouble that that prat Thad had caused.

Alec looked to Kevin. "Methinks she wants that feather too much."

Kevin nodded. "Yep."

Alec moved closer and murmured against his lips. "No feather until you confess what's troubling you."

"Not fair." She looked from man to man, and when they presented a united front, she sighed. "Okay. I'm worried that you won't want me anymore, not after Thad burst in here and roughed you up."

Amazement jumped into Alec's eyes. "Not want you! Daft cow! How could you ever imagine anything so incredibly backwards? You're everything I've ever dreamed about in a woman...and more."

Kevin nuzzled her ear and pressed his warm body to hers. He put his other arm around Alec. "We're a family. We're lovers. No one, especially not that wanker, is going to split us up. *Cappice*?"

She almost cried in relief and nodded. Her heart felt incredibly, miraculously joyous and she flung herself into their arms. "I love you more than I thought I could ever love anyone. I think I always have. I just didn't realise how much."

"So you'll have our child? You'll stay with us? Forever? Please make us the happiest men alive." Kevin spread his palm over her belly. So did Alec.

Wanting nothing more, she nodded. For all she knew... She looked down and put her hands over theirs in the perfect triad. "Forever and ever. You're my best mates and I'm totally, completely in love with you." She corrected one more thing. "I'll have your 'children'." Hopefully, a whole house full, several with Alec's soulful eyes, and several with Kevin's incredible lips and beautiful blond hair. "It's a good thing you'll be able to feed us all," she said with a mischievous grin directed to Alec.

A primitive growl arose from Kevin's loins, and he swooped her into his arms and deposited her back on the bed. "Children, huh? Guess we'd better get started."

She patted her belly. "Maybe we already have."

Kevin's hard cock pointed at her pussy and moved in for the kill. As he straddled her, he murmured against her lips, "Just in case, we'll just have to keep making love until there's no doubt. Insurance."

She smiled, thinking of life with her best mates. "I like insurance very, very much."

THE WAGER

Dakota Rebel

Dedication

To my friends, who have supported me above and beyond belief. To Beth, my unexpected muse, to Joe M, my personal reader, to Dave and Angela who believe in me, to Chris and Jenny, who love to make me laugh. And as always, to Mr. Rebel, for everything.
XoXoXo
D

Chapter One

I ran into Maxiel, our local vampire pub, at eight-fifteen PM. I was late, as usual, but he would be expecting that. I had never yet been on time for this weekly date. He might even worry if I got there on time or, heaven forbid, early.

I scanned the few occupied tables and found Will in the corner already nursing a beer. And even from across the room I could tell the waitress was flirting with him. But I couldn't blame her. I'd been with Will for twenty years, and I still flirted with him every chance I got.

He looked up, saw me watching him and flashed me a grin. I did a little finger wave and started towards him. The waitress disappeared quickly, which also didn't surprise me. I'm not known as an understanding girlfriend. And I like it that way. It keeps the skanks away.

Not that I ever really worry Will would stray. I believe I keep him plenty happy.

"Hey Sadie." He wrapped his arms around my waist and kissed me deeply. I ran my fingers through his hair and kissed him back just as hard. The feel of his skin against mine never failed to send little shocks through my body. I could spend eternity with him and he would still make me shiver in anticipation of what was coming. Because with Will, something was *always* coming. Luckily it was usually me.

I heard a loud thunk and turned to see the waitress had brought the beer Will had ordered for me. Foam ran down the side of the bottle from the force with which she'd slammed it on the table. I hissed at her through my fangs. She rolled her eyes then walked away.

"Bitch," I muttered. "Why don't you come back here and fucking try me, you American twat?"

"Shh. She's not worth it. Besides, she'll probably be gone by the end of the week anyway. Just let it go." He nuzzled my neck, his fangs just barely scraping the skin.

I smiled. He was probably right. Most of the waitresses who had problems with me disappeared before too long. We were very good customers at this pub and the owner liked to keep us happy. And what made me happy was being able to spend time in public with Will without having to worry about waitresses making unwanted passes at him.

"Do you want to rack?" Will asked, motioning towards our pool table.

"Do I ever?" I replied before sitting at our table and taking a long swig of my beer.

"You know, if you don't start showing up on time, I am going to make you start racking. Where were you anyway? You were awake when I left the flat, so I know you didn't oversleep this time. What did you have to do that was so important?" he asked, walking towards the table with the tray of balls he must have gotten before I arrived. I am sure the waitress was only to happy to grab his balls for him.

"There was a sale." I raised my leg to show him my new shoes. "I was only going to pop in for a second, but it was a really good sale."

"And how much did that cost me?" He glanced down at the shoes, obviously not really even seeing them.

"Aren't they cute?" I bounced my foot impatiently while ignoring his question.

He shook his head laughing. He looked again, this time taking my ankle in his hand and pulling my foot closer to his face, almost pulling me off the barstool in the process. "They are adorable. And I am glad to see that kept me waiting for a good cause then."

"Besides, if I had been here on time you would have missed quality flirting time with your future ex-girlfriend." I pointed the neck of my beer in the direction of our bitchy waitress.

"That's true," he said, dropping my leg and doing a convincing leer at her. "It would have been a shame to miss such fascinating conversation."

"Oh really? And what did Ms. Skeezy have to say that was so great?"

"The usual," he said walking back to me. "Why am I wasting my time with a woman who obviously doesn't appreciate what she has? When am I going to find a real woman to satisfy my needs?"

"She has a point," I said, draining my bottle and motioning for another. "When she comes back with my beer you should take her up on it."

"Maybe I should," he said with a smirk. "I'll chat her up, and you can rack."

"Bite me." I couldn't fight the smile enough to make any false anger believable.

"Gladly." He moved between my legs and nuzzled my neck, his fangs rubbing against the skin again, this time with more pressure. I gasped at the feel of it. It was a small prick of a bite, just barely breaking skin, but enough that when he licked the wound he came away with a small drop of blood on his tongue. Which he was kind enough to stick out and show me.

I pushed him away and swatted his ass.

Running my tongue over my fangs, I watched him bend over the pool table. He was racking the balls for our weekly billiards game at Maxiel. I'd always told him I wasn't any good at racking, but to be honest, I just liked the way his jeans hugged his arse when he was bent over.

The waitress dropped off two more beers, more softly this time, then walked away with out a word. I smiled to myself, figuring someone had "talked" to her about her attitude towards me.

"So Sadie, what's the wager this week?" Will asked, straightening up and hanging the rack over the table. He walked over to me and put his hands on my hips.

"Why do I have to decide?" I asked. "Don't you always pick?"

"I'm starting to feel bad about this game." He kissed the tip of my nose. "I always win and you always have to pay up. So I thought if I let you pick what you want to do when you lose this week, I can alleviate some of my guilt."

"What a gentleman," I said smiling up at him. "What was the bet last week?"

"Forgotten already?" he asked. "I would have thought your arse would still be sore after the whipping I gave you." He ran his hand over my bottom making me shudder for him.

No, I hadn't forgotten the lashing I had gotten after losing last week. Just like I hadn't forgotten the week I had spent as his slave when I'd lost the week before that. Or the week of blow jobs I had given him the week before that. He continued to get more and more creative with his wagers, and I had been looking forward to him picking the wager this week as well.

"I don't mind if you pick," I said. "I kind of like it when you do."

He smiled and kissed me deeply, pulling my body tight against his. The kiss was so forceful he nicked me with his fangs again. I growled low against his mouth when I tasted the sweet metal of my blood in our mouths.

He didn't usually draw blood in public. Even in a vampire safe pub like Maxiel it could be considered tacky. But he had already done it twice and I was going to start wondering why if the behaviour continued.

I wanted to think it was because he just couldn't resist me. But I had a feeling the waitress may have come on to him a little stronger than he would ever admit to me.

"Excuse me, are you two going to play or are you going to shag? Cause there are people waiting to use this table." A male voice broke up our moment.

I spun around with my best glare on my face, but it wilted when I saw our friends, Tony and Dave, standing there smiling like idiots. It had been weeks since we had seen them. We all took turns hugging, shaking hands and doing that guy thump on the back thing.

Will and I had known Tony and Dave for many, many years. Dave and Will even had a "thing" together for a while, though neither of them ever talked to me about it in detail. All I really knew was that they were living together before Will met me, then Will moved in with me and no one was ever hurt or bitter about any of it.

The four of us had even caused quite a bit of havoc together in our younger years. We all got along really well and had the same sense of inappropriate fun.

Our parties used to be notorious. All the vampires in town wanted to be there, and humans wouldn't come near the neighbourhood. It had been great fun for a while. Then Will and I sort of grew out of it...but Tony and Dave never really did.

"So, is this the only vampire pub in town where you two are still allowed?" I asked them.

"No," Dave said, pretending to sound hurt. "We are still allowed at Draper's too."

After vampires "came out" Parliament had gotten together to find a way to protect its citizens from "our kind." They decided there would be pubs where all the patrons understood the rules of blood sucking. Women and men who wanted to be bitten could come to these establishments and offer themselves to us. In return we promised not to kill them or take unwilling victims off the street.

Tony and Dave weren't as quick to take to the new ways as some of us were. And while they never took "victims", trying instead to stick to groupies, they sometimes used a little more coercion on the humans than allowed by law if they wanted one who didn't seem to want them back.

I never really understood that. The bars in the vampire district were crawling with humans begging to be bitten. The arrangement had been made so that everyone could get what they wanted, vampires could get their fill of blood anytime they wanted it, and humans who wanted to be bitten would have cool scars to show their friends.

For the most part this had all worked out great, except that vampires didn't have anywhere to escape the groupies. That is until Maxiel opened.

There were no humans allowed in here and it was the busiest of the vampire pubs. But on Thursdays, when Will and I had our weekly game, Maxiel's was usually slow. And skanky waitress not withstanding, they treated us really well there.

"Do you guys want to play teams?" Tony asked, interrupting my thoughts.

"This is kind of our weekly date," Will said, looking at me.

"You guys can hang out with us if you want to, but we are playing for some pretty high stakes tonight," I said.

"Oh yeah?" Dave asked. "Money?"

"Not exactly." I hoped I wasn't blushing as I said it.

"Oh," the boys said together, so much for hoping.

"That's enough." Will's voice held the hint of anger.

"What have you told them?" I turned to Will and could feel my eyes narrowing.

"I didn't have to tell them anything," he said. "They're deviant enough to figure it out on their own. Besides, if you are going to blush every time a guy wiggles his eyebrows at you, you're going to give away a lot more than that about us."

"Your break," I said to Will, shoving him away in false anger.

He walked around to hug me from behind. "We still haven't decided what the wager is yet," he whispered in my ear.

"Then you had better start thinking quick."

"I do have one idea," he said, his voice husky and low against my ear.

I turned in his arms and looked at him expectantly.

"If I win, I get to watch you have sex with Dave and Tony."

"Interesting," I said slowly. I didn't blink. I didn't even move. I tried to keep my body as neutral as possible. Will knew I had been with both of them before, though never at the same time. The idea had possibilities. "And if I win?"

"It's your call," he said.

It didn't take me long to decide what I wanted from him, but I wasn't sure if he would go for it. It wouldn't be the first time for him, but it would be the first time in a long time.

"Okay. If I win, I get the same thing," I said softly.

"If you want to have sex with them for me, we can just skip the game and go home now," he said, his eyes wide with surprise.

I laughed. "No sweetie. If I win, you have sex with them while I watch."

He didn't even pause, "Okay."

"That was fast," I said a little shocked. Even if he had been with men before, hell even though one of them had been Dave, I wasn't expecting such a quick affirmative reaction from him.

"I've seen you play," he said, as if that explained everything. "No offence, Sadie, but I'm not really worried."

"I'll break." I hoped my voice sounded as indignant as I felt at his reaction. He had no idea what he had just done to himself.

I took the cue from his hand and walked to the table. I ran it through my fingers a few times and bent over the rail. I pulled back and slammed forward hard. The balls flew across the felt, three solids going in the corner pockets. I aimed and took my second shot. One then two more balls fell into the pockets before I missed and it was Will's turn.

He looked at me stunned when I handed the cue back to him. I smiled and kissed his cheek.

"Did I mention I always lose on purpose?" I asked. "Usually the bet is something I really want to do for you or to you. But tonight I am feeling a little inspired to win."

Will walked slowly to the table and I headed back to watch him with the boys at our table. I ordered a couple more drinks, but I didn't have long to wait before it was my turn again. I had apparently thrown Will completely off his game. His first shot was good, but he missed the second and I was up again.

I couldn't help but smile as the truth of my words sunk in. I had never tried to win before, and he had never really seen me play. But now that the wager held something interesting for me to win, I wasn't about to miss the opportunity.

When Will stepped up to take his turn again, I turned to the boys.

"Hey, you guys, do you want to help me with something?"

"Sure," they said together.

"Will decided to include you two in our bet tonight and I figure I should get your permission before the game is over."

"What kind of wager?" Dave asked.

"Well, he decided if he wins I will have sex with you two while he watches," I said.

"Yeah, I think we could agree to that," said Tony quickly.

"Fantastic. Thanks guys," I said and turned back to watch Will take his shot.

"Wait a minute," Dave said. "You seem to be kicking his arse though. What happens if you win?"

I knew that wouldn't really work, but it was worth a shot.

"Oh, well, I get to watch you two shag him. If that's okay I mean." I knew Dave hadn't been horribly upset by Will leaving him for me, if that is even what happened, but I wasn't sure he would be willing to jump into bed with him again.

Tony and Dave glanced at each other then at Will as he missed another shot. They looked back at me and grinned. I never understood how they managed to move in unison like that. I always assumed they had some kind of mind link, like twins separated at birth or something. It was spooky sometimes.

"Okay," Tony said. "But I don't want his dick in my arse."

I laughed and told the boys no one would be asked to do anything they weren't comfortable with. It was all agreed by time my turn came around again.

The game went quickly after that and when only the eight ball remained on the table it was Will's turn. He walked around the table looking for his angle. Finally he called a pocket and took his shot.

We all watched the cue ball skip off the rail then land in the pocket and the game was over. I smiled up at my men and fought the urge to jump up and down clapping and cheering. I had won for the first time ever. And oh what a prize I won.

Will drained his drink and shook his head. He walked over to me and gave me a congratulatory kiss.

"I guess you won," he said. "But how do you know the guys will go for it?"

"Don't worry sweetie. I already cleared it with both of them, and they are fine with it. So I guess we'd better get going. We have a long night ahead of us." I kissed him again and dropped some pounds on the table. I even left a tip for the skeezy waitress. Karma points for me.

Will looked at Tony and Dave, and they grinned back at him.

I shook my head and led the strange group of vampires to the parking lot. Yeah, it was going to be a very long night.

Chapter Two

Tony and Dave followed us back to our flat. Will stayed silent the entire ride home and I let him ponder the events that were about to take place. I fought to keep a grin off my face, not wanting to spook him out of paying up. Not that he was spookable.

And it wasn't like he had never had sex with a man before. In fact before he and I had gotten together he was living with Dave. I didn't know if he had ever slept with Tony, but from Tony's earlier comment I had to assume not. Though it was hard to imagine Dave doing anything without Tony.

I was kind of excited. I had never won before and I was just dying to gloat. I resolved to control myself until later though. I stole glances at Will once and a while, searching for signs of his feelings towards the situation. Unfortunately he just seemed to be his normal, stoic self. He didn't look upset, or happy, or anything at all really. Sometimes it gets annoying dating someone who doesn't have facial expressions when he doesn't want to.

My face is an open book. I never learned that particular vampire skill. The blank stare, the smooth face, nope. If I was thinking it you could see it plastered all over me.

When we got to the flat I poured everyone some wine, and we sat on the patio talking. Well, the boys and I talked. Will remained silent and killed off the bottle of wine by himself. He wasn't drunk, but I suspected he had a good buzz going. He still didn't seem upset or uncomfortable with the situation though.

After about an hour the mood had become thick with everyone's anticipation. We stole furtive glances at each other during every break in conversation, and I figured it was time for Will to pay up.

"So," I said. "Shall we go inside?"

"Sure," Tony said. "The night's not getting any younger."

Will drained the rest of his glass and stood up, swaying slightly, then led the way into the flat. We all followed him into the living room.

"How do you want to do this," Dave asked Will when we were all seated around the room. "I mean, what are the ground rules and stuff?"

"Well it's usually up to the winner of the wager. But there have never been other people involved in the payoff, so I'm not really sure," Will said then looked at me expectantly.

"I agree. I don't feel completely comfortable telling others what to do."

Now that the moment had arrived, I was a little nervous. Not enough to let Will back out, but enough that I wasn't sure how to proceed. I didn't want to bring up their past relationship, but I guess I just expected them to know what to do and do it for me. I hadn't thought about the part where I would be directing my own private porn show.

"You? Not comfortable telling people what to do," Dave sniggered.

"Yeah, that's a little hard to believe Sadie. I mean, you are the most stubborn, outspoken…beautiful woman we have ever seen and we're lucky to be allowed in your presence," Tony 's tone changing at the look on my face.

I laughed in spite of myself. They really were adorable boys.

Dave leaned over to Tony and whispered in his ear for a minute, then looked at me, his face serious again.

"How about this, you dictate what you want, and we will go along with it? If any of us, including Will, have a problem with what's happening we will speak up and decide at that time what to do about it," Dave said.

I nodded. "I'm okay with that. Will?"

"That sounds fair to me. Though to be honest, I don't know that I should really get a say in it since I lost the bet. I never let you back out of anything we wagered."

"I think you should," I said. "You would have let me stop if I wasn't comfortable with something we've done. I won't let you completely back out, but if it gets to be too much we can work something out. We're all kind of in new territory tonight. I don't want to spoil our friendships and make things weird because things end up in a place where someone isn't comfortable."

They all nodded and I smiled. If everything worked out, this was going to be a night none of us would ever forget. And we might end up with an even closer friendship. Hopefully.

"Should we move to the bedroom?" Tony asked.

"No," I said. "I think there's more room for everyone to manoeuvre in here."

After sharing a glance, they all stood to faced me.

"What does my Mistress desire of us?" Will asked, his voice surprisingly steady.

And the games began.

"Tony, Dave, would you undress Will please?"

Dave dropped to his knees to unbutton Will's jeans while Tony started undoing Will's shirt. They had him naked in seconds and I smiled my approval.

"Good. Now undress yourselves, please," I said. "I want Will to see what he has to look forward to." I was pretty sure Will remembered what Dave had to offer, but since I wasn't sure about him and Tony, I figured I would act like this was everyone's first time together.

They quickly stripped off their clothes and soon they all stood naked in front of me. I worried that I wouldn't be able to stay out of the action for long. Looking at the hard, naked flesh in front of me made me want to drop to my knees and fondle all of them.

But tonight, I had someone else to do that for me. I wondered if I would regret asking Will to do this. If seeing him with someone else would bother me more than I could handle. We had been each other's one and only for a long time. I guess I would find out soon enough.

"Will, drop to your knees and touch them. Take their cocks in your hands and stroke them, slowly," I rose to my feet and starting to walk towards them.

Will fell to his knees with a quickness that made the floor tremble. He took a deep breath and reached for both Tony and Dave. I walked behind them so I could see Will's face as he stroked them. He stared at me while he pumped his hands up and down the hard lengths of their cocks. The fire in his eyes made my nipples twinge almost painfully. I rubbed them absently through my shirt while I watched my lover's face.

Then I moved around to see Tony and Dave. Their eyes were burning too. Both of them stared down, watching Will's hands manipulate them. I didn't need to have the same equipment to know what they experienced. And I couldn't help being jealous now. I'd had Will's calloused hands caress my skin so many times that I'd memorised the feeling. His skin was rough, but his touch was feather light. He had a way with flesh that was amazing. Some nights he had brought me off with just one touch.

"Enough," I said, shaking myself from my thoughts. "We don't want the boys spent too early, darling."

Will dropped his hands to his lap, watching me and waiting for my next command. I looked down at him, pleased to see that he was as hard as they were. I knelt behind him and whispered in his ear.

"Look at how hard touching them has made you already. And look at how hard they are for you, baby. Look at how much they loved the feel of your hands on them. Their beautiful cocks are waiting for you. They're waiting for my next order as anxiously as you are. They want me to let you make them explode. They are watching us, hoping I will let you touch them again, let you make them come for me. But we have all night, my love. Tonight is for *my* pleasure. You will do as I tell you, and only I have the power to release them. But it will be through your actions. Your hands and mouth and flesh will bring them for me. Do you understand?"

"Yes Mistress," he said. "I understand."

"Do you know yet why I love to make you happy? Do you feel the power that you have as my slave?" I asked.

"Yes Mistress," he breathed. "I do know. Thank you."

"Good boy." I nipped his throat lightly with my fangs, making him hiss through his own. "Next time you make me your slave perhaps you will remember the power you give me." I licked the small pin-prick size drops of blood I had left on his neck before standing again.

Will groaned as his muscled cock twitched in anticipation of my next order. I glanced at Tony and Dave, finding them staring at Will's naked body. At that moment, I knew that no matter what I commanded tonight, none of them would call the game. They were all getting into this, and we had only just begun.

"Tony, kneel behind Will," I said.

Tony walked around to take my spot on the floor behind Will. He was close to Will's naked back but did not touch him.

I nodded then looked up at Dave. "I want you to stand directly in front of Will." He shuffled to his left moving a few inches closer to Will.

"Will, I want you to very slowly lick Dave's cock. I want you to start at his balls and lick up to the tip. Just once, don't suck, just lick," I said.

Will moved his head forward and, as instructed, licked a single line up Dave's dick making the man shudder.

"Good boy. Now, swirl your tongue over his tip. Lick the beautiful juices you're making him seep," I said. "Taste him. I know you want to." Watching Will's mouth on Dave, seeing the matching looks on their faces as they stared at each other, quickly reminded me that this was not their first time together. They had known each other a long time, longer than I had known them. I couldn't help but feel slightly jealous of the bond they had. Not enough to make them stop, it was too fucking hot for that.

Will put his tongue on Dave's tip, licking circles around the small hole in it as if Dave was an ice cream cone. Dave groaned loudly and pushed his hips forward.

"Not yet," I said sternly. "Let him remember the taste of you first. It's been a long time since Will has had a cock in his mouth." I ran my hand through Tony's hair. "Don't worry, lover. I haven't forgotten about you. Just give them a moment."

Tony nodded, but he didn't seem to mind watching. His eyes were focused on Will's mouth working the tip of his best friend's cock like it was the most amazing thing he had ever seen. I watched as Tony reached for his own dick, but he must have thought better of it because he moved his hands back to the floor, clenched into fists so tight his knuckles turned white.

I knew the feeling. The crotch of my panties was drenched, and I ached to touch myself, as well, or to at least, touch them. I wanted flesh in my hands, and I wasn't too picky about whose it was. But this was not about me, not really, not anymore. This was about the three beautiful naked men in front of me.

"Will, I want you to take as much of Dave's cock into your mouth as you can. I want you to suck his dick the way you love me to suck yours." I gripped my hands tightly into Tony's shaggy hair as we watched the other men.

Will nodded and opened his mouth, sliding it down Dave until he almost met Dave's body with his lips then pulled back. Dave's fists clenched at his sides, and I knew he fought slamming his hips forward to fuck Will's mouth.

Tony's hand was on his cock now. He stroked it hard, his eyes never leaving the beautiful sight in front of him. I let go of his head so I could bend down to whisper directions in his ear.

Will jerked slightly when Tony's hands ran up his back, but he didn't stop what he had been told to do. Tony's fingers wound their way into Will's hair and grabbed two fistfuls, the way I had just done to him. He used Will's hair to control the speed of his mouth. Slowing him down so each stroke stretched for many seconds.

Tony edged forward so his cock rubbed against Will's back and all three men moaned softly. Tony rocked slightly to increase the friction against his frustrated cock and Will's hand moved to the base of Dave's dick so he wouldn't accidentally gag if the speed of his head was increased by either of the other men.

I didn't want to stop them, they looked so beautiful like that, but I was afraid that one, or more of them, would come too early.

"Enough," I said loudly.

They stopped, but the reluctance from all of them was apparent. I tried not to smile at the sight of their disappointment. I was glad they were all as into it as I was enjoying watching them.

"Don't worry boys. Everyone is going to get what they want tonight." *Including me,* I thought. Watching them all together like that was driving me crazy. I wanted so badly to be in on the action. I could only direct for so long. I could feel my need building every time they touched each other.

Chapter Three

"Will, get on all fours for me," I said.

He looked at me with his eyes wide, and for a second, I thought he was going to argue, but he shook his head and did as he was told.

"Good boy," I said. "Tony, kneel in front of him so he can suck that beautiful cock of yours. Dave, come over here and take off my clothes please."

I wasn't going to interrupt their action, but if I didn't get someone to touch me I might combust. Dave walked behind me so he could remove my clothes while he watched Will go down on Tony.

We both stared at the two naked men in front of us while Dave's hands ran over my breasts to reach the buttons on my shirt. He pulled the cloth apart and reached to pinch my nipples through my bra. I leaned against him, feeling his cock press against my arse. I considered bending over when he got me naked and letting him alleviate the pain between my legs. But I knew I couldn't. Not yet, there were too many possibilities left to explore before I joined in the mix.

Will was sucking Tony's cock with so much force I could hear the wet sucking sounds his mouth made. Tony's eyes were slits and his hands wound their way back into Will's hair while he fucked his mouth as Dave had wanted to.

Dave had removed my jeans and moved so he could crouch in front of me. He pulled my panties down my legs, leaving me naked in front of him. He pressed his cheek against my upper thigh then inhaled deeply through his nose.

"You're enjoying yourself then?"

"Cheeky monkey," I whispered to him. "Give me your hand."

He reached his hand up to me and I sucked his finger into my mouth and pulled it out again. I ran his hand between my breasts, over my stomach and between my legs. He let me manipulate his finger into my soaking wet slit while I watched my lover suck our friend's cock in a frenzy.

I wanted to come against Dave's hand so bad, but I knew I shouldn't. If I let myself come now then the night I'd imagined would be over and I would be the only one getting fucked by them. So after a minute I pulled his hand away and pushed his finger into his mouth.

"Maybe when you three are finished we can all have some more fun. But for now, I want my pay off," I said. "Go to your friends."

Dave nodded and pulled his finger out of his mouth. He ran it over my lips then walked to Tony and Will. I licked my lip and groaned. Watching them all and not being in the middle of it was going to be more difficult that I had originally thought.

"Stop," I said, the command coming out a little harsher than I'd meant for it to. But my frustration was peaking and someone needed to come soon if I wasn't.

They all looked at me waiting for what I wanted next. I shook my head and walked towards them. I knelt in front of Will and kissed him, forcing my tongue into his mouth, cleaning Tony's musky taste from it.

I pressed my tongue against the points of his fangs until I could taste my hot, coppery blood mixing in our mouths. Will growled into my mouth, pressing himself as tightly against the front of my body as he could.

My clit felt as if it would actually explode and I wanted to touch myself, to make them touch me, something, anything to make the pain stop. I was beginning to wish I had lost the game now. At least then I would be in the middle of these gorgeous men. But I'd won, and I was the Mistress. They were waiting for me to give them their orders, not to act as their slut for the night. Not yet anyway.

"Am I behaving to your liking Mistress?" Will asked when I pulled away from his lips.

"Yes slave, you are a good little cock sucker. I think you deserve a reward for your skills. Boys, would you agree that Will has earned a little treat?"

"Yes Ma'am," they said together.

"Would you two be willing to suck on Will now?"

"Yes Ma'am," they said again.

"Dave, I want you to lay next to him and take his cock in your mouth. Tony, I would like you suck on his balls. But he is not allowed to come. Do you understand me?"

They both nodded. I pushed Will onto his back and the boys took their positions. I sat on the floor and watched them manipulate my lover. Their faces were so close, and the sight of Will's cock disappearing into Dave's mouth was almost enough to put me over the edge.

I watched Will's face and knew that no one would mind if I sat on his face and made him eat my pussy until I came. I inched closer to him and his head turned towards me. His eyes were wide and his chest was heaving.

"I can smell you," he whispered.

"The sight of you three together like this is amazing," I said. "I feel like I am going to die just watching. I cannot imagine how you feel." I ran my hand through his hair. "You're a very good slave, my love."

"Thank you Mistress," he said. "Would you like me to service you now?"

"Not yet." I smiled. "But thank you for the offer."

"Mistress, I believe he may be close," Tony said.

They both pulled away from Will and looked at me.

"Good boys," I said. "And thank you for your help."

I stood and looked down at them again. They were fucking beautiful. My brain worked a mile a minute trying to figure out what I wanted to see next.

"Both of you, up here by Will's face please," I said.

They scrambled forward and sat on their heels on opposite sides of my lover.

"I want to watch you rub your gorgeous cocks all over Will's face. Try to drip yourselves on him. I want to see thick trails of your pre-cum staining his beautiful face for me. Rub your cocks together for me too. Run them over his mouth at the same time. Will, I want you to look at me while they do this."

He nodded and focused his eyes on mine. But I looked back at his occasionally, just to make sure he was following my orders. I wanted to watch Tony and Dave's cocks.

They did exactly as I asked. They rubbed against each other and dragged the tips of their cocks over Will's cheeks and mouth and nose. I wondered if Dave and Will had done this before. I also began to think that Dave and Tony had history too. Their movements together were too comfortable, too familiar to be the first time. And as far as I could tell without watching his eyes the whole time, Will never looked away from me, as if he had been waiting for me to put it all together from the beginning.

My cunt was so wet watching all of this that my juices started to flow down my legs. I finally gave in and rubbed my soaking wet slit. I avoided my clit, because I didn't want to come yet, but I had to be touched. Will started to reach for me, but I slapped his hand away.

"Bad slave," I said. "I did not give you permission to touch your Mistress, did I?"

"No Mistress," Will said quickly. "I am sorry Mistress."

"That was very naughty, slave. I'm afraid that now you must be punished. You two stop please. You will all wait here and not touch each other until I return. Do you understand?" I asked.

"Yes Mistress," they all said.

I stood and walked quickly to the bedroom. My heart pounded in my ears. Will had to know what I was going to get, but I had never used it on him before. He had used it on me many times though. It was what happened to naughty slaves, and he knew that.

I closed the bedroom door behind me and thought about the three of them sitting silently in the living room waiting for my return. I replayed in my head the events of the night so far.

Will looked even more gorgeous than usual with a cock between his lips. I laid on the bed and thought about the boys rubbing their cocks all over Will's face. My fingers slammed between my legs as I imagined how their fluids were drying on my lover's cheeks and lips while I lay on my bed fingering my aching pussy.

My fingers tapped against my clit and stars exploded behind my eyelids. I wanted to let them wait for a few minutes. Anticipation was always so exciting for Will and me, and I had a feeling Tony and Dave were appreciating it too. I wanted to give them time to cool down, as well, because when the time came for them to fuck Will, I wanted to be sure it lasted long enough that I was as satisfied as they would be.

I lay on the bed for another minute, waiting for the throbbing in my stomach and pussy to subside. I went into our bathroom and cleaned up a little, wiping away the juices that had dripped down my thighs and cleaning off my fingers. It was more for my comfort than to hide what I had done.

Vampires have a very keen sense of smell, and they had probably known the instant I'd come, even from down the hallway. I grabbed the cat 'o nine tails punisher from the closet and a bottle of lubricant from the bedside table then walked back to my men.

Chapter Four

I walked back into the living room with the cat o' nine tails in my hand. Tony and Dave smiled at me with knowing eyes.

"Does our Mistress feel better now?" Dave asked.

"Yes thank you," I said. "And how is our slave feeling?"

"I am ready for my punishment, Mistress," he said.

"Cheeky monkey," I snapped. "You do not ask for your punishment slave. You just take it."

"Yes, Mistress," he said unapologetically.

I smiled in spite of myself, and Tony and Dave broke into wide grins.

"Get on your feet." I stood over Will, staring down at his beautiful face, wishing I could be looking down the length of my own body at it pressed between my thighs instead.

Will rose, turning to face me with his arms at his side. I ran my hand up his thigh and over his hip then reached around him to cup his arse in my hand.

"Turn around," I whispered.

He turned showing off that lovely behind to me. I raised the whip and ran the leather straps down his back. He shuddered for me as I drew the straps over his shoulders, ran them up his spine, then over his arse. I ran my free hand between his thighs, urging him to spread his legs further apart.

"Count," I said sharply as I brought the whip across his back with a loud crack.

"One," he yelped.

"Two," he said as I brought it down again.

I cracked it across his arse and he jumped slightly.

"Three."

I snapped it against the back of his thighs.

"Four."

"Five," was gasped as I let a few of the straps clip him between his legs. I knew at least one had grazed his balls.

"Six" was hard enough to draw blood at his shoulder.

I dropped the whip and licked the line of blood that pooled to the top of the razor thin cut. Will collapsed to his knees and Tony and Dave drew closer at the scent of his blood.

I looked at them and nodded. They each took one of Will's wrists in their hands and bit down as I dug my fangs into the gash in his shoulder to open it further. Will cried out his pleasure as we drank from him. The smell of his cum shooting from him burned my nostrils and I was momentarily sorry I was drinking from his upper body instead of lower things.

We all released him at the same time, and he fell forward, catching himself on his hands. His body still shook and Tony and Dave stroked their cocks again watching him.

"I think our slave is ready for you," I said to them. I picked up the bottle of lube I had brought back from the bedroom and held it up. Dave and Tony looked at each other for a moment, then Tony moved to take it from me.

I looked up at him, and he bent down, placing a soft kiss on my forehead—an unspoken promise not to break my lover. I nodded and walked around to look at Will's face.

"Yes?" I asked him just to make sure he was still okay with what was happening.

"Yes, Mistress," he said, his voice hoarse.

I nodded and moved out of their way. Dave knelt in front of Will and pushed his cock into Will's mouth. Tony positioned himself behind Will and placed the tip of the bottle into Will's ass.

My clit began to ache again in anticipation of what I was about to witness. Since I'd seen Will sucking cock earlier, I moved behind them to watch as Tony stretched my lover's arse with his finger.

Tony slowly finger fucked Will with one finger. When Will started pushing himself back against his hand Tony added a second. He was going slow, but his cock dripped with his excitement. He added a third finger, drawing as sharp gasp from Will's mouth that was slightly muffled from Dave's large cock moving in and out of it.

Before I could admonish him for his outburst Tony brought his hand down on Will's arse with a loud crack. I smiled my approval at him and went back to watching him loosen Will's hole.

I knew they could smell how wet my pussy had become, but I could smell them too. Their musky scent stronger than my own, filling my senses. Once again I wished it was me on the floor between them. Wished Tony's fingers were working me loose, wished my mouth was stretched wide around Dave's cock.

Tony seemed satisfied that Will was ready for him and moved to position himself at Will's entrance. I stepped forward and grabbed his cock in my hand. I guided him into my lover's hole. I watched as Will was stretched wide to wrap around Tony's large dick. I stared in disbelief as Tony worked himself deeper into Will. He went slowly, letting Will adjust to every inch he gave him.

Dave slowed the pace at which he'd been fucking Will's mouth too. His eyes met Tony's over the man between them and they gave each other little half smiles. It almost seemed like a private moment between the two of them, and I wondered again if this wasn't the first time they'd shared another man.

When Tony had sheathed his entire cock in Will's arse, both men paused, letting Will completely adjust to the feeling. Will shifted his hips slightly, and Tony brought his hand down on his arse again.

"I think our slave is impatient for his fucking, boys," I said. "Is that it, baby? Do you want to be fucked so bad you don't want them to be careful anymore? Your cock is hard again. You love this don't you? Do you like being a slut for your Mistress and her friends? Do you want these two huge cocks to rip you apart? Have you missed the feel of cock filling you up? Or are you just that big of a whore for me?"

He mumbled around Dave's cock, and I smiled.

"That's a good slave. You've been so good tonight, baby. We'll have to give you what you want then. This is your final reward for being such a good little man-slut for me. Boys, fuck him. Fuck him hard. Fill his ass and his mouth and make him come again," I said.

Tony and Dave started moving in time together, they started out slow, but didn't wait long before they slammed their cocks so hard into Will it was as if they tried to break through him and meet in the middle.

I smelled Will's scent leaking from his cock. I watched the men fucking my lover, and I didn't think I had ever loved Will more.

"Does it hurt, baby? Being filled by two men? Or do you like having your arse and your mouth full of cock? I'll bet you do. It looks like it feels amazing. But I'll bet your cock hurts. I know my pussy hurts. I want to come so fucking bad, baby. After you three come, I want you all to make me come. Will you do that for your Mistress, baby? Will you all fuck me until I come, too?"

I was on the floor next to him now, whispering to him, but I knew the other two could hear me. I didn't care. The sight of these men fucking each other for me was too much. And if I didn't get their cocks inside me too I might throw a fit. This was too much flesh to let out of my house without feeling it inside me, as well.

It wasn't long before Tony cried out. Right after that, Dave filled Will's mouth with so much cum it spilled from the corners of his lips. They continued to pump into Will for a minute before they each pulled out. I had stood behind Will again so I could watch Tony pull out his cock. Tony's cum oozed out of Will's arse, and my knees almost buckled at how fucking hot it was.

Will collapsed completely to the floor, his breath ragged. I laid next to him again and looked into his eyes.

"Slave, you didn't come," I said softly.

"I cannot come until I have pleasured my Mistress." His voice was hoarse, but he looked quite pleased, like the cat with the proverbial cream.

I shook my head and smiled at him. He smiled back and snaked his tongue out to lick a drip of cum off of his lips. I shuddered at the sight, and he grinned harder at me.

"How long do you boys need before you are ready again?" Will asked, his voice stronger.

I raised an eyebrow at him.

"Our Mistress has made a request, and we are duty bound to obey," he said.

I smiled and glanced up at Tony and Dave. They looked down at us stroking themselves. Both were already becoming hard again.

"But I want to be the slave," I said with a small pout. Being bossy had been fun, but at heart I will always bottom for Will. I love him, and he loves me. I trust him even more than I trust myself to know what my body needs.

"As my Mistress commands," Will said, then crushed his mouth against mine.

Chapter Five

"I cannot have my slave distracted though," Will said after breaking our kiss. "I'll have to take care of your pussy before we do anything else."

He raised himself over me and slid down my body. I watched him snake his head between my legs. He raised my legs over his shoulders then buried his face in my soaked pussy. The first time his tongue ran over my clit I came hard. My whole body shook, and I scraped at the carpet with my nails.

He slammed his tongue in and out of my pussy, fucking me with his mouth. He nicked my clit with one of his fangs and I came again, screaming his name and burying my hands in his hair.

Tony and Dave had moved closer to us. They each took one of my wrists, and as they had done when it was Will at their mercy, they bit into me. Will moved his head so he could bury his fangs in my thigh. I screamed, and I came over and over again. Waves upon waves of pleasure and muscle spasms overtook my body. When they released me, I couldn't move. I was drenched with cum and sweat. And I wanted them. I wanted all of them on me, inside of me.

But I was the slave now, and I couldn't command. I was at their mercy, and Will knew it, even if the boys didn't understand how the game had changed.

"And now I can play with my slave any way I wish," Will said, wiping my juices from his chin. "I am your Master. And I will take my pleasure as I see fit from you. Do you understand that, you naughty little slut?"

"Yes, Master," I said with a whimper.

"You have been a very bad girl, Sadie. Playing Mistress with me. That has never been allowed, and you're going to pay for it. Do you understand?"

"Yes, Master," I whispered.

Will shoved two fingers into my pussy and finger fucked me hard, his eyes never leaving mine. When he was satisfied, he brought his fingers up to my lips and forced them into my mouth.

"Clean yourself off of me," he snapped.

I sucked his fingers clean, staring into my Master's eyes with a contentment I could never have felt when I was Mistress. This was where I belonged. Obeying my Master like a good girl. Doing as my lover wished me to do for him.

"Good girl," he murmured, removing his fingers. "You will not need quite as much time for adjustment as I was afforded. You seem quite ready to submit to our pleasures. You are ready to be our slut now, aren't you Sadie?"

"Yes, Master. Please let me be your slut. Please do as you wish to me. Please," I begged. I usually wasn't allowed to beg, but I thought tonight he would be more lenient on the rules of our game.

"Dave, where do you want her?" Will asked him.

"I have been wanting to fuck her pussy all night. Her scent has been taunting me since we got here," he said. "I can smell her from here. I want to bury my cock inside her and let her squeeze me dry."

"Tony, do you want to fuck her sweet little arse?" Will asked.

"You know I do," Tony growled.

"Then I will allow her to suck my cock," Will said.

The plan was decided as if I wasn't even in the room. The walls of my cunt contracted forcefully at the thought of them treating me as their whore. I loved it. I wondered for a moment if Will had felt this good, but the thought was brushed away at the feel of their hands.

There were hands all over my body. Fingers pinched my nipples roughly, and someone massaged my clit and fingered my pussy. Then Will's face was over mine, and he kissed me. The finger on my clit was replaced by a mouth that began sucking on me. And one of my nipples was also pulled into a mouth, fangs nipping gently at the hardened skin. The sensation of their hands and mouths on my body shut down my brain, and I gave myself over to the moment.

Will pulled away from my mouth and looked down at me.

"Are you ready to have all of your holes filled, baby? You asked what it was like to be stretched open in every way by huge cocks, and now is your chance to find out," he said softly. "Are you ready for us baby? Do you still want to know how it feels?"

I nodded and took a shaky breath. The hands had all left me and I looked around to see where the boys had gone. Dave was laying on the floor next to me and Tony was sucking his cock. My pussy clenched at the sight and I noticed Will's dick twitch when he looked at them, too.

"You need to ride Dave's cock first, slave. Get up," Will ordered.

My body was still a little shaky so Tony moved away from Dave to help me to my feet. I straddled Dave's hips and Tony guided Dave's cock into my soaking wet pussy the way I had helped Tony ease into Will's ass. I slowly slid up and down a few times until I felt hands on my shoulders.

"Hold still for Tony," Will whispered softly.

I felt something cold filling my arse and bent forward on Dave to allow Tony access to my hole. I relaxed as much as I could as he slid two fingers into me, working me open as he had done for Will. Somehow I knew they were not going to start out quite as gently for me as they had for Will though. And I was secretly glad. I wanted them to take me. I wanted it rough and violent. I wanted to beg them to hurt me.

Will knelt over Dave's face and placed his cock on my lips. I opened my mouth for him and closed my eyes as I felt Tony press his cock into my arse. I slid Will further down my throat, and we all stayed still for a moment so I could get the full effect of all three of them inside me at once.

But I was only given a short moment, then they were fucking me. Hard. They found a rhythm quickly and slammed themselves inside me so hard I was afraid they really could break me. And I almost wished they would.

Will's cock hit the back of my throat and I felt Tony and Dave's cocks rubbing against each other between the walls of my pussy and arse. Someone reached between my legs and pinched my clit and I came.

I couldn't scream around Will's cock. The force of the orgasm that ripped through me caused my eyes to tear up and my throat to contract around Will's dick, and I broke nails into the flesh of whoever's arm was in reach. It must have been Will's because as soon as I felt blood trickling over my fingers, he exploded into the back of my throat. I couldn't swallow because he was still hitting the back of my throat with his thrusts so I just tried to relax and let his cum run down my oesophagus.

Dave and Tony seemed to come at the same time, filling my pussy and my arse with so much cum it was hard to believe they had both come inside my lover not twenty minutes earlier.

We lay in a heap together for a few minutes, then Will and Tony peeled me off of Dave. We collapsed to the floor and caressed the skin of the people closest to us. The men recovered much faster than I did. I wasn't sure I would ever recover. They pulled themselves together and Tony and Dave went to clean themselves up in our bathroom.

Will moved to lay next to me and raised my head up to lay on his chest. I smiled up at him and entwined my fingers with his. He kissed my head, and I smiled weakly.

"I love you, Sadie," he whispered.

"I love you, too, Will," I whispered back.

"We love you guys, too," Tony said, walking back in the room.

"Yeah, thanks for a lovely shag," Dave said. "We should do it again sometime."

They were both dressed and somewhat pulled together.

"Sure," I said weakly. "Not tonight though."

Tony chuckled. "No. Not tonight."

They both walked over to us and we shared kisses and hugs then they left. The sun would be up soon, and we all should have been in bed already.

Will kissed my head again and slid me off of him. He walked down the hall. A while later, he returned and shook me awake.

"Come on, sleepyhead," he said, picking me up and carrying me to the bathroom.

I snuggled into his arms, happier than I had been in a while. I loved him. I would do anything for him, and after tonight I knew that he would return the favour any time.

He had drawn us a bath, and he carried me into it. I lay against his front, letting the warm water relax my muscles. He wrapped his arms around me and held me up in case I fell asleep in the water.

"So, how does it feel to be the winner?" He placed a soft kiss against my temple.

"Sticky," I murmured.

He laughed and hugged me tighter against him.

"Will?"

"Hmm?"

"I don't understand something," I said.

"What's that darling?" he asked, his voice slow and heavier than it had been a few minutes earlier.

"Your last shot at the pub. I have seen you make that play a million times. Were you just nervous tonight or something?"

"Well. To be honest, I may have lost on purpose," he said.

"Cheeky monkey. I knew you did," I said, settling deeper into his arms.

"Yeah, well the guys and I might have talked about our wagers before," he said.

"Ah, so it wasn't so much my blushing that gave us away. It was your big mouth," I said. I brought his hand up to my lips and kissed it.

"Maybe," he said, pretending at sheepish. "We may have had this week planned for a while. Though it was originally going to be you in the middle."

"Why did you change your mind?" I asked.

"Because you seemed to want to win so badly. And you do everything I ask you to do. So I thought this was finally something I could do for you. It was a small sacrifice to make you happy," he said.

"You didn't act like it was much of a sacrifice once you had a cock in your arse," I said.

"Well, it's been a while. I've never hidden the fact that I have been with Dave. Granted I've never been with two men at once, but it surprisingly wasn't that bad."

"I noticed," I said with a small smile. "I know I enjoyed this evening very much."

"I'm really glad, Sadie," he said. "So, what's the wager for next week?"

"I'll have to think about it," I said, closing my eyes. "Today, I just want to sleep."

"You know those two are going to be at every game we play from now on, don't you?" Will asked, his voice thick with sleep, too.

"Let's hope so," I said. "I love you, Will."

"I love you, too, Sadie."

"We love you guys, too," Tony said from the doorway.

I turned to look at him. Tony and Dave were standing just outside the bathroom door looking a little embarrassed, yet incredibly pleased with themselves at the same time.

"The sun's coming up. Can we crash here?" Dave asked from behind him.

"Your room is always ready," Will said. "Just don't wake us up tomorrow."

"We know the rules, lover," Tony said. "Don't worry. We wouldn't dream of making any noise before seven-ish. Though, if you hear screaming or groaning or even a little moaning and cursing, don't worry. We'll just be re-enacting something amazing that happened to us last night."

"Oh yeah?" I asked.

"Yeah, it was pretty hot," Dave said, his arm snaking around Tony's waist.

"Mmm, you'll have to tell us about it," Will said, his fingers sliding over my chest and reaching between my legs.

"Tomorrow," I said, pushing his hand away. "Okay? Tomorrow, please?"

"It's a deal," Tony said.

"It's a date," said Dave.

They walked towards their room hand in hand, and I wondered if they really would have sex again before going to sleep. I was too exhausted to even think about having sex again, let alone to actually do it.

I closed my eyes then groaned when Will shifted to wake me up again.

"You don't want to wake up in an ice bath tomorrow, do you?" he asked, helping me out of the tub.

"Maybe," I mumbled, clinging to him for support. "That might feel nice. You know, refreshing."

He picked me up and carried me to our bed. Carefully, he laid me down and crawled in beside me. We snuggled into each other, still damp from the tub, and I felt a small twinge between my legs as I fell asleep thinking about what tomorrow would bring for me, my lover, and our best friends.

FOURPLAY

Desiree Holt

Dedication

To all my friends from RT who so enrich my life. You know who you are. It was a great time.

Chapter One

Holly Martin climbed out of the big four wheel drive vehicle, looked around her and let out a long breath. A heavy breeze lifted strands of her auburn hair and whipped them across her creamy cheeks. She pulled her jacket a little tighter around her small frame and looked at the man who'd arrived with her.

"Oh, Michael. It's beautiful." She stretched out her arms and turned in a circle. "Just absolutely beautiful. It reminds me of my grandparents' place in Maine."

And so it did. This cottage just outside of Glendale, in the Isle of Skye, looked as if it had been set down in paradise. Made of stone and wood, it perched on a windswept bluff overlooking the Atlantic Ocean. Surrounding it were acres of natural grounds. Michael had told her it was a wildlife habitat, and this was the only house that would ever be built here. It made a perfect, private setting for the outrageous sexual adventures in which Duncan McLaughlin and his friends engaged in on a regular basis.

Holly had been looking forward to this visit ever since Michael had approached her about it. She'd met Duncan McLaughlin when he'd come to Denver on a business trip and stayed with the two of them. By then ménage with closely selected friends had become a regular occurrence, something she'd grown into and not only felt comfortable with but thoroughly enjoyed. The memory of the week the three of them had spent together sent shivers through her.

The thought of another week alone with both men spent entirely in sexual activities had given rise to many nights of erotic dreams. All through the long plane trip, the connecting flight and the drive, her body had tingled with anticipation, knowing what she was stepping into.

She and Michael had been together for four years. Tuning in to her natural submissive desire on their first date, he'd brought her along carefully to the type of D/s relationship he liked, introducing her to things she'd never thought she'd dare to try. By the time she'd experienced her first ménage, she'd been willing to try anything as long as it gave him pleasure, knowing that she was the one who controlled that pleasure. It was both freeing and empowering.

But lately she'd wondered where this...thing...between them would go next. Never the clingy type, she still wondered what the future held for them. Several times on the plane trip, she'd thought of casually asking him then bitten her tongue. She didn't want to destroy the mood of this trip and what they would all experience. She tucked her question in a corner of her brain, packing it away until they were back in their own place.

She lifted her face to the sun and let the strong breeze caress her skin. Everything smelled fresh and clean and looked freshly washed. A painting would not have done it justice.

Michael came up behind her and wrapped his arms around her, his hands sliding under her sweater to cup her breasts.

"It's been in Duncan's family for years," he told her. "I spent a summer here years ago. Look." He pointed with one hand. "Over there, across the sea, is Dunvegan Head and beyond that the Hebrides, "

"It's like being on another planet," she told him. "And so isolated."

"That's the point, my love." He kissed her earlobe. "You can even stand out stark naked on that deck that runs around three sides and no one will see you."

"Did you do that?" she asked.

"Mm hmm. And a lot of other things. Wait until you see the inside." He nipped at the side of her neck. "Nervous?"

"A little." Holly leaned back against him as his thumbs rasped her hardening nipples. "But not a bad nervous."

"Good, because we have a special surprise for you this week."

She turned to look back at him over her shoulder, one eyebrow quirked. "A surprise?"

"Mm hmm. One I think you'll really like. A little extra spice in the stew, as it were. Oh, yes. I can tell that excites you. Your nipples are like pebbles," he murmured, brushing them with his fingers. "Let's see how the rest of you feels."

He dropped one hand to gather up her skirt and slide his fingers into her naked folds. She never wore undies anymore—no bra, no panties. Not even a thong. He'd given her strict instructions that he wanted access to her any time, any place, and she had become anxious to comply.

"Ah, there you are, nice and wet." He pinched her clit, then drove two fingers into her slick vagina. "You really are getting turned on. Good."

Holly wiggled against him, feeling her pulse accelerate and the walls of her pussy quiver. Just the slightest touch of his hand got her hot these days, and the expectation of what awaited her made her cream even more. The fact she trusted Michael implicitly took the edge off any reservations she might have about the coming week.

"Playing with the goodies already, are we?"

A booming voice startled them. Neither had heard the door to the cottage open. Duncan moved towards them, grinning, his large body a study in fluid grace. Like Michael, he was well over six feet, lean and muscular, but where Michael's hair was a dark blond, Duncan's was a rich black. And where Michael's eyes were hazel, Duncan's were a blazing emerald green. Otherwise the two men could have been twins.

"Just getting an early start," Michael joked.

"How are you two? And Holly, welcome to Scotland and my humble hideaway."

Totally unselfconscious about her condition, Holly smiled up at him. "Thanks. This place is absolutely gorgeous. And far from humble."

"Maybe not so humble but truly secluded." He winked. "Michael, you're supposed to share with the host, remember?"

Michael laughed, hoisted Holly up and draped her legs over his arms so she was spread wide open. "Have at it."

Holly was sensitive to smells, turned on by so many of them. When Duncan came closer to her, she caught the scent of the outdoors and wood and fresh air. She inhaled deeply, her pheromones on a rampage.

He smiled at her as he caught her own special bouquet and his mouth widened in a feral grin. "It's the Scottish air that does it to them," he told her. "It gets the lasses every time."

Duncan pulled Holly's skirt up even further and pressed his warm hands against the insides of her thighs, petting them, then used his thumbs to open her labia. "Mmm. Looks delicious." He slid two fingers inside her hot sheath and wiggled them back and forth. "And feels terrific. I've been hard as a rock just thinking about this for the last two days. I can't wait to get started on our fun and games."

He removed his hand and Holly wiggled her hips as much as she could. "You don't need to stop," she told him."

He threw back his head and laughed again, "Let's get your things inside and get the party started where it's more comfortable."

He set her down on the ground, then he and Michael each pulled one of the large suitcases from the vehicle and the three of them trooped into the cottage, although Holly thought "cottage" was too small a word to describe the house. The central room was huge, with high beamed ceilings. A wood burning fire place filled most of one wall and two other walls were floor to ceiling windows. One end of the room was a granite and steel kitchen.

The furniture was dark wood and upholstered in leather, the pieces looking large and comfortable. What caught Holly's eyes, however, were the additions not usually found in a cottage. In the centre of the room was a massive bed on a raised platform, obviously custom made. On one side of it was a spanking bench, well padded with holes cut into it for

a woman's breasts to fit into. A long table on the other side held Duncan's collection of toys—handcuffs, dildos, vibrators, floggers, and a few things even Holly didn't recognise. As she cast her eyes over them she felt liquid seep from her cunt and trickle down one thigh. Yes, this was definitely the place where Duncan came to play.

He opened a door to one side of the fireplace. "I'll put your luggage in here," he told them. "It's just a small changing room, if you ever feel the need for privacy" he grinned. "Although I sincerely hope not. And you'll find a bath through the other door." He turned to Holly, who was still taking in everything. "Now, lass, let's get you more comfortable.

He peeled off her coat and hung it on an antique rack by the door, then bent to capture her mouth. His tongue, bold and swift, scoured every inch of her mouth. He slanted his head to gain a better angle, his big, warm hands resting on her shoulders before they slipped down to cup her breasts. When he broke the kiss her body was humming.

"I've missed you, lassie. A great deal. And dreamed fantastic dreams about you."

She smiled. "Me, too."

"I'd planned for us all to have a great visit. My dick has been hard as stone just thinking about this. And you. I know you've had a long trip but I cannot wait. Let me see what's hiding under those clothes."

"It's all right," she grinned. "I slept on the plane. I'm eager, too, Duncan."

That was all the encouragement he needed.

Michael leaned back against the counter, observing with interested eyes, as Duncan peeled Holly's sweater over her head and tossed it to him. The big man's breath hissed through his teeth.

"Your tits are just as gorgeous as ever, Holly mine. Nice and plump, with rosy nipples that tempt a man's mouth." He leaned down and placed a kiss on each of them. "I have some fine jewellery for them later on."

"Take off the skirt, Holly," Michael told her, "and give Duncan a view he's been waiting for."

Hands trembling slightly, Holly unzipped her skirt, shimmied out of it and tossed it to Michael to put with her sweater. Then, knowing what he expected, she turned around,. spread her legs and bent over to grab her ankles.

"Oh, that's a very excellent sight." Duncan's voice was thick with lust. "Such a tempting cunt and a tempting asshole. I don't know which one to plunder first."

His hands trailed over her wet slit, pinching her clit lightly, then dragging the moisture back to her anus, lubricating it just enough to insert the tip of his finger. "Very tight. Oh, yes, this will be too fine. Stand up now, lass. I have something for you."

He picked up a narrow collar from the table and linked it around her neck. "You know this means you're ours for the week," he murmured.

Holly nodded. Whoever would have the thought she'd embrace the D/s life as wholeheartedly as she had, but Michael was such a strong, caring Dom it had been easy to tumble into it with him.

"Whatever you ask or tell, I'll do." A thrill of excitement ran through her.

Duncan placed a kiss on her forehead. "She's well trained, Michael. Even better than the last time we were together."

"She's made for the life," he replied.

"Well. I have the single malt Scotch waiting. Shall we have a drink to toast the week?"

"You bet," Michael agreed, rubbing his hands. "I've been tasting it all the way over here."

When Duncan had poured drinks for each of them, they clinked glasses and took their first sip. Even Holly, who usually liked her drinks mixed, savoured the smoky taste of the liquor as it slid down her throat.

"And now, my lass," Duncan said to her, "while Michael and I finish our drinks, I think it would be nice for you to start the week's activities with a little entertainment."

She raised an eyebrow, waiting.

Duncan put down his drink. "Remember the first night I was in Denver, when Michael had you put on a little show for me?"

How well she remembered. Michael had placed her on a raised table and had her finger herself while they watched. It was the first time she'd done it with more than him watching, and the intensity of the climax had stunned her.

She nodded. "I remember."

"I've had visions of that rosy cunt of yours since I got on the plane to come home. I can't get the image of you stretched out on that bench at your place fingering yourself to climax out of my mind. I've been waiting all this time to watch it again."

Holly blushed and took another sip of her drink. "You want me to do that now?"

"Yes, indeed. And I've got something to add a little spice to it." He put down his drink, took hers from her and lifted her easily in his arms.

In seconds, she found herself lying on the bed, pillows under her ass. She'd done this so many time before for Michael. Bending her knees, she moved her legs wide apart and planted her feet firmly on the bed. Her mind already drifted to what she'd do.

"Let's help her a little, shall we?" Duncan asked Michael, then turned back to Holly. "We want to make sure you don't close those gorgeous thighs of yours, m'love, and hide the view from us."

He lifted something from the table next to the bed and she recognised it as a spreader, the long bar that locked around knees or ankles to prevent the woman from closing her legs. Holly wet her lips. Michael had just begun using one like this. The feeling of helplessness it gave her was more stimulating than she could have imagined.

When Duncan had the instrument locked in place around her ankles, he and Michael trailed their fingers over her skin, dancing on the soft insides of her thighs, stroking the crease between thigh and hip, caressing the bare skin of her mound, lightly pinching her nipples.

"All right, sweetheart?" Michael asked. "I know we're getting off to a fast start here."

She tossed her head. "No, it's fine. *I'm* fine. I want to do this."

Michael bent to kiss her, his tongue probing the inside of her mouth, skimming the roof, then licking her lips as he retreated.

Holly felt heat rushing through her blood and her nerve endings fired.

"How about a little atmosphere, dear lass?" Duncan smiled at her, then let his fingers trail over each of her breasts. "Something to put you in the mood? Let's see what we can do."

He picked up a box of matches from the counter and lit the candles placed around the room. Then he opened an armoire on the far side of the fireplace. In moments soft music drifted into the room, its melodic sounds blending with the seductive scents of the candles to tease at her senses. She felt soothed and relaxed and her eyelids fluttered.

Drinks in hand, Michael and Duncan seated themselves on a bench at the foot of the bed.

"All right, sugar," Michael said in his deep, low voice. "Let's see you pleasure yourself the way you do for me."

Holly took a deep breath, closed her eyes and let it out slowly. Her hands drifted down over her stomach until they reached her freshly waxed mound. With one fingertip she traced her plump outer lips, enjoying the feel of the naked skin. Since she'd been waxing, her body had been so much more responsive to stimulation.

As she moved her finger down and around, she felt liquid already gathering in her cunt and trickling out. Gathering it on her fingertips she rubbed it into the soft inner lips guarding her vagina, stroking up and down in a slow rhythm. Already the walls of her pussy quivered, demanding more.

She rubbed the soft skin of the inner lips, teasing herself by deliberately avoiding that hot little bundle of nerves at the top of her slit, as well as, the hole itself. As the rhythm of the music increased, so did her strokes, and liquid arousal dribbled onto her fingers.

"Touch that clit," Duncan urged. "Peel that little hood back and rub it for all it's worth."

Obediently she used two fingers of one hand to expose her clit and with the other hand began circling it and teasing at it. Streaks of lightning spiked through her. Clitoral stimulation always sent her to unbelievable heights. Michael knew this, and often used it to show his control over her. He'd gotten her off in the movies, in a restaurant, once on a bus with a blanket over her lap, and sometimes when she was on business calls at home and he knew she couldn't say anything.

Michael leaned forward and slipped one finger into her cunt, stroking in and out just twice.

"You're soaked, sweetheart. But you were already hot when we got here."

She nodded and moved her fingers faster. The tension built in her body, gripping her, pushing at her, and she knew she was very close. Still rubbing her clit, she used her other hand to slide two fingers into her dripping pussy, but long, hard fingers closed over her wrist.

"No." Duncan's voice was gentle but firm. "I want to see everything."

He climbed up onto the bed so he could lean over the spreader and pulled the lips of her pussy as wide as he could get them. He licked his lips at the sight of her puffy, rosy cunt lips gleaming with dew, so much of it that he saw it trickle from her hole down into the crack of her ass.

Holly opened her eyes and saw that both he and Michael had shed their clothing. Michael stood beside the bed, stroking his engorged cock, his eyes on her and Duncan.

"Now, lass. Have at it. Make yourself come."

Holly badly wanted something in her grasping vagina or else to be able to squeeze her legs together but she knew that wasn't going to happen. Gritting her teeth she rubbed her clit harder, faster, as Duncan opened her even wider. She was almost there. Almost there. She pinched her clit, hard, and the orgasm rushed over her. She felt the walls of her vagina spasm, sucking on air, demanding to be filled.

"Good God." Duncan's voice was almost reverent. "Look at that cunt. I can see it pulsing, see her cream pouring out of her. Michael, you are indeed a lucky man."

Michael took one of Holly's nipples in his fingers, rolling and pinching it. "Isn't that a sight to behold?" he agreed. "Kind of spoils you for anyone else."

By the time the spasms had subsided Holly was covered with a fine layer of perspiration. Her pulse finally settled down and she drew in a great lungful of air. She hoped they had a lot of other things planned for her, because while the orgasm was intense it had left her unfulfilled.

When she opened her eyes again she saw Michael and Duncan holding their cocks with one hand and their drinks with the other.

"You didn't…"Her voice trailed off.

"Come?" Michael shook his head. "We're saving ourselves for later, sweetheart."

Duncan tossed back the last of his drink then bent down to unlock the spreader. He kissed the inside of each knee and ran his tongue up one thigh and down the other.

"Very good, lass. Top drawer." He moved over her and kissed her pussy. "In a minute we'll have the sumptuous feast I've laid in for us, but first I have some things to get you ready for the evening."

He was busy at the table, then Holly felt him spreading the lips of her cunt again and sliding something hard and cold into it.

"A wand," he explained. "It will help to keep you on edge until after dinner. Don't want you to lose that level of arousal, sweet thing."

He pressed the bottom of it once, and it began to vibrate gently. Holly's eyes flew open wide. "Are you…are you planning to keep it buzzing like this?"

Duncan laughed. "Of course. I promise you'll love what it does to you. Now turn over on your stomach, there's a good girl."

Used to obeying her Master's commands, Holly rolled over, trying to adjust to the vibrator.

"Michael, how about a little help here? Can you lift her onto her hands and knees for me?"

"My pleasure."

Before she knew it, Holly was on all fours, the vibrator humming away and hands separating the cheeks of her ass.

"Holly, sweetheart?" Michael's voice was soft, soothing. "We need to prepare you so we can both fuck your ass later. You know the drill. Okay?"

Another deep breath. Another nod.

Fingers spread cool gel up and down the cleft of her buttocks, then other fingers probed inside her rectum, spreading more gel liberally, stroking the hot, dark tissues.

"I have some oil I've been saving," Duncan told her, his mouth close to her ear. "But that's for tomorrow. I promise you'll love it."

The next thing she knew something hard pressed against her anus. Steady pressure continued until the tight ring of muscle popped and the butt plug slipped inside.

"Beautiful," Michael breathed. "Only I wish that was my cock inside you."

"All right, folks. Time for dinner," Duncan announced.

He and Michael lifted Holly from the bed, rubbed her muscles so she could stand and walk. They led her over to one of the chairs at a huge granite table. The plug stretched her unbelievably and the vibrator buzzed away, keeping all her senses on edge. She gritted her teeth, knowing that no matter what, she couldn't come again until one of these men gave her permission.

"Okay, Duncan." Michael poured himself another drink. "I think we're ready for dinner."

Chapter Two

The dinner was a gourmet feast. They sat at the carved table near the crackling fire, sipping fine wine and enjoying the five course meal. Duncan and Michael, who had known each other since college, exchanged stories that made Holly laugh. They could have been any three people spending an evening at dinner, if not for the fact they were all stark naked.

Frequently either or both of the men would lean back in their chairs, wine glasses lifted, lightly stroking their swollen cocks. When a drop of fluid would seep from the slit, the man in need would nod to Holly and she would drop to her knees, taking the head in her mouth and licking the pearly drop from the soft skin.

And then, of course, there was the butt plug, which stretched her so much she wondered if the men planned to invade her back channel with both cocks at the same time. And the vibrator, always there, buzzing away at low speed, except for the times Duncan would press the remote. Then she had to hang onto the sides of the chair to keep from falling. Vibrations would spike through her body and juices would flow from her stimulated cunt.

By the time the meal was finished, Holly would have done anything if only they would let her climax.

Duncan changed the music to something with a more driving beat. That and the wine had her blood heating in her veins. Now she watched him sit at the edge of the bed, legs splayed, cock bobbing.

"All right, love," Michael said, guiding her to the bed. "On your knees. Let's see you take Duncan's penis in your sweet-sweet mouth. He's fed and watered us, and I think he's waited too long for this."

Obediently she dropped to the carpet, hands behind her back, and looked up at Duncan. Lust burned in his eyes and his chest rose and fell rapidly. She licked her lips, anticipating the taste of him.

"One more thing," Michael said, slipping padded cuffs around her wrists and locking them into place at the small of her back. "Now I think we're ready."

Holly bent her head forward as Duncan guided his cock to her mouth, rubbing the head across her lips.

"Lick it, lass," he commanded. "Let me feel that wet tongue on it."

She stretched her lips wide and slowly slid them over the stiff cock, caressing the velvet skin with her tongue as she took each inch into the wet cavern of her mouth. He was hard as steel covered in rough satin, and she traced every ridge and vein. The flat head hit the roof of her mouth and she moved back and forth to rub it against her palate.

She sensed Michael behind her, kneeling and bracketing her with his thighs. Without warning the speed of the vibrator increased and her body jerked in response. Michael reached around her to pinch her nipples and she knew her cream was running down her thighs.

Duncan leaned forward and took her head in his warm hands, moving it this way and that to get the proper angle. He began to slide his hips back and forth, his cock moving deeper and deeper into Holly's mouth. When she relaxed her lips slightly and bit down just a little bit he shuddered.

She felt Michael's lips on her shoulder, then sliding down her back, nibbling at her skin, licking wherever his teeth touched her. He wrapped one arm around her waist, the only thing that kept her from falling forward as he kicked the vibrator up another notch.

Duncan was urging her to suck harder, moving her head faster, and his hips thrust in cadence with the music as he fucked her mouth.

"Oh, God, lass. Oh, Jesus, that's so good. Yes, suck me, Holly. Suck me hard. Take me deep."

He tensed, his grip on her tightening, and then he was coming, spurting thick hot jets of semen into her mouth and down her throat. She swallowed convulsively, determined not to lose a drop of it.

At last, his hold loosened, his body began to relax and slowly he drew his penis from her mouth, moaning in satisfaction. He lay back on the bed, one arm over his forehead, his breathing uneven.

"Michael, old man, I do envy you, having access to that mouth twenty-four-seven."

Michael gave a low chuckle, still stroking Holly's breasts and placing kisses on her back. "I wouldn't trade it for anything," he said.

"Then I'm damn glad you're willing to share."

"Ready for me now, sweetheart," Michael murmured against Holly's neck.

She had barely caught her breath from the blow job she'd given Duncan. And the vibrator was driving her crazy, but she nodded her head.

"Let's get you up here, then."

With Duncan's help, he lifted her to the bed, again placing her on her knees, leaning her forward against Duncan's big body.

"Deep breath, honey," and he slowly drew out the butt plug.

In seconds Holly felt more gel being spread along the cleft of her buttocks and into her asshole. First one finger, then two probed and rubbed inside her. Duncan shifted her slightly so she was further up on his body.

"I think we're good to go," he told Michael.

He pulled one nipple into his mouth and began sucking on it, then used both hands to spread the cheeks of her ass as wide as he could. He held her like that as Michael's penis probed at the tight ring of muscle. The plug had loosened and stretched her enough that in just seconds he was all the way in, his breath hissing in satisfaction.

"Oh, God, honey, that little hole feels better every time I stick my dick into it. So tight and hot. You feel like you're burning me alive."

Holly tried not to think about the vibrator driving her crazy, or Duncan's strong mouth pulling at her nipple, or the tight feel of Michael's cock plunging in and out of her ass. She was so close to climax. Yet she knew she dared not come unless either of them gave her permission.

"She's damn good," Duncan panted, releasing her nipple. "I can't believe she can hold off all this time."

"She knows the punishment if she loses control," he replied between strokes, his breathing laboured. "Right, Holly?"

She nodded her head, barely hanging onto control. Duncan was sucking her nipple again and Michael's cock pounded in and out of her to the beat of the music. With the wine coursing through her system, she was on sensory overload. Suddenly the vibrator was pushed up to full speed and she screamed at the intensity of the sensation.

"Please," she cried. "Oh, please, Michael. Duncan. Please, please."

"Please what, lass?" Duncan asked, his tone guttural.

"Please let me come."

"In a minute," Michael panted. "Hold on for just one moment, sweetheart."

He gave one last thrust and she felt him spilling inside the hot tunnel of he rectum, spurt after spurt of semen filling her, his balls slapping against her as he gave his final thrust. Then she felt herself turned over so she was lying on top of Duncan, facing Michael.

"Now, baby," he commanded. "Now you can come."

Duncan's fingers pulled at her nipples and Michael pinched her clit between thumb and forefinger, pulling and stretching it. His forearms kept her thighs wide apart.

"Come on, lass," Duncan encouraged. "You can let go now."

She thought the orgasm would shatter her, spasms gripping her so hard that every muscle jerked and twitched. The vibrator drove her higher and higher, Michael's fingers on her clit kept pushing her from one plane to the next. Her cunt pulsed around the vibrator, gripping it, while more liquid spilled from her.

Finally, when she was sure she'd lose her mind, Michael turned the vibrator down to low and turned it off. He eased it out and tossed it to the side, unlocked the handcuffs then rearranged her on the bed so she was lying on the fluffy pillows. Hands massaged her aching arm muscles and the line of her jaw, easing the after effects of strain.

When she was sighing in contentment, fingers probed in her vagina, sliding gently in and out.

"Juicy," Duncan said. "I love a juicy lass."

"And tasty," Michael agreed. "She always tastes like ambrosia." He placed a kiss on her clit, then lifted his head and kissed her on the lips. "I think you need to rest a while, sweetheart. We don't want to wear you out the first night."

"Mmm," she murmured, a satisfied look of bliss on her face. "It's okay." And then her eyes fluttered closed.

She had no idea what time it was when she awoke. The music playing had changed again, back to something soft. The candles were all out, but the fire continued to blaze and crackle, casting a warm glow over everything. She realised what had awoken her was movement on the bed. When she turned her head, she saw Michael lying on his stomach, hands gripping his pillow, while Duncan stroked his cock in and out of Michael's ass.

The firelight gave a bronze glow to their skin and outlined the musculature of their bodies. Holly felt herself getting wet just looking at them. Although Michael had shared her in a ménage with special friends like Duncan, this was the first time she had seen him in a sexual situation with another man. She couldn't believe how turned on it made her.

Her eyes caught Duncan's as his body moved in the age-old rhythm. The heat in his eyes nearly burned her, and the smile he gave her was one of hunger and need and pure desire.

"Would you like to play along with us?" he asked, his words uneven.

"Yes." She nodded, now fully awake. Her gaze was drawn back to where the two men were joined, to Duncan's thick penis ploughing into Michael up to the hilt. All her pulse points throbbed.

Michael turned his head to look at her. His eyes burned as hot as Duncan's.

"Finger fuck yourself, Holly," he commanded. "Let Duncan see you while he fucks my ass."

Obediently, she bent her knees, spreading her legs wide and planting her feet on the mattress. One hand separated the folds of her cunt while the other began the familiar stroking motion, over her clit and along the wet flesh. As Duncan increased his pace, so did she, her fingers moving faster and faster. Sliding two fingers into her already quivering pussy, she rubbed her thumb over her clit.

"Faster, sweetheart," Michael gasped. "I want you to come when Duncan does."

Her eyes still glued to the sight next to her, Holly increased her movements. She felt the orgasm building in her belly, tightening her muscles low in her abdomen. She was almost there. Almost...there. She clamped her teeth on her lower lip and began thrusting her hips in time to her movements.

"Duncan?" Her voice was strained.

The muscles in his neck were corded, and his face was taut with sexual tension.

"All right, lass."

He gave a last final thrust, and his big body convulsed, shuddering as he shot his semen into the tight grasp of Michael's rectum. Holly pinched her clit and scraped her fingernail over it then exploded along with him. The bed shook with their spasms, hips jerking and thrusting, cries of completion filling the air.

Then they all collapsed, the sounds of air being dragged into lungs a counterpoint to the snapping of the logs in the fireplace. Holly felt the sheet beneath her soaked with her cream, the last little droplets pushed out by the final pulsing of her vaginal walls. No one spoke for several minutes, drained as much by physical exertion as by the intensity of the situation.

"Such a responsive girl," Duncan crooned to her as he pulled away from Michael. "I can see why Michael takes such pleasure from you."

He reached over to touch her pussy, scooping her liquid with his fingers then licking them with slow swipes of his tongue. His eyes never left hers, but when she finally tore them away to glance at Michael, she saw he was watching her with the same intensity.

Duncan reached down beside the bed and lifted a wet cloth he'd obviously had ready. Very carefully he cleaned both himself and Michael. When he was finished Michael flipped over onto his back, a huge erection jutting from the thick nest of curls at his groin.

He grinned at Holly. "It seems someone isn't quite finished."

"I'd have to agree." She reached out and ran a fingertip over the head of Michael's cock, spreading the tiny pearl-like drop at the slit over the soft skin.

"What say we take good care of him, the two of us. All right?"

"Oh, yes," she breathed, touching her collar. For Michael anything. "Please."

Duncan wrapped his fingers around Michael's shaft and began to stroke it up and down, while Michael watched through half-closed eyes. Holly reached down and cradled his balls in her hand, loving the soft feel of the fine hair covering the skin. She massaged them while her tongue slipped back and forth across the dark purple head of his cock. He tightened his hands into fists and closed his eyes, giving himself over to the pleasure.

Holly licked the satiny skin as Duncan rubbed it, turning her head so she could watch Michael's face. Each time she squeezed his balls or nipped at the head of his shaft, his jaw tightened and a soft groan escaped his lips. As aroused as he was, it wasn't long before the muscles in his abdomen tightened. Holly felt his balls draw up, and with a thrust of his hips and a shout, his orgasm took him.

As the jets of thick white cum spurted from him, she licked them rapidly, catching it almost before it touched his skin. When he was finished and his body relaxed, his breathing finally slowing, she moved up to kiss him, her tongue slipping into his mouth.

"I taste myself on you," he murmured, then smiled. "I think I like your taste a lot better."

"I think we need to get some sleep," Duncan told them, "or we'll be wasting the whole day tomorrow."

"You're right," Holly agreed.

In a moment, she was sandwiched between the two men, facing Michael, her back to Duncan. Michael reached down and lifted her leg over his hip, slipping two fingers into her drenched cunt. Duncan cradled her head on his shoulder, then slowly pushed one finger into her very tight asshole.

Holly sighed. "Good night." And she promptly fell into a deep sleep.

Chapter Three

Holly leaned back on the padded lounger on the deck, sipping from a mug of hot coffee and enjoying the view across the water. She wore only a knee length sweater and the sun warmed her face and her legs.

The atmosphere in the cabin had changed subtly since they'd arrived the day before. The three of them were much more aware of each other, and in a new and different way. Each time Holly looked at the two men, the scene from the night before flashed in her brain and arousal spread through her body. It was the same with the men when they looked at her or each other. Their cocks instantly sprang to life.

Duncan had fed them royally this morning. Stoking their energy, he'd called it. She could hardly wait to see what today would bring.

The door behind her slid open, and the men moved out onto the deck. They were dressed in shorts and t-shirts and each carried mugs like hers. Michael had a small canvas bag in his free hand.

"Enjoying the scenery?" he asked, sitting down next to her on the edge of the lounger.

"You bet. I can't believe how wild and beautiful it is out here."

"I always hate to leave it to go back to the city," Duncan told her.

Michael slid one hand up the length of her leg and under her sweater, pinching each of her nipples in turn. "I think we need to prepare for the day's activities, don't you, gorgeous?"

"Whatever you say." She lowered her eyelashes demurely.

Although they incorporated many of the aspects of BDSM into their lives, and she wore his collar, he'd never had any desire to have her call him Master. And even though she was still wearing the one Duncan put on her at arrival, no one had insisted she use that form of address. Her comfort level was just as important as her submission.

"I like the way you say my name," he'd told her. "As long as you obey, Master is just a word."

Now she waited to see what he'd ask of her.

"Let's see that luscious ass," he said, taking her coffee mug and setting it on a small table.

Holly obligingly turned over and draped herself over his lap. She glanced sideways and saw Duncan watching avidly. At the look in his eyes, she felt liquid seep from her cunt and wet her thighs.

Michael slid the sweater up so her entire ass was exposed, caressed the globes with his hand then let his fingers trail through the cleft. The tip of one finger pressed against her anus, rubbing it gently.

"I expect this little hole to get a lot of attention today," he told her. "Let's make sure it's ready for whatever comes along."

She saw Duncan bend over her then heard a zipper and realised Michael was opening the little bag he'd brought out with him.

"Shall I give you a hand?" Duncan asked.

"Absolutely."

Hands separated her buttocks, pulling the cheeks wide and she felt the breeze drift over her sensitive skin. She waited, expecting the gel she was so familiar with, but instead a warm liquid drizzled onto her hole and Michael worked it into her with one finger. The minute her tissues began absorbing it, her clit started to throb and the walls of her pussy quivered.

"This is a special oil I got hold of," Duncan told her. "Not only will it ease the passage for whatever you take here but it will keep you constantly aroused." He placed a kiss on each of her ass cheeks. "And we want you to be aroused, lass. Really aroused."

As Michael continued to work the oil into her and the throbbing in her cunt accelerated, she heard the door open again onto the deck and a strange voice said, "Am I too late to join the party or too early?"

Holly tensed and tried to shift from Michael's lap.

"Michael, what's going on here?" she asked nervously.

Duncan's hands released their hold on her, and in an instant, Michael's open palm came down in a slap, then again, once on each cheek. And again, her flesh stinging at the touch.

"Bad girl," he told her. "Remember. You don't question anything I ask of you. Right?"

She swallowed hard. "Yes, Michael. I'm sorry. I forgot."

"I think we need to make sure you don't forget again."

He spanked her again, five, six times, until her flesh was burning. Between the heated special oil and the slaps, she was nearly ready to come, and she didn't even know who the new person was.

"I think she's got it now," Duncan said. "Holly, this is Jim Grainger. He went to university with Michael and me and the three of us spent many an interesting evening together."

"Hello, Holly," a deep male voice said, and fingers trailed over her buttocks.

"Duncan and Jim have been spending time together over the past few years," Michael explained. "We thought this would be a good time for us all to get together again." He kissed her thighs. "And I wanted to show off my most prized possession so Jim could tell me what a lucky bastard I am."

"Since Jim didn't get to play last night," Duncan said, "why don't we let him do the honours this morning."

"Good idea," Michael agreed.

Holly glanced sideway from her position on Michael's lap and saw him hand a butt plug to Jim. The embarrassment of having a stranger do something so intimate to her was washed away in the erotic excitement of the action. Once she would have been humiliated by something like this, repelled by it. Now she found herself eagerly anticipating it.

Michael brushed her hair aside and kissed her cheek. "I'm moving you onto your knees, sweetheart, so Jim, can get a good look. Then he's going to put in the plug, all right?"

She nodded, her breathing jerky and uneven.

In a moment, she was on her hands and knees, legs spread wide. Fingers teased at her vagina. One slid easily inside while a thumb rasped against her clit.

"A prize, Michael," Jim said, working his finger in and out of her. "So tight and juicy. I can't wait to fuck her."

Hands spread her ass wide again and more oil drizzled into her anus. Then she felt the pressure of the plug against her hole, pushing, pushing, then popping through the tight ring of muscle and easing inside. She had to bite her lip hard to keep from coming there and then.

Then Michael helped her up, and she raised her eyes to see a tall, heavily muscled man with an engaging grin, warm brown eyes and thick sandy hair standing beside the lounger.

"Nice to meet you, Holly, " he grinned. "All of you."

"Here you go, pal." Duncan had disappeared inside and now returned with a mug of coffee for Jim. "I think you have too many clothes on."

"Get naked, and we'll let you see just how good Holly feels," Michael told him. "Right, sweetheart?"

"Whatever gives you pleasure," she told him.

"Can't get better than that."

By the time Holly had turned around, moving gingerly as the butt plug pinched slightly, Jim had stripped off all of his clothing, piling it on a chair and stretching out on another lounger. He patted his thighs. "Come on, sweet stuff. Let's get acquainted."

Duncan had picked up his coffee again and was sitting in a wide chair, watching while Michael helped Holly climb onto Jim.

She balanced herself with her hands on his shoulders. He was bigger than either Duncan or Michael, broader, with thicker muscles and wider, and a thick mat of sandy hair on his hard-muscled chest. His skin was warm and had a faint spicy scent from whatever cologne he used. When she leaned forward her breasts brushed against him and even with the fabric of the sweater separating them, tiny jolts of heat sparked through her.

He lifted his head fractionally and captured her mouth, his tongue plunging deep inside. His big hands held her head, slanting it to give him greater access to the wet cavern as he greedily drank from her. His kisses were drugging, taking

Holly to the next level of arousal. With the tiny functioning portion of her brain she thought, *It's only morning and all I can think about is how many different ways we're going to fuck.*

"Taste those nipples," Michael urged. "They feel like ripe strawberries."

Jim cupped one breast and pulled the nipple into his mouth, sucking on it and grazing it with his teeth. Holly felt more liquid release in her cunt and the flutters in her vaginal walls threatened to erupt into full blown spasms. Jim's mouth was soft and his tongue like liquid heat on her, his teeth sending sparks of electricity straight to her womb. He worked on one until it felt hard and swollen, then switched to the other one. By the time he'd worked both of them to a point of almost painful arousal, she wanted nothing more than his cock inside her.

"Let me," she whispered, positioning herself over him.

"My pleasure." The tone of his voice reflected his need.

Slowly she lowered herself onto him, one inch at a time, until he was so far inside her she could feel him prodding at her womb. His penis was thick and ridged, and she felt every tiny bump against her tender skin.

Jim's big hands settled at her hips, steadying her. He released her nipple from his mouth and raked his eyes over her.

"God, you've got the tightest cunt I've ever fucked." His voice was low and hoarse. "I can feel every inch of that plug in your ass."

Michael had moved around to stand in back of Jim, and now he leaned over him and palmed Holly's breasts, scraping his thumbs across the hot, hard nipples. "Lean forward, sweetheart," he commanded, "so Duncan can play, too. Jim, make room for him."

Jim spread his legs on either side of the lounger, his hands holding Holly firmly in place on his cock. Duncan knelt behind her and reached around to pinch her clit between thumb and forefinger.

"Ride him, lass, and we'll make sure you go off good."

She began to move up and down on the stiff penis, Jim's hands guiding her and holding her steady. The oil in her rectum spread its stimulating heat throughout her body, driving her with an incredible force. Michael toyed with her nipples and Duncan with her clit, settling into the rhythm of her movements. Every time she lifted and settled back down, skin rasped against her clit while fingers rolled and pinched the hard, beaded points of her nipples.

Duncan's mouth fastened on the spot where her neck joined her shoulder, nipping and licking as she rode Jim's cock. Michael leaned his head further over Jim's and took her mouth, teasing her with his tongue, licking the insides of her cheeks and the roof of her mouth, coaxing her own tongue to tangle with his.

The need that had been rising inside her began to spread outward through her body, heating her skin and sending wave after wave of her cream onto Jim's pulsing cock. With her vaginal muscles clamped onto him, she squeezed him and milked him, pulling every ounce of response from him.

When his body tightened and his hands gripped her harder she knew he was close.

"Now, sweet cheeks." His voice was ragged and uneven. "Make it happen now."

Fingers pinched and dragged at her clit as she rose and fell twice more, and then she was there, falling over the edge and taking him with her. Their bodies shook and shuddered together, their groans intermingled as the orgasm tossed them in its clutches. Michael's hands moved to her head, holding it in place so the kiss was never broken. Duncan nipped at her shoulder again, then licked spot to soothe it.

At last, the aftershocks dissipated, and she collapsed forward onto Jim, his arms wrapped around her as Michael backed away. Duncan's fingers probed to where she and Jim were joined, rubbing the stretched lips of her cunt and running his finger up and down the cleft of her ass.

"Ye don't know how gorgeous ye look with that plug in your dark hole," he told her, his brogue thickening. "The only thing that would be better would be if it was my dick inside you there."

Michael clapped him on the shoulder. "Later, old man. Meanwhile I think our little girl needs some rest, don't you? We have a big day and an even bigger evening planned."

Holly felt limp as a noodle as hands lifted her from Jim's body, then placed her on the empty lounger. Duncan returned and pressed a fresh mug of coffee in her hands.

"This'll help you get your strength back," he grinned. "I added just a touch of brandy to it."

The three men sat around unselfconsciously with their own drinks, chatting as if they were in a local pub. The only difference was they were all completely nude and idly stroking their cocks with their free hands, Jim's still only semi-erect after his climax. Holly couldn't take her eyes away from them, curiosity consuming her.

Michael got her look. "You like watching us, sweetheart? You've seen me do this before."

"I know." She sipped her coffee. "And one or two of our friends. It's just, well, after last night…"

Duncan threw his head back and laughed. "I take it she's never seen any of your male friends fucking you before."

Michael grinned and shook his head. "No but did you see how fascinated she was?"

Holly felt heat suffuse her face. She was sure her entire body was blushing.

"Maybe we should put on a show for her while she's resting," Jim suggested. "Would that turn you on, sweet cheeks?"

Unbelievably Holly felt the pulse beating in her vagina and cream running onto her thigh. And the oil Michael had rubbed into the tunnel of her ass still stimulated her, maintaining a level of arousal that the climax had barely taken the edge off. She squeezed her legs together, hoping everyone would buy her air of nonchalance. But Michael knew her far too well.

"Look at her eyes," he said, stroking his cock a little harder. "You bet it would turn her on. Why, sweetheart, if I'd known that, we could have been doing a lot more things in our threesomes all this time."

"I think Jim needs to be the man on the bottom," Duncan said. "He already got his rocks off today while the two of us just got to watch."

"Fine by me," Jim said. "Who's got the lube?"

Holly knew by the condition of their penises both Michael and Duncan were already fully aroused. They wouldn't take much preparation. She watched avidly as Duncan fetched a large tube of gel from the cabin while Jim slouched down in the chair, throwing his legs over the arms to expose his anus.

Duncan took one of the extra canvas pads and placed it on the deck to kneel on. Then, squeezing a large dollop of gel on his finger, he inserted it into Jim's ass, stroking back and forth as he did so, wiggling his finger. He did this twice more and Holly watched Jim's brown eyes darken almost to the colour of coffee. A muscle jumped in his cheek. She gripped her mug and forced herself to take a calming sip of the cooling liquid.

Duncan liberally slathered his cock and passed the tube over his shoulder to Michael. Taking his shaft in his hand, he pressed it against Jim's asshole and slowly pushed it inside. Jim's sudden intake of breath was the only signal that something had invaded his body.

Then Michael repeated the process with his dick and Duncan's ass, balancing himself on the cheeks of his buttocks and pushing himself inside with one strong stroke. Duncan groaned and tightened his grip on the arms of the chair.

Every pulse in Holly's body throbbed, harder and harder. No matter how tightly she squeezed her legs desire thrummed through her, threatening to consume her body. The sight of the three men was the most erotic she had ever seen.

Slowly they began to move as one unit, cocks moving in and out as if the bodies were all fused together. It was like a choreographed ballet, each man performing his role perfectly. Their groans mingled as the passion grew. Duncan's hips increasing their speed, and Michael's keeping right up with him.

Holly saw muscles tighten, heard their cries increase in intensity. She was afraid to touch herself for fear of her own reaction so she just gripped her mug and crossed her legs. But when the men erupted, their orgasms loud and violent, her own body reacted by itself, a climax rolling through her like an immutable wave. Everything contracted—her vagina, her womb, the muscles low in her abdomen. She rubbed herself back and forth across the rough canvas of the chair mat as if she was actually fucking someone, unable to control her response.

When the men had pulled out and collapsed on the deck, Michael happened to glance over at her and a wide grin split his face.

"I think that's a first, sweetheart." The words were uneven as he still fought to control his breathing. "If I'd known you could get off without touching yourself just buy watching, I'd have done this a long time ago."

All the men were smiling at her now as they sprawled in the aftermath of sex. She didn't know what to say. Her thighs were soaked and she knew the chair mat beneath her was, also.

"I think it gives us some ideas for the rest of the week," Jim pointed out. "But first, I know I'm not the only one who needs a shower right now."

Michael came over to the lounger, set her mug aside and helped her up. "I think we can take that shower together, don't you?"

The shower took much longer than usual because the men couldn't keep their hands off each other or Holly. Michael removed the butt plug from her and Duncan provided a light anal douche to rinse out the oil. Then each man took his turn to clean up the after effects of their combined orgasms.

Holly was soaped, rinsed, rubbed, her rectum and her cunt thoroughly examined and washed as they prepared her for the rest of the day and the evening. Halfway through the process they were all so consumed with a need for her that they insisted on a break in the bathing process.

Duncan sat on the bench in the corner holding her on his lap and draped her legs over his thighs. His hands reached around and opened her cunt as wide as possible, leaning back to give the other two the best possible access. Jim, who had not looked his fill earlier, sat on the floor of the shower, leaned forward and began lapping her and shoving his tongue into her tight canal.

Michael stood just to the side and turned her head enough to slip his cock past her lips. While Duncan stimulated her clit and Jim fucked her with his tongue, Michael slid his cock in and out of her mouth. Despite his very recent climax, he was already hard and swollen. Holly knew he had incredible stamina and could go more times in a short period than any man she'd ever met.

And despite her own climax before, she felt the heat spiking through her again, reaching out to every inch of her body. She lifted her hand to curve her fingers around Michael's penis. The faster Jim moved his tongue, the harder she sucked. Fire raced through her igniting every nerve and setting every muscle to convulsing.

When her orgasm hit, she tightened her grip on Michael and screamed her climax around him as thick jets of cum spurted into her mouth. Duncan manipulated her clit, prolonging her release, as Jim drank and drank from her.

At last, she was left draped across Duncan, thoroughly exhausted.

Michael leaned down and kissed her, a gentle, affectionate kiss. "I think the baby needs a nap," he said in a very soft voice. "Play time's over for now, gentlemen."

Chapter Four

For the rest of the day, they might have been any four friends off on a holiday at a cottage in Scotland. They drove into Dunvegan for lunch, and Duncan gave them a tour of the village. Holly, who loved architecture, adored the mixture of traditional stone houses with the modern.

"It's yesterday and today all mixed together," she commented, staring out the window, eyes alight with interest.

When they passed Dunvegan Castle, she made him stop at the roadside so she could take pictures.

"This place is home to the Clan Macleod," he explained. "They've occupied the castle continuously since the thirteenth century."

"I wish we could get inside," she told him wistfully.

"Maybe on another trip, when they're having a public function."

They ate a late lunch at a local pub, dawdling over their food and drinks, the men telling one bawdy joke after another. By the time they returned to the cabin, they were all pleasantly mellow, the edge of the morning's activities gone but anticipation for the evening ahead gripping them.

The weather was pleasant, the blowing breeze fairly mild, and the scent of the water crisp in the air. Duncan served drinks and snacks out on the deck, the party mood of the afternoon continuing. But when the last of the day's light had faded, they moved indoors and the eager expectation of what lay ahead was thick in the air.

In their own rooms, everyone shed their clothes and showered. Holly sprayed perfume Michael had given her liberally on her body and brushed her hair until it shone.

"You look beautiful." Michael kissed her on the tip of her nose, then took her mouth in a deep kiss.

Holly was startled at first by the unexpected possessiveness. This wasn't like Michael at all. They were a couple. It was understood. And no matter what activities they engaged in, everyone knew that he was her Master. So what was going on? When he finally drew back she raised her eyebrows.

"Michael?"

He gave her ass a gentle slap. "This week's going to be hot and heavy. Four instead of three, for example. I 'm just making sure you know who you belong to. "

"I wear your collar, don't I?" She was puzzled by his attitude.

"Yes, but—"

"Ready in there?" Duncan called, interrupting whatever he was going to say.

"All set," Michael called, then put his mouth close to Holly's ear. "Just remember. Mine."

When they entered the great room, Jim and Duncan were lounging on the couch, naked, their hands nonchalantly rubbing their cocks. Their eyes were dark with sexual expectation and the heads of their cocks already purple and swollen. Holly felt the heat they radiated reach out and envelop her.

Music played again, this time a combination of something soft yet with a steady beat, and candles burned on every surface of the room. Duncan had stoked up the fire so the room was toasty warm, and the fragrant scent of the burning wood blended in the air with the vanilla and jasmine of the candles.

A tray of drinks stood ready on the bar. Michael took one for himself and handed one to Holly.

"To a great week," Duncan toasted.

They all raised their glasses and drank.

Duncan rose and came to where Holly was standing, a large square of silk in his hand. "Holly, my love, we thought it might enhance the experience for you if you were blindfolded. Makes it more arousing,"

She and Michael had used the blindfold many times, so she just nodded her head and stood quietly while he folded the silk and tied it firmly around her head.

Someone's hands pulled at her nipples until she felt them harden and distend. A tiny pinch made her gasp.

"Nipple clamps." Jim's voice. "My contribution to the assortment of toys for the week. They look gorgeous on you, sweet cheeks. You have nipples made for sucking and tormenting."

Thin shards of pain shot through her breasts, like tiny icicles. But then lips pressed each pebbled bud in turn and the pain was subdued by the pleasure. Her body began to ready itself for whatever was to come.

Someone took her wrists, wrapped leather, fleece-lined cuffs around them and tied them together. An exciting feeling of helplessness overwhelmed her. She'd learned long ago she loved being at the mercy of her Master and whoever he chose to include. It was a big part of the trust she gave to Michael, and he never abused it.

Hands rested on her shoulders and a hard mouth came down on hers, a tongue rubbing across her lips. She opened at once, admitting the tongue, and it brushed against hers in an intimate kiss. The kiss was neither voracious nor demanding, just heavily seductive, and it seemed to go on forever. When it ended, her head was spinning slightly but before she could recover, another pair of lips took their place.

It was hard deciding which mouth belonged to whom. Even Michael, whose taste and touch were so familiar, was lost in then merry-go-round of one set of lips after another. When one kiss ended another took its place, until her lips were puffy and swollen from the attention paid to them.

She was still reeling from the most recent assault on her mouth when she heard a voice—Jim?—saying, "I wonder if you all noticed when the three of us were getting it off this morning that our little sweet cheeks here treated herself to her own orgasm without permission. I think that calls for a little punishment, don't you?"

"Oh, Holly." Michael's voice, edged with authority laced with a little humour. "You know that's a no-no. I guess we'll have to teach you a lesson." He chuckled. "All three of us."

Before she knew what was happening she was lifted and carried and found herself face down on what she knew was the padded spanking bench. Her breasts hung through the opening provided for them, the clamps pulling on her distended nipples almost painfully. Her arms stretched out in front of her, the locked wrists resting at the end of the bench. Hands separated her legs and placed them on flat extensions, locking manacles in place around her ankles.

Michael's head leaned close to hers. She knew it was him by his special musky scent. "I think we won't tell you who takes which turn, sweetheart. That will heighten the anticipation."

He'd barely finished speaking when the first slap hit her buttocks. Not hard, but enough to sting. A pause and then another slap. Then they came in rapid succession, some harder than others, with no defined rhythm. She felt the heat from her ass spreading to her thighs and straight to her cunt, where her juices were already gathering. She tried to wriggle but she was held firmly in place.

The next slap landed on the lips of her pussy and she jerked, as much from pleasure as pain, and now excitement coursed through her like hot liquid. Another slap. Then she felt something soft trailing across the backs of her thighs.

A flogger!

Only Michael had ever used it on her before.

She turned her head, trying to sense where he was.

"Michael?"

He was beside her in an instant, his lips trailing along her cheek and jaw line, his hand smoothing her hair.

"Shh, it's all right, honey. You know how hot it gets you."

As he was talking to her in soft, gentle tones the first lash struck the backs of her thighs. Not hard, just enough to enhance the pleasurable pain. Then it struck again, the pace increasing but not the strength behind it.

She lost count of how many times the suede straps caressed her skin, hitting her ass, her thighs, her cunt. And all the while she knew her juices were running copiously from her vaginal hole, soaking the table beneath her and wetting her thighs.

Suddenly it all stopped and fingers slid into her cunt.

"Soaked, she is." Duncan, his voice unmistakable. "I think she's had her punishment."

"Let's get her on the bed, then," Jim said. "I'm hard as hell, here. I can't wait to play."

Holly felt herself lifted and carried again. They placed her on the bed on her hands and knees. Fingers separated the cheeks of her ass and the oil Duncan had used that morning was rubbed into her rectum. Her buttocks and thighs were already hot from the spanking and flogging. The addition of the special oil sent her body into overdrive, her womb clenching, the walls of her vagina fluttering.

But it was nothing compared to the feeling when fingers rubbed the oil into her pussy and her clit. She was afraid she would come right then and there, with no added stimulation and worse, without permission. She bit her bottom lip to force some kind of control over her body.

"Remember that double dildo we had such a good time with at your place, lass?" Duncan asked, very close to her.

Holly nodded, her teeth sinking deeper into her lip, her body quivering with expectation. She could visualise the toy now, long and thick with a copy of the head of a penis at each end. The one they'd used when Duncan had visited was also a vibrator. He and Michael had enjoyed teasing her with it every night.

"She remembers." Michael said, his voice low. "Let's show Jim how good it works."

"If it works too good," Jim said, "I might find myself in major agony just watching."

"We can fix that easily enough."

The words created images in Holly's mind, memories of the morning's activities, and more bolts of pleasure shot through every part of her body. Her pussy was begging for something to fill it. Her ass, too.

She held herself patiently, and in seconds, one end of the dildo pressed into her cunt, its entry made easy with all the cream collecting there, not to mention Duncan's oil. When it was fully seated, the other end pressed through the sphincter muscle of her anus and slid inside her hot rectum almost as easily.

Someone showered tiny kisses on her buttocks, then the switch for the vibrator was flipped on and the dildo began to fuck her in both holes. Lightning swords of pleasure shafted through her, setting every nerve afire and making her entire body quiver. She rocked back and forth on her hands and knees, the tight coil of need low in her belly unwinding and spreading through her womb and into her breasts. Her nipples, securely clamped, ached for someone's mouth on them.

The bed next to her dipped, and she felt the brush of bodies, just the briefest kiss of skin.

"We're going to fuck right next to you, Holly." A whisper. Whose voice? She could hardly think, let alone decipher identities.

Male groans echoed in her ears, and one hand reached beneath her to abrade her demanding clitoris.

"Don't come," the voice whispered again. "Not until we tell you to."

As the bed began to shift, Holly could imagine the two male figures next to her, faceless in her mind, one's cock impaled in the other's ass, beginning the familiar movements. Was the man on the bottom face down? Face up with his legs thrown wide? Was his entire asshole exposed the way hers was?

Duncan was right. Not being able to see anything only enhanced the eroticism and its effect on her. She clamped down on her lips again as carnal images teased at her and the dual vibrator hummed away.

The movements next to her increased in speed, and the moans increased in volume.

Where's the third man? Is he just watching or is he jacking off? Oh, God, I wish I could see them. No, no, it's better this way.

Then her brain shut off as all her energy was focused on containing her orgasm.

"Please," she cried.

"Please what?" Another whisper.

"Please let me come. I have to come."

"Not yet."

She could feel a fine sheen of perspiration covering as her body strained with the effort at control. Someone turned off the vibrator and there was jerky movement next to her followed by a lusty cry.

Well, someone got to come, damn it.

"Holly?" They were still whispering, unwilling to let her identify who was doing what.

"Yes?" She was moving mentally into subspace, that place where she could exist almost indefinitely and control the reaction of her body to a degree.

"Would you like to be fucked now, sweetness?"

"Oh, yes. Yes, do it." She began to rock back and forth again.

"We couldn't decide who should go first, so we're all going to."

"But..." *What about the man who just came?*

As if deciphering her mind, the voice whispered, "He can go again. Just let us guide you."

Hands lifted her as a body slid beneath her and her arms were tugged forward, hands looped over someone's head. Her hips were lifted as fingers caressed her cunt, scooping at her cream and massaging it into the tissues. Then, with great care, a thick penis was guided into her tight channel. The man beneath her moaned in pleasure, then captured her mouth in a hungry kiss.

"Okay?" a whispery voice asked.

Holly nodded.

"Deep breath, then, sweetheart."

More hands separated the cheeks of her ass, thumbs pressing to widen the cleft, and a second cock began to enter her, pressing into her rear channel with a steady stroke. She felt pinched, full, and cried out at the pressure.

Hands stroked her back. "Shh. You can take it. You have before. Just relax. Breathe through your mouth. That's a girl."

Holly forced herself to take deep breaths. The voice was right. This wasn't the first time she'd had two cocks stuffed into her at the same time. The man beneath her took her swollen nipples in his fingers and pinched them gently, pressing the clamps into them, distracting her.

And then it was done!

They were both in!

"My God," a voice whispered. "What a sight."

A hand cupped her chin and turned it sideways. Before she could get her mind straight, a third cock slipped slowly into her mouth. She was helpless, impaled fore and after, hands bound, a rigid shaft filling her mouth. Then they all began to move. As if at some secret trigger to her body, she was suddenly wrapped in a sexual haze, where all she could think of was three large penises fucking every one of her openings.

Her cunt clamped down on the one rasping the inner walls of her vagina and her rectum tried to squeeze the one filling its hot depths. Her teeth scraped lightly on the one in her mouth. And then it was all movement and shifting and sliding. Hoarse male groans filled the air, the beat of the music reverberated through their bodies and the thick scent of candles and fire teased at her nose.

Holly lost time as the men fucked her body. She was only aware of the intense sensation of the cocks and the spiral of need winding out of control inside her. She found the rhythm of the men beneath and behind her and moved her hips in cadence with them, urging them to push harder, deeper, even as she sucked the cock in her mouth far back into her throat.

She tried to stop the orgasm when it took hold of her but it was beyond capture. Then someone whispered in a guttural voice, "It's all right. You can let go now."

At the first splash of semen in her asshole she began convulsing, the shaft in her mouth spurting against the back of her throat and the one in her pussy shooting a stream into her. The orgasm shook her so hard she was sure she'd fly apart. She rocked and clenched and shivered, her womb contracting, her pussy muscles clenching, her juices bathing the cock in it with liquid heat.

She flew on a sexual carpet, moving from one plane to another. One minute she was slowing down, the next she was thrown into a spasm even greater, even stronger. The pressure on her nipples stimulated every nerve in her body. When at last the cock slid from her mouth, she threw her head back and screamed her satisfaction.

She had no idea how long it was before she finally fell forward, limp and spent. She was awash in a sexual haze, her head and mind somewhere on a different plane. Being blindfold, not knowing who was doing what, had enhanced every act and carried her to heights of arousal she'd never reached before.

Hands shifted her body, sliding the cocks from her, turning her to her back. A soft, warm cloth cleaned her pussy and her ass, wiping the excess from her thighs. Hands removed the nipple clamps and two different mouths licked and sucked the hard distended buds now throbbing hard with the sudden flow of blood. Then an arm lifted her, propping her up and holding a glass to her lips.

"Drink," came the whisper.

The smoky taste of the single malt Scotch whiskey felt good as it worked its way into her bloodstream, reviving her and smoothing out the rough edges. Three or four sips and the glass was removed, her head lowered to the pillows.

"Rest," the voice whispered. "Soon it will be time to play again.

Chapter Five

"You think it's time to wake her again?" Jim asked, looking at Holly.

Michael checked the clock on the mantle and nodded. "She doesn't need more than half an hour to revive." He grinned. "She's developed a healthy appetite over the past couple of years."

"I'll say it again," Duncan told him. "You are one lucky bastard."

"I agree." Jim lifted his glass in a toast. "May we all be as lucky as you in finding a sub as perfect as Holly."

"Remember," Michael reminded them. "This isn't a full blown D/s relationship. That wouldn't work for either of us. We take from it what makes our relationship satisfying and fulfilling."

"I realise that. And it obviously works very well for you. I'd hang onto this one, Michael."

Michael looked at both of them. "I plan to. Let's all remember that." He put his glass down and moved to the bed. "I think it's time to wake Sleeping Beauty."

"Michael?" Holly roused as Michael's hand caressed her cheek and his lips brushed over hers. She still wore the blindfold.

"Time to wake up, sweet thing. Play time's far from over."

She came fully awake at his words, her lips turning up in a smile. "More fun for me?"

Michael laughed. "For all of us. Lie back, honey, spread your legs and bend your knees. Jim's going to make sure you're plenty wet for round two."

He and Duncan knelt on either side of her, holding her legs apart as Jim opened her cunt lips with his fingers and lapped her slit from top to bottom. Her hips jerked in response, but two sets of hands held her in place while Jim ate at her with steady strokes. His tongue swirled around her clit and licked her inner walls. Tasting her as she spilled lightly into his mouth.

He looked up at Michael. "I think this is the most perfect cunt I've ever seen. Pink, pouty lips. Rosy tissue. A clit that's a hot bundle of nerves. And absolutely delicious cream."

At this words Holly tried again to thrust her hips upward, and again she was restrained.

"I think she's ready," Jim told them, hardly able to take his eyes away from the beckoning hole.

Michael reached over to the little table beside the bed and lifted a tiny device that looked almost like a butterfly.

"Is that what I think it is?"

"Aye, it is," Duncan answered. "I picked it up special for this week." He held out his hand. "May I?"

Michael shrugged. "You're the host."

They watched as Duncan peeled back the little hood protecting the clitoris, now ruby red, and fastened the tiny butterfly to it. A thin wire led from it to the remote in his hand. He looked at Jim. "Ready?"

"Without a doubt."

Michael and Duncan each took one of Holly's legs and placed it on their thighs, spreading her as wide open as they could. Jim scooted forward, pushed two pillows under Holly's buttocks, then prodded at her opening with his penis. The other two men watched as the thick cock eased its way past the puffy pink lips, into the waiting channel, one inch at a time.

At the first intrusion Holly began to moan, a sensual sound, escaping from her lips on puffs of air.

"This is a beautiful sight, sweetheart," Michael told her. "We can see every bit of your pussy and watch Jim's cock ease its way inside you. God, this is gorgeous. You have no idea what a turn-on it is to watch him fuck you this way."

Duncan reached over and stroked her distended nipples, lightly scraping the surface with his nail. "And such gorgeous breasts. What a feast."

At their words they could see her liquid spilling out onto Jim's cock, bathing him with her juice. Her hips tried to move but the men held her fast.

"No, no," Michael told her. "Stay absolutely still. We want to see every bit of this without you moving." He bent down and kissed her lips with a light touch. "In a minute you'll want to move even more, but if you hold still the reward will be worth it. Okay?"

She nodded, her breath hitching, the pulse pounding harder at the hollow of her throat.

Duncan pressed the button on the remote and the butterfly began to do its dance. Holly cried out at the sensation and her body began to quiver.

"Oh, God," Jim cried. "The minute you turned that thing on those tight little cunt muscles began to squeeze me. Oh, Jesus, don't stop."

Duncan laughed. "Don't worry, we won't."

Jim began to thrust his cock in and out of the opening, the other two men watching avidly, seeing every bit of Holly's outer lips, watching their friend fuck that delectable little hole. As he increased his pace, Duncan increased the speed of the butterfly and Holly began to moan louder, her body flushed a bright pink, her breathing more erratic.

"Oh God oh God oh God," she cried out. "Fuck me hard. Harder. More. Deeper. Do it. Do it. Do it."

The muscles on Jim's arms where he braced himself bunched, and he rolled his hips, pushing into her as deep as he could go.

"I'm taking it to the top," Duncan told him.

"I'm ready," he gasped.

The butterfly began to hum at top speed, Holly's body bowed under its effect, and with three more powerful thrusts Jim threw back his head and cried out as he jetted his release into her. Duncan and Michael continued to hold her wide open, watching Jim's cock jerk inside her, feeling her spasm against their hands. Long after Jim was finished, Holly continued to rock and shake, hunching as much as she could, until there were only aftershocks.

And then she was still.

The two men watched as Jim slowly withdrew his cock, gathered in a deep breath, and backed off the bed, collapsing at the foot of it. Duncan removed the butterfly and he and Michael stroked Holly's cunt, pressing their fingers into it side by side, feeling the wetness and scooping it out to lubricate her ass. Then they, too, released their hold, and Michael brought the drink to her mouth again.

"Mmm." She licked her lips. "Yummy." She sighed. "Whoever that was, you're damn good at it."

They all broke out in laughter, easing the sexual tension so thick in the room.

None of them slept that night. They each wanted their turn plundering Holly's ass, Duncan's special oil stimulating her and easing their passage. Then Duncan and Jim held her while Michael used the wand on her clit and her pussy, driving her to incredible heights, then holding her cunt lips open as she came so everyone could see her orgasm for themselves.

One time Michael got on his hands and knees next to Holly and accepted Jim's cock into his ass while Duncan's slid into Holly's, then the two couples fucked in almost simultaneous rhythm. There was never any question of sexual identity. Each of the men was secure enough in his own masculinity to enjoy the benefits of a session like this, and always fully in control of the situation. It was, after all, only another way to stimulate the senses and reach unbelievable orgasms.

At dawn, Duncan stoked the fire one last time, turned down the music, extinguished the candles and they all crawled into the huge bed to sleep. Unlike the first night when Holly had slept with Duncan and Michael's fingers comfortably lodged in her rectum and her vagina, tonight Michael tucked Holly's head into his shoulder and placed his hand wide and flat on her ass. It was a subtle and silent declaration. Play time was over for the night. She belonged only to him again.

* * * *

One day blended into the next as the week progressed, with the routine seldom varying. As Duncan pointed out in his rough way, "If it works, don't screw with it."

The weather continued to hold, so mornings they ate breakfast out on the deck, then each one would get to choose the first sexual activity of the day. When it was Holly's turn, she always chose to have one of the men fuck her while someone else fucked him. She was mesmerised by the sight of it and so turned on she often had multiple orgasms.

The men all had the same favourite choice. Two of them would sit beside Holly on the double wide lounger, holding her legs wide over their thighs as they watched the third man fuck her. Sometimes they used the butterfly to make her come harder. Sometimes they inserted the vibrating butt plug to give her anal stimulation. But always their eyes were focused on that cock moving in and out of her rosy, puffy cunt.

Then they would all shower together, a lengthy process because it had become a contest to see who could make Holly come the fastest in the shower without using any of the toys.

About the middle of the week, when they stepped into the huge shower for water play time, and Jim moved close to her, she shook her head, her mouth curved in a secret smile.

"I think I should get to turn the tables on one of you." She looked up at them through lashes lowered seductively. "You know, bathe you the way you have me."

When they all simply looked at her, she said, "Oh, come on, guys. I promise you'll enjoy it."

Duncan stepped forward, his eyes darkened to the colour of rich coffee, cheek muscles taut. "You can bathe me, lass. I'd consider it a real treat."

Holly grabbed the bottle of fragrant soap, squirted a large dollop of it into her hands and began to work it into a rich lather. Jim and Michael watched with heated looks in their eyes.

"Let us know if we can help," Jim commented, a carnal grin turning up the corners of his mouth.

Holly spread the lather over Duncan's large body, working it into the hard muscles of his chest and pausing to tweak his dusky male nipples, noting his eyes darkened even more. He shifted slightly, his body tense as he waited for each place her exploring fingers would touch.

When she washed his legs, she was careful to stay away from his balls until the last moment then cupped them in both hands and spread the soap over the soft skin. A tiny moan floated past his lips, and she saw his fists clench, but otherwise he gave no indication she'd aroused him at all. His cock was still semi-hard.

"Turn," she told him.

Obediently he faced the wall of the shower and leaned his hands against it. Jim and Michael were mesmerised watching her ministrations and Duncan's reaction to it. She poured more soap into her hands and paid the same attention to his back as she had to his front. But when she reached his ass, she slid two soapy fingers into the cleft and pressed against his anus.

His breath hitched, and his buttocks clenched.

"Let me make you feel good," she told him. "You know, the way you all do for me. Relax, Duncan. It's better than being fucked by either of these two he-men."

Michael had discovered how much he liked it, and it had become a part of their regular routine. Now she wanted to share it with Duncan, who had already given her so much pleasure.

He swallowed, and she felt him forcible relax under her touch.

She glanced at the other two men. "I could use a little help here, please."

Obligingly they each took one cheek of Duncan's ass and pulled it so his anus was fully exposed. Holly added more soap and pushed both fingers in to the bottom knuckle, then began stroking the hot channel and scraping the tissues with her little nails.

Duncan's cock sprang to full erection, and his breathing got heavier.

Holly worked his ass the way they did hers, finger fucking him with a steady rhythm.

Duncan's entire body tensed, then began to shake.

"Why, Duncan," she teased. "I do believe you're going to come."

She looked over at Michael who obligingly wrapped his fingers around Duncan's bobbing cock and stroked it rapidly from root to tip, up and down, keeping time with Holly's fingers in the man's asshole.

When she reached down and cupped his balls, squeezing them gently, his whole body shook.

"Oh, Jesus," he cried between clenched jaws, and his cum spurted in a thick stream against the shower wall.

Holly worked him with her fingers. Michael gripped Duncan's cock until the last spurt had pumped from him, and he collapsed against the wall gasping for breath.

"You're a little minx, lass," he panted, when he could speak. "Did anyone ever tell you that?"

Michael snickered. "Too often. Not that she ever does anything but smile when I say that."

Jim leaned down and put his lips to her ear as she was lathering herself up. "Just be sure I get my turn, minx."

They finished cleaning themselves off and staggered to the bedrooms to dress.

Like every other afternoon they trooped into the village for a late lunch and drinks at the pub, followed by a nap before the evening's activities. One day later on in the week Michael insisted she wear the silver vibrator. Once in the pub, tucked into a corner booth with the three of them surrounding her, Michael played with the remote. He teased her by turning it on and off, just enough to keep her on edge, to see her eyes glaze over and her hands clench into fists as she tried to hold back her response. By the time they got back to the cabin, she was ready to attack the first naked man.

It happened to be Jim, who sprawled on the bed with Holly tumbled over him. He tested her wetness, then lifted her and plunged her down onto his shaft with one quick movement. She was so aroused that in seconds she came, her pussy muscles clamping around his cock, milking him, her hips lifting and falling as she rode him for all she was worth.

She came so quickly Jim hadn't yet found his release, and she knew she'd be in for a punishment session later on, but she didn't care. She leaned forward, draping herself over his chest, and panted, "Just give me a minute, okay?"

As she lay there, gathering herself, knowing Jim was still struggling to reach his climax, she felt hands at her buttocks, cool gel at her anus, and a plug steadily inserted until it was in all the way. When it began to buzz, her depleted body sprang to life. She pushed herself to an upright position. Jim's smoky eyes fastened on her as he reached for her clit.

She looked to the side and saw Michael watching her, a sensual look on his face. She raised her eyebrow and he nodded, and she began to ride Jim's cock again.

This time she held herself off until she felt him ready to come, then let her liquid release and soak him as he spurted into her. When she fell forward this time his hands came around to caress her back and shoulders. His lips traced tender kisses across her forehead, and he crooned soothing words to her.

But always, when they crawled into bed to sleep, Holly lay cradled in Michael's arms, the position of his hand on her a definite Keep Off sign. There were no restrictions during play time, but when it was over, she was all his.

More than once Holly wanted to ask him if this meant their relationship was truly permanent, but she bit her tongue. Time enough for that when they were back in Denver.

On the last night everyone seemed more intense than usual, the imminent conclusion to their week of high-flying, supercharged sex and unbelievable eroticism kept them all in a state of perpetual arousal. They had all climaxed at least twice. Now Holly was on the bed face down, wrists cuffed and attached by a thong to the headboard, the spreader bar holding her legs wide. Duncan had just applied a liberal amount of oil into her pussy. Tonight she would take two cocks in there while the third man fucked her mouth.

When Michael looked at her, he saw the dark excitement shining in her eyes and kissed her so hard he stole her breath. He had insisted on being one of the two men, and now he helped Duncan finish preparing her.

Holly clenched her hands as Michael's shaft worked its way into her, and he rolled his hips, seating himself to the balls. Then he leaned forward to make room for Jim who crouched down behind him. One tiny movement at a time, Jim pressed into the waiting vagina, his oiled shaft sliding tightly against Michael's.

"Breathe, honey" Michael said when Holly tensed. "Breathe so you can relax."

She tried to take deep breaths but she felt so full she didn't think she could do it. Then Duncan released the thong, sat cross-legged at her head and cupped her cheeks in his hands, guiding her mouth to his penis. He nodded at the two men behind her who began moving slowly, together, stretching her unbelievably. Impossibly.

And she stopped thinking.

It was all sensation. The friction in her mouth. In her cunt. Everywhere. Her body was on fire. Heat sparked through her everywhere. That dark spiral of need uncoiled again, unwinding its way through her, grabbing every nerve ending and muscle.

When their orgasms hit them all it was more cataclysmic than any they'd experienced all week. They shook and shuddered in a jerky rhythm, cries filling the air, hands grasping and clutching, Holly's cunt milking the two shafts filling her while she hollowed her cheeks to suck the last bit of cum from Duncan.

When it was over no one wanted to move, but Jim and Michael forced themselves to crawl away from Holly, knowing they were too heavy for her. She lay there totally limp, unable to move a muscle. The room was redolent with the scents of the blazing fire, Scotch, musk and sex. Holly wondered if she could bottle it and sell it. They'd make a fortune.

"Well, kids," Duncan said at last. "Michael and Holly have an early plane to catch so I guess we should try to get at least a little sleep."

Jim lay back against the pillows, his cock limp against his thigh, his body completely spent but a smile on his face. "I have to say thanks for inviting me here this week." He shifted position and groaned slightly. "It was great seeing you guys again. And Holly, my darling, it was more than a treat getting to know you."

"You, too, Jim." She fluttered her eyelashes at him. "All of you."

"Ah, sweet cheeks, you make me blush. Well. I hope we can do it again. Soon."

Duncan looked at Michael. "I'm game. What about you two?"

Michael dragged himself off the bed and managed to stand up. "Maybe. But I have something to ask Holly first, and you can both be witnesses. Then we'll see after that."

Holly wrinkled her brow at him. They had released the spreader and cuffs and she lay curled on her side on the bed. "Is this another surprise?"

"Mm hmm. One I hope you like. Don't move, okay?"

"Like I could," she chuckled weakly.

Michael disappeared into the room where they'd left their things and came out minutes later with his hands behind his back.

"Holly, my love, we've been together for four years. They've been the best four years of my life."

Holly felt a knot in her stomach. Was he saying goodbye to her? Passing her off to one of his friends here? No, Michael had more class than that.

"Mine, too," she agreed, her voice tremulous.

"I want to make sure the rest of my life is just as good." He brought his hands out, one of them holding a small black jeweller's box. When he opened it, an emerald cut solitaire diamond winked in the firelight.

Holly was glad she was lying down, otherwise she was sure she'd pass out. "Michael." She wet her lips. "Are you asking me…that is, are you…"

He took pity on her then as she stumbled over her words. Naked, his cock even now semi-erect, he dropped to one knee at the side of the bed and reached for her hand. "Say you'll marry me. I love you more than I ever thought I could love a woman. And I promise to make you happy."

Tears were rolling down her cheeks. "Oh, Michael, you already do."

She held out her left hand, and he slipped on the ring. A perfect fit.

"I was actually going to wait until we were on the plane to do this," he said. "But I thought after the intimate week we've all shared, you guys might want to be part of this."

"Not to mention staking your claim," Jim commented. "Right?"

Michael winked at him. "You're damn right."

"Well, kiss her, you fool," Duncan roared. "Then let's all have another drink."

Michael stood and pulled Holly up with him, his kiss at once both tender and demanding. His tongue was a caress and a flame, his lips like velvet and rough silk. He held her as if he'd never let her go, and she wrapped her arms around him tightly.

"I love you," she whispered. "I've worried for weeks you were getting tired of me."

"Never, sweetheart," he murmured in a low voice. "I can't imagine my life without you."

Duncan opened a bottle of his best wine and passed around the glasses.

"I know we'll be invited to the wedding," he said, "but what about the wedding night?"

Holly held her glass and looked at Michael, then the other two. "After this, could we possibly have one without you. But gentlemen, you'd better get plenty of rest beforehand."

They laughed lustily as they toasted the couple, their erotic thoughts reflected in their eyes and Michael hugged her close to him.

"Just remember. The groom gets first dibs."

MONSOON FEVER

Lisabet Sarai

Dedication

To Das

Chapter One

The rain drops are Lakshmi's tears. That is what Lalida had said — tears of pity wept by Vishnu's consort at the sad state of mankind. From the sheltered veranda, Priscilla watched sheets of rain sweep relentlessly across the land. The silver curtain alternately hid and revealed the shapes of the green hills rising in the distance.

Priscilla swallowed the last of her biscuit and leaned back in the rattan chair, drawing her shawl around her shoulders. She knew, from the past week's experience, that the downpour would end in a few hours. The lush wet bushes would sparkle in the sun, as though someone had scattered handfuls of jewels over their leaves. For now, the muted hues of the landscape matched her mood.

"More tea, Madam?" Lalida stole up behind her on bare feet, her orange sari like a streak of fire in the grey morning.

"Not for me, but please bring a fresh pot for Mr. Archer."

"Yes, Madam." The maid hurried away, leaving Priscilla alone again with her reveries.

Had it really been only a month ago that they had arrived in India? It seemed like a lifetime. She could barely remember the streets of London, the bustle and the noise, the clatter of hooves on the pavement, the horns and the backfiring engines of the autos vying with the carriages for space. It was so quiet here on the plantation. All she could hear was the hiss of the rain sluicing down.

The first week she had been busy, working with Lalida and a few of the village girls to clean up her father-in-law's bungalow and sort through the untidiness of two decades of bachelor living. She'd met Jonathan's father only once, at the wedding six years ago. Her confused recollection was of a jovial, but somewhat distracted man with eyes younger than one would expect from his seventy four years. He had travelled five weeks to see his only son married, yet he stayed in London only four days. India was his home, he'd told her. He couldn't bear to be away for long.

Once the house was in order, Priscilla had little to occupy her. Jonathan's days were full, managing the plantation and trying to figure out his father's tangled affairs. He had little time for her. Not that this was so different from her life in London, but there she had friends and diversions. Here she had no one to talk to but Lalida whose English was hardly adequate for a conversation of any depth.

The door hinges squeaked. Priscilla turned, expecting the servant, but instead she saw the trim, erect figure of her husband.

"Good morning, Jon. Did you sleep well?"

"Well enough. I hope that my tossing and turning didn't disturb you."

"Not at all." Priscilla couldn't tell him the truth. Often she lay awake for hours, staring at the pale mosquito netting looped above their bed, listening to his muttering, wanting but not daring to wake him. Dying for him to touch her. "Sit down and have some breakfast. Lalida's coming with a fresh pot."

"I'm really not hungry. I'll take a flask of tea with me. I want to get out to the north slope as soon as I can and see how the plucking is coming along. Suresh told me that normally the second flush harvest should be completed before the rains begin. The longer we take, the poorer the quality will be."

"Please, sit down for just a minute. Have a biscuit. These days I hardly see you!"

Jonathan rested his hand on her shoulder. He brushed his lips across her ginger curls. The brief touch made Priscilla shiver with delight. "I'm sorry, Pru. I know that this must be hard on you. As soon as the harvest is finished, we'll start looking for a buyer. We'll be back in England before Christmas, I promise."

He straightened up, a resolute look hardening his youthful features. "Right now, though, I'm facing something of an emergency. I hope that you can understand. Lalida, put that in a Thermos for me. I'll be back for lunch, around one." He reached for the oilcloth raincoat hanging by the door post.

Priscilla rose and put her arms around his waist. His body had changed in his few weeks of physical exertion. She could feel the hard muscles shifting under his shirt. Her own body sparked awake, suddenly aware of the texture of his skin, the scent of his soap. "I'll miss you, Jon." She tried to kiss him, but he twisted away, only his moustache brushing her lips.

"Priscilla, please! It's broad daylight."

"There's nobody around. No one would be out in this deluge. Do kiss me, please." She rubbed her body against his, deliberately trying to rouse him. "Anyway, you didn't mind before, when we first got married. Do you remember that time, when you met my train at King's Cross? You were so desperate for me, you slipped your hand under my blouse, right there on the platform!"

"That was a long time ago," Jon's face was grim. Tears gathered into an aching lump in Priscilla's throat. "We were young and irresponsible."

"I liked being irresponsible," she declared, putting on the bratty air that used to amuse him. But she couldn't bring a smile to his face. Firmly, he put her aside and pulled the oilcloth over his head.

"We'll talk about this later, Priscilla. I've got to get to the fields." She knew, though, that this conversation, like all the others about their private life together, would not be continued.

She watched him stride down the path, heading for the paddock. Before long she heard the clip-clop of his horse fading into the misty distance. She sighed, leaning on the railing and peering out through the shifting veils of rain.

Priscilla had been crazy for Jon when they met. She couldn't get enough of him. She'd been a virgin when they wed, but before long she was as randy and ready as any woman of the street, or so he claimed. Back in those days her sexual audacity had excited him. Memories of their early adventures made her cheeks burn and her thighs dampen.

Somehow, though, his early ardour had cooled. It could have been the increasing weight of his business concerns, or the terrible hardships of the war years. It might have been due to the fact that, despite frequent and vigorous efforts, she could not seem to conceive. They both wanted children. In the beginning, the notion that they were creating a child together added a special thrill to their lovemaking. As the years went by without her becoming pregnant, they stopped talking about children. Silently, each of them oscillated between guilt and blame. When they made love, the unspoken recriminations made it more and more difficult for them to connect.

If only they could try again...but Jon hardly touched her now. She could easily remember the last time, on the steamer a few days out of Portsmouth, when she had been seasick and Jon was trying to comfort her. She hadn't been in much of a condition to enjoy herself, but still his attentions had been welcome.

Nearly two months ago! Priscilla was frustrated beyond belief. Being here in India made it worse. Assam was much cooler than Delhi or Calcutta, but inevitably, in this climate, they wore fewer clothes. The native food, with its spices and chillies, tended to stir the blood. And the native people were far less circumspect than the English about their bodily functions.

Once, walking past the village on an errand, she had come across a man and woman coupling in the shade of a huge *bo* tree. Hidden behind a brake of bamboo, embarrassed but unable to look away, Priscilla had watched their mating. The man pulled the woman's sari aside and bared her lower half. She spread her thighs wide, wrapping her legs around his waist as he drove his organ into her sex. He shrugged off his simple cotton garment as he churned on top of her, each thrust eliciting a deep moan of pleasure from his partner.

Priscilla could see sweat glistening on his mahogany skin. She was close enough that she could smell them, sweat and musk, garlic and palm oil. Gold bangles gleamed on the woman's ankles, which were hooked around the man's hips. She rocked back and forth seeking her pleasure. The man finally growled and ground his pelvis savagely into the woman's depths. She answered with a keening cry that certainly must have been audible in the village a hundred yards away.

Priscilla hurried back to the bungalow, locked herself in the bedroom, and plunged both hands into her knickers, desperately trying to assuage the hunger between her legs.

In fact, that was one way she had been passing the time over the past weeks, in frantic self-pleasuring. No matter how often she brought herself to climax, though, it did not relieve her need. Her own touch left her empty and cold. It was Jon's touch that she craved, his skin and his scent, his gentle hands and his fierce penis.

Relentless rain still pounded the earth. Priscilla felt a sudden wild desire to tear off her clothes and run off the veranda into the rain. She didn't move, of course. But she saw herself in her mind's eye, dancing naked in the deluge. She could almost feel the cool rivulets sluicing down over her bare skin, tickling her nipples, flowing into the crevice between her thighs to quench the constant fever there.

All at once, through the hazy curtains of rain, she saw something move. Down below, on the path that led up to the bungalow from the government road, there was a dark shape. As it came closer, it resolved itself into a huge black umbrella. By the time it reached the steps, Priscilla could see that the umbrella was carried by a tall, formally dressed, extremely wet native.

"Good morning, Madam," he called. "Are you Mrs. Archer?" His English was near-perfect. The lilt of his accent just made his speech more melodious.

"Yes, I'm Priscilla Archer. Can I help you? Please, come up out of the rain. You're drenched."

The Indian scrambled up the steps with his portmanteau, struggling to shut his umbrella on the way. He smiled, his teeth even and brilliantly white against skin the colour of milk tea. "Thank you, Madam. I am indeed wet. The carriage from the station left me at the foot of the hill. I had no alternative but to walk to your door, and in this wind my umbrella is hardly effective." He leaned the umbrella against the railing and reached into his jacket pocket for his visiting card. "Allow me to introduce myself. I am Anil Kumar. I am — that is, I was — your father-in-law's solicitor."

Priscilla took the card, noting the Calcutta address. "You've come a long way, Mr. Kumar. Please, sit. I'll ring for some tea."

The man beamed and grasped her hand, "Thank you so much, Mrs Archer. Tea would be very welcome. But perhaps I should change my clothing, rather than causing your furniture to become as wet as I am."

"Of course, how inconsiderate of me. Lalida, show Mr. Kumar to the guest bedroom and bring him some hot water for washing."

"Right away, Madam. Sir, please follow me." The two natives disappeared into the house, leaving Priscilla alone again on the porch.

She sank down into one of the chairs, staring blankly at the card, seeing its owner in her mind's eye. Anil Kumar was a native, true, but clearly a gentleman. His clothing, even when wet, showed signs of custom tailoring. His bearing was regal, his face both comely and intelligent. Heavy eyebrows arched over deep eyes the colour of teakwood. His high forehead was crowned by lush black hair, cut neatly but with a tendency to curl. His long, straight nose and square chin were balanced by a set of lips full enough to belong to a woman.

A handsome man, yes, but more than the sum of his parts. Even in their brief interaction, Priscilla had sensed something, some energy or life in him that made him doubly appealing. He exuded confidence but without a trace of arrogance. The English had learned the hard way to be wary of the natives. Nevertheless, Priscilla could not help trusting Anil Kumar.

She heard the squeak of the door, looked up and caught her breath. It was Kumar returning. He was dressed all in white, in loose cotton trousers and a gauzy kurta that bared his throat. A gold amulet hung around his neck. His skin seemed darker, his face more exotic. Priscilla was reminded of the statues of Krishna she and Jonathan had seen in Calcutta, on their way to the plantation. Her heartbeat surged. Wet heat gathered between her legs. Before, he had looked like a gentleman. Now, he seemed a god.

"Please forgive my state of undress, Mrs. Archer, but I'm afraid that these are the only garments I have with me that are not soaked through. Your maid has kindly taken my suit for cleaning. As soon as it is dry, I will dress myself more appropriately. Meanwhile, I hope that I do not offend your sensibilities."

"Not at all," Priscilla waved off the concern with a smile. He certainly affected her sensibilities, but she was far from offended. "We all have to muddle along during this infernal rainy season. It's difficult to imagine being completely dry."

"Ah, but the monsoon is a blessing from the Mother Goddess. Without it, all India would starve."

"Yes, I'm sure that you are right. It's just hard for me to imagine living with this for another three months."

Anil leaned toward her, his face earnest. Priscilla caught a hint of sandalwood essence wafting from his warm skin. A wave of dizziness swept over her. "It must be difficult for you, being so far from your home. I think, though, that if you allow yourself, you will come to love India."

Priscilla struggled to control her physical reactions, "Perhaps. Certainly, the rain is very beautiful. It softens the rough edges and makes everything seem dreamlike, insubstantial. Sometimes you can see the hills. Sometimes it's as though they are not there."

"Yes, exactly. The monsoon reveals the truth, that all is Maya, illusion. Our bodies, this world, pleasure and pain, it is all a dream of the gods."

For Priscilla at that moment, nothing seemed more real than the demands of her body. Anil's closeness stirred her to extremes of desire she hadn't experienced since her first weeks with Jonathan. Her nipples were aching knots pressed against the muslin of her shirtwaist. She could feel the juices leaking from her sex and soaking her skirts. She thought of Jonathan, tried to smother her lust in guilt, but failed utterly. Jonathan had neglected her. He had left her alone to suffer this awful, delicious temptation.

She called on her reserves of British propriety to help her through the moment, "So, Mr. Kumar, what has induced you to undertake the long journey to this remote place?"

Kumar sat back in his chair, "Business, of course. Your husband's father made a variety of investments in India in addition to this tea plantation. I have been gathering information on their status. Now I have come to give your husband a report and to execute the various documents necessary to transfer ownership."

Priscilla couldn't bear it any longer. She had to get out of this man's intoxicating presence, back to the safety of her room. She rose, careful not to reveal the damp patch at the rear of her dress.

"Well, Jonathan is currently out in the fields supervising the workers, but I expect him for lunch, around one. I hope that you'll join us."

"That's very gracious of you, Mrs. Archer."

"Not at all. It's a pleasure for us to have company in this isolated spot. Meanwhile, I hope you'll excuse me while I retire. The humidity often gives me terrible headaches. Make yourself comfortable; I'll have Lalida bring out the tea."

"Thank you, Mrs. Archer. I hope that you feel better. I will see you at lunch."

Priscilla choked out some response and fled to the bedroom. She threw herself face down on the bed, hands between her thighs. A single touch, through the soaked fabric of her knickers, was all it took. She screamed her release into her pillow, surrounded by the fragrance of sandalwood.

Chapter Two

Jonathan leaned back in his chair and looked around the table, highly satisfied. The curry had been delicious — he'd begun to realise that skipping breakfast was a mistake sometime around ten thirty — and he'd enjoyed two hearty helpings. The workers were nearly done with the north slope, and his overseer Suresh estimated that the entire harvest would be complete by the end of the week. Then perhaps he could spend a bit more time with Pru.

Poor woman, she was looking paler than usual, in her place at the foot of the table. She hadn't spoken much at lunch either, leaving him and their guest to carry the conversation. Perhaps she was angry with him for resisting her advances this morning. *I haven't been the best husband*, he thought. *First I drag her out here to the wilderness, and then I reject her.*

He didn't completely understand why their private life had become so dismal. He still found her attractive. With her red-gold ringlets, creamy complexion and lithe figure, she was highly desirable, even if she was no longer the innocent young creature for whom he'd fallen. She was still the woman he imagined on the rare occasions when he masturbated. Yet when she sought physical affection from him, he froze up and lost all interest.

Part of it was guilt. He knew that he was responsible for failing to give her children. The physicians had certified that she was completely healthy, that her cycles were normal and she should be able to conceive. It had to be him. He'd been with some whores before he met Priscilla; perhaps, unknown to him, he'd contracted some disease that left him sterile. Or maybe it was hereditary. After all, in the twenty-two years of marriage they'd shared before his mother died, his father had sired only a single child.

Jonathan pushed the thought of his father away. He didn't want to ruin his good mood. Instead, he tried to pick up the thread of Kumar's conversation.

"There are rumours that Montagu and Chelmsford will introduce a bill that offers far more self-government to the provinces and repeals the 'official majority' provision. Have you heard anything about this, Mr. Archer?"

"Nothing at all, but you must remember that we're very isolated here. We don't even have a working wireless. Being in Calcutta, I'm sure that you're much better informed than we are."

Kumar smiled. He really did seem like a decent chap, quite charming in fact. Jonathan was glad for his company. "I cannot evaluate the truth of the many rumours that I hear. However, I think that the Crown is finally coming to understand that India is not a country of savages, and that we have the ability, and the right, to govern ourselves."

"Be careful where you voice those sentiments, Mr. Kumar. Some people would label them as seditious."

"I understand your point. However, I feel that I can trust you with my honest feelings. Your father was my close friend for nearly a decade. I look forward to having the same sort of relationship with his son."

"Of course," said Jonathan, finding himself for some reason embarrassed. How like his father, to take a native as his bosom comrade! His father, who fled to India after his mother's death, leaving his ten year old son in the care of his spinster sister. Who became so attached to his adopted country that he'd been cremated there, instead of having his body sent home to be buried in England! His father had no sense of propriety; based on her hints, Jonathan suspected that the old man had actually taken swarthy Lalida as his mistress.

On the other hand, it wasn't fair to take all this out on Kumar. He was an innocent bystander. "I look forward to working with you, Mr. Kumar."

"Please call me Anil, as your father did."

"Very well, Anil. We can review the papers this afternoon, if that would be convenient for you."

The handsome solicitor gave one of his dazzling smiles. "That would be perfect, Jonathan. However, what about our fair hostess? What will she do while we're working?"

"Don't worry about me, Mr. Kumar—" Priscilla appeared uncomfortable for some reason. A red flush crept into her pale cheeks.

"Anil."

"Um—Anil. I manage to keep myself occupied. Fortunately we brought a whole trunk of novels with us on this trip."

"Reading is an excellent pastime. But have you visited any of the famous sites in the province?"

"No, not really. There's a local shrine above the tea fields that Lalida showed me, but that's about all."

"Ah, you must take advantage of your leisure and see some of our wonders. For example, you might visit the ruins of the temple/city of Madan Kamdeva, world famous for its graceful erotic sculptures."

Priscilla's blush deepened.

"Unfortunately, Madan Kamdeva is quite a distance," Anil continued, seeming not to notice Pru's discomfort. "However, I could take you to Kamakhya Temple. It is one of the holiest places in eastern India, and extremely interesting. The temple is set high above Gauhati city on Neelachal Parbat. Only a few hours drive, if we can secure an automobile ."

"The Resident at Cachor has a brand new Bentley," said Jonathan ." But I don't know how you'll persuade him to part with it, even for a day."

"Robert Stevens? I know him well. If you can get someone from the village to take him a message, I think I can manage it. What do you say, Priscilla? Shall we make the trip tomorrow, assuming I can influence Mr. Stevens to loan us his car and driver?"

Jonathan felt strange, hearing the native use his wife's Christian name.

"I—I don't know. I'm a bit nervous. I haven't really been out on my own here…"

"You won't be on your own, Pru. I'm sure that Anil will serve as both guide and protector. Look, I'm going to be out all day anyway, making a last push before moving to the southern fields. You should go and enjoy yourself."

"I hate to leave you by yourself, Jonathan. What if there were some accident?"

"I'll have Suresh and Lalida, not to mention the workers. I'll be fine."

"Well—I'm not sure…"

"Let me see if we can get the car,"Anil offered. "We will let the gods decide for us."

Priscilla was silent, but she still looked uncertain. Jonathan rose from the table and circled to her chair, helping her to stand. From behind, he bent, a bit awkwardly, and kissed her cheek. "Go ahead, Pru. I want you to go."

Jonathan could not understand the wild, desperate look she gave him.

Chapter Three

Jonathan threw open the louvered shutters in the bedroom that his father had converted to his office and library. The rain had trailed off during lunch, and now the early afternoon sunshine streamed in. The fresh-washed air smelled of the earth—mown grass, ripe fruit, animal dung. From here, he could see the tea fields a mile away, the rolling land brilliant emerald after its drenching. He caught a hint of movement, a rippling across the hillside, as if the bushes were rustling in the breeze. But the air was still. It was his small army of workers, filing along the ranks of tea plants, carefully plucking only the top buds and leaves.

Why did he care so much about this harvest? His London factories produced machinery, the engines and boilers that were powering the new century. He was no farmer. Somehow, though, it was important that he complete this task, bring this final harvest to a successful conclusion before selling the plantation. A last symbolic effort to win his father's approval, perhaps? But his father had never really disapproved of Jonathan. He had merely been absent when Jonathan needed him.

A knock drew him away from the scene at the window. "Come in," Jonathan called. Kumar glided in on sandaled feet, his casual native costume an odd contrast with the heavy lawyer's satchel that he set on the desk.

"Am I disturbing you?"

"No, not at all, Please, make yourself comfortable," Jon gestured at an armchair at the side of the desk.

Kumar seated himself, and began pulling folios of papers out of his case. He did look comfortable, perfectly at ease despite his attire. Jon shrugged off the jacket he had donned for lunch and hung it on his chair back. No cause for formality here.

"So. You said my father had other business interests. I'm a bit surprised. This plantation was all that he ever mentioned in his letters."

"The plantation was his home, the focus of his life. He loved it here. However, he also owned a jute factory, a cotton mill, and several apartment buildings in Calcutta, as well as a pilgrim's hostel in Varanasi."

"A pilgrim's hostel?"

"Your father went to bathe in the Ganges every year."

"You can't be serious! I've heard that it's unbelievably filthy…"

Kumar smiled gently. "Earthly concerns such as hygiene are not a concern of those seeking enlightenment."

Jon snorted his astonishment. "Enlightenment? My father? He was a businessman, not a mystic. "

"The two are not necessarily mutually exclusive." Kumar laid a long-fingered hand on Jon's arm. "India changes people, Jon. It reveals their true natures."

Jon found himself caught in the Indian's beneficent gaze. The man's eyes drew him in more deeply. He searched Kumar's face, trying to understand the odd stirring in his heart and in his loins. The man was bloody beautiful, that was the truth of it, with that noble brow, those liquid brown eyes, that ripe mouth. His height, his broad shoulders, and the muscled curve of his bare forearm were undeniably male, but in his face Jon found something feminine, something exquisitely desirable.

With an effort, Jon tore his eyes away and forced his mind back to business. He reached for a handful of papers. "Let me see the details."

Kumar laid out the first folio in front of Jon. "Here are the accounts for the jute company. As you can see, it has been a moderately profitable enterprise. Last year it cleared forty percent more than in 1917."

The Indian leaned over to point out the relevant figures. Jon couldn't help but notice the man's scent, some spicy, aromatic perfume that made him momentarily light-headed. The scent was somehow familiar. It had the strange and alarming effect of causing Jon's penis to harden.

"Well—the war..." Jon struggled to retain his composure. "I'm sure that the international situation..."

"Of course, you're right," Kumar agreed smoothly. If he noticed Jon's discomfiture, he did not show it. "Do you want to see the detailed revenue and expense statements?"

"No, no, I'll take them and look at them later. Just give me the ownership transfer documents for now."

Kumar leaned closer, leafing through the folio until he reached the last page. Jon shrunk away, afraid that the native's body would brush against his own, terrified of his own response if it did.

"Sign here, please," said Kumar, so close now that Jon could feel his breath. "And initial here, with the date." Jon followed instruction, giving a sigh of relief when Kumar moved away to put the papers back into the satchel ." The ownership transfer will not be official for at least a month — the English have done what they can, but trying to rationalise Indian bureaucracy is a losing battle — but you can take possession of the factory any time."

Jon tried to slow his racing pulse ." Well, I expect that I'll be occupied here at the plantation for the next two weeks at least."

"Quite so. Well, what would you like to deal with next?"

"Can you give me a moment?" Jon pushed himself back from the desk. "I think need a bit of air; I'm feeling a bit ill." He turned to the window, gulping in the moist, fragrant air. His cock was still swollen, harder in fact than before. What was going on?

"Can I do anything to help, Jon?" The Indian stood behind him, lips close to Jon's ear. "Should I call Priscilla?"

"No! No, please, don't bother, I'm sure that won't be necessary." Jon could just imagine Priscilla's reaction, finding his cock wakened by the presence of this native stranger, when he had just turned down the offer of her body. "I'll be fine in just a minute."

Kumar snaked his arms around Jon's body, pulling it back against his own. Jon froze. His cock jerked skyward. "Let me help you, Jon. You are so tense. You need to relax."

One of Kumar's hands stroked Jon's pectorals. Jon's nipples spiked up into tight triggers that shot incredible pleasure through him when touched. The native's other hand reached between Jon's legs to cup the bulk of his erection.

"No," Jon moaned, but at the same time his engorged cock threatened to explode in response to the intimate caress.

Kumar squeezed the rigid organ, and Jon groaned again. Please, I can't…"

Kumar nibbled Jon's earlobe. Sparks flashed down Jon's spine to ignite in his groin ." Why not?" he murmured, his voice rich with encouragement. "Why not allow yourself the release you crave, that you need?"

Nimble brown fingers unbuttoned Jon's trousers. Jon gasped at the first touch of Kumar's bare skin on his own. He slumped back, letting Kumar take his weight as the Indian fondled his aching cock. Jon could feel the hard bulk of Kumar's own erection pressing into his backside. Panic seized him. He had to escape.

At the same time, the rock-hard evidence of the other man's arousal nearly took him over the edge. He leaned against the other man, not daring to move, trying to ignore the insistent tease of Kumar's cock, knowing that with the slightest provocation he would experience the ultimate shame. Yet the humiliating image of his seed shooting out all over Kumar's hand only drove him closer to that extreme.

Kumar slid his thumb back and forth over the exposed and sensitive bulb. Jon gave a strangled cry of pleasure and anguish. "Don't resist it, Jon. Why not enjoy the flesh that the gods have given you?"

"But—it's an abomination. You, me…"

"Perhaps in England. Here we know that male and female are merely two aspects of the One. Turn around now, and I will show you such pleasures that you will not doubt they come from the gods."

Jon could not help himself. Kumar steered him around until the two men were face to face. The Indian fastened his ripe lips on Jon's mouth in a sweet, deep kiss. He crushed Jon's exposed cock to his own groin. Through the thin cotton trousers, Jon could feel the native's rigid cock, duelling with his own.

The heat of the kiss stole Jon's breath. He had never before kissed a man, but now something was loosed in him. He opened his mouth to Kumar's agile tongue, welcoming the foreign sensation of being invaded, savouring the exotic taste of anise and coriander. He wrapped his arms around the Indian's muscled frame. Kumar's light cotton garments were no barrier to sensation. Jon could feel everything—the heat coming off the native's silky skin, the dampness near his armpits and his groin, the stony pillar of flesh rising between his thighs.

The Indian finally broke the kiss. Before Jon could sigh his regret, Kumar had slipped to the floor, kneeling in front of the Englishman. Before Jon could think about propriety or shame, Kumar had sucked Jon's cock into his mouth.

Wetness, heat, pressure—the sensations were incoherent but overwhelming. Jon threw back his head and howled as he rammed his cock down Kumar's throat. His seed gushed into the other man's mouth; he felt new pleasures as the man swallowed, then opened wide for more.

Like an earthquake, the climax was followed by weaker aftershocks. Finally, Jon collapsed to his knees, totally spent. Kumar had to hold his shoulders to keep him from sinking onto the floor.

"I—um—you," Jon began, trying to reclaim the sanity that had so precipitously deserted him.

"Hush," whispered Kumar, kissing him lightly and leaving a distinctive bitter aftertaste on Jon's lips. "Don't think about it. Just enjoy." He pulled the Englishman to his breast, cradling him gently. "Don't worry, Jonathan. All will be well."

All at once there was a frantic knocking. "Sir! Sir! Do you need help? I heard a scream."

Jon scrambled to his feet. He grabbed his jacket to hide his bare, drooping penis ." Never mind, Lalida." The servant's broad, dark face appeared at the half-open door. "I managed to slam my finger in the desk drawer, but don't worry, I'm fine." The woman looked dubious, but she nodded.

"Very well, Sir. Will you take afternoon tea on the porch, as usual?"

"Yes, that would be excellent, thank you. In about twenty minutes. You might want to let Mrs. Archer know."

"Ah, Madam went out walking, Sir, about half an hour ago. She said that you should not wait for her to have your tea."

Walking? That was an unusual thing for Priscilla to do. Normally she spent afternoons indoors, reading or handling correspondence, and walked after tea when the weather was cooler. On the other hand, she had not been herself at lunch. Perhaps she had felt a need for some air.

Perhaps they were both suffering from some kind of fever that was affecting their senses and their judgement.

"Alright, then." Jon was desperate for some privacy so that he could put himself back together, but the servant remained stubbornly in the doorway. "Is there something else, Lalida?"

"Yes, Sir. The boy came back from the Resident's compound. He says that the Resident will send his driver with the car tomorrow morning at ten."

Jon glanced at Anil Kumar, who grinned with just the slightest hint of cockiness ." It seems, Jon, that the gods have smiled." Anil gestured at the pile of papers. "Should we see if we can get through these before tea?"

Chapter Four

Priscilla woke before dawn from dreams that she could not recall. They must have been concerned with sex, given the stickiness she felt between her thighs. Whatever the content, they had not brought her satisfaction. The bud at her centre throbbed, demanding stimulation. She was aching, hungry and empty.

She stole a look at Jonathan, curled up on his side next to her. For once, he was not tossing about and moaning. With his knees pulled up and his fist curled under his chin, he looked peaceful and young, his worries erased by sleep. His tousled blond curls and the cupid's bow mouth below his silly little moustache made him seem like some innocent youth pretending to be a man.

As if he sensed her attention even in his sleep, he sighed and shifted onto his back. Priscilla wanted to throw her body on top of his, to mash her breasts against his chest, to feel his strong arms encircling her. She noticed that his pyjama bottoms formed a tell-tale peak at his groin. Some dream image had aroused him. She imagined what it would be like to loose his cock from his clothing, to scatter light kisses over the swollen bulb, to wake him with the heat of her mouth engulfing him. Perhaps that was what he was dreaming of, her swallowing him as she used to in the early days, when she could drive him crazy with her lips and tongue.

The picture was vivid enough to make her sex throb with new hunger. One move, one touch, and she could make her vision real. But something held her back. She remembered Jon's coldness the previous morning. It was not she whom he desired. Whatever his dreams, it seemed that they did not include her.

With tears in her eyes, she turned her back on his tempting form and sought solace in sleep.

* * * *

It was past nine when Priscilla woke again. Jonathan's side of the bed was empty. Unexpected sunlight filtered through the slats in the shutters; normally at this hour it should be raining. She felt groggy and lazy. She even contemplated going back to sleep. Then she remembered the planned excursion to the temple.

She rose in a hurry, splashed some water on her face, and, after some deliberation, dressed in her twill riding skirt with its front buttons and a long sleeved cotton blouse. She really had little idea what to expect, but she knew enough to shield her English skin from the fierce Indian sun.

Anil was waiting for her on the veranda, drinking tea. He was once again wearing his formal lawyer's garb. There was no sign of Jonathan.

"Good morning!" His smile was as brilliant as the sun riding high in the cloudless sky.

"Good morning. I'm sorry to have slept so late. Do we still have the time to get to Gauhati city and back today?" Priscilla found herself hoping that something would derail the plans for the expedition. Although Anil was charming, she was not at all sure that she wanted to spend the day alone with him.

"Certainly. There is no problem. The car and driver are already waiting down at the gate."

"Oh dear! Let me just have a bite of breakfast and we can be on our way."

"There's no need to hurry, Priscilla," Anil poured her a cup of tea, as deftly as any British matron, and offered her a roll. "This day is devoted to your enjoyment." As he handed her the porcelain cup, his fingers briefly brushed hers. Electricity charged through her. Her nipples tingled; her sex clenched, then relaxed, flooded with moisture. "Take your time."

Her enjoyment? Her whole body hummed with excitement. She felt light-headed, girlish. Guilt and fear were not sufficient to weigh her down. She sipped her tea, trying to regain her composure, wondering what it was about this stranger that drew her so.

"Where is Jonathan? Perhaps I could persuade him to join us."

"I haven't seen him today. I assume that he is in the tea fields; he was already gone when I woke up around seven. He is very diligent."

"Maybe too much so."

"Well—perhaps. But his father would have been pleased. As I told Jon yesterday, his father loved this plantation very much."

Priscilla wondered what Anil would think about their plans to sell it. She took another swallow, and then put down her cup. "There, that's enough. I'll just get my bag and then we can leave."

"Be sure to bring an umbrella."

Priscilla squinted up at the turquoise sky. "Actually, it's strange that it's not raining. Since the monsoon started, the rains have run like clockwork. Every day, it pours from seven until noon. Then it clears and the rest of the day is fair. Surely the rainy season can't be over already?"

Anil laughed, the sound warm and smooth like a subtle caress. "Hardly. It will rain until at least the end of September. However, as the monsoon progresses, the rain becomes less predictable. Nevertheless, I can guarantee that we'll see some rain before we return this evening. So, as I said, I recommend an umbrella, and also a hat."

"I will be right back. Lalida, would you please clear the table?"

"Yes, Madam."

Back in her room, Priscilla gathered a shawl, a comb, her diary, some toffees and her money purse, and swept them into a leather satchel. She stopped in front of her mirror, surveying herself critically. Her hair was an unruly shock of ginger curls. Her cheeks were rosy and her eyes sparkled. She looked younger than her twenty seven years, and incredibly excited. *Too excited*, she thought. *I must not forget that I am a married woman, and that my husband trusts me.* The girl in the mirror, though, did not look married.

Anil took her arm to guide her down the steep path to the road. Priscilla had to fight to keep from swooning at his touch. Just outside the gate, the luxurious burgundy and chrome auto gleamed in the sunlight. The native driver, who wore a spotless white uniform, gave them a brisk salute. Anil handed Priscilla into the open back seat, then spoke to the driver in what Priscilla guessed was Bengali.

"The driver says that the road to Gauhati is open. Last week, it seems, a landslide closed it for two days."

"A landslide? Perhaps we should not undertake this trip after all."

Anil took her hand. Warmth crept through her body, starting at her extremities but eventually settling in her sex. "Don't worry, Priscilla. The terrain for most of the trip is quite flat and poses no danger. The English have sent in men to reinforce the site of the previous slide."

Priscilla extricated her hand from his. Her reactions were so intense, she couldn't bear his touch for long. "Are you sure?"

"Trust me, Priscilla," Anil replied, holding her gaze for just a moment longer than was proper. "All will be well." She turned her head to stare at the passing scenery, afraid of what he might read in her face.

There was little traffic on the packed dirt highway, aside from a few carts drawn by bullocks or water buffalo. Twice they had to stop and wait while a cowherd drove his handful of scrawny animals across the road, but generally they made good time. The location of the landslide was obvious. The road ran through between two hills, the raw sides of which were bristling with labourers digging ditches and building retaining walls.

By noon they had reached the outskirts of Gauhati and were driving through a sprawling maze of wooden shacks intermixed with stuccoed official buildings and verdant plots overgrown with banana plants or sugar cane.

"Are you hungry?" asked Anil. He had been quiet for most of the drive, allowing Priscilla to pretend fascination with her surroundings. In fact, she hardly noticed the picturesque scenes of native life as they passed. She was too busy trying to ignore the heat emanating from the lean, masculine body seated beside her. "We could stop at the Hotel Nanda for luncheon before proceeding to Kamakhya."

"No, I'm fine. Let's just head for the temple."

"Very well." Anil leaned forward and exchanged some words with the driver, who headed into the city proper.

After a month of near isolation at the plantation, Priscilla found Gauhati somewhat overwhelming. The twisted streets were crowded with carts, carriages and the occasional automobile. Porters, vendors, school children and beggars all darted around the traffic, working to avoid being crushed. The air rang with the cries of hawkers, the hammering of construction, the wail of some native song coming over the wireless. She smelled charcoal smoke and fenugreek, jasmine and manure.

They emerged out of the tangled streets facing the mighty river. A broad promenade followed the river's course. They turned to follow it westwards, crossing the railroad tracks. Before long, Priscilla caught sight of a steep outcrop jutting up from the green fields.

"Neelachal Parbat," Anil explained. "The temple is perched on top. We will have to leave the car below and climb by ox cart."

The rough wooden cart lurched up the winding road to the summit, repeatedly casting Priscilla's body against Anil's, then away. After several tooth-rattling cycles of this, Anil circled her shoulders with one arm, pulling her to him and holding her steady. "I hope that you do not mind, Priscilla," he said, smiling down at her. "I don't want you to be thrown out of the cart."

Mind? she thought, her heart beating as twice its normal speed, *I don't think I have any mind left.* In truth, her physical reactions and sensations drowned out coherent thought. She huddled against him, happy for an excuse to be so close. His sandalwood fragrance surrounded her. She could only hope that it would cover up the scent of her arousal. Her thighs were slippery with the juices leaking from her sex. Her taut nipples ached, dying for stimulation. Surreptitiously, she rubbed her chest against his coat and was rewarded with a sharp spasm of pleasure both above and below.

Despite the jolts and bruises, she did not want the ride to end. All too soon, though, they reached the temple precinct. Seven beehive-shaped towers of stone rose above the vault of the main building, each one topped with gold. Ancient trees shaded the complex. A white-robed priest reclined in the shade of one. A colony of monkeys squealed in the branches of another. The place was crowded with worshippers carrying garlands and sacrificial vessels. Still, it was oddly peaceful.

Anil took her hand to lead her through the throng. Somehow, this seemed completely natural. "This temple is sacred to Sati, the wife of the Lord Shiva. When her father insulted her husband, the goddess committed suicide. Shiva, in anger and desperation, danced the Tandeva to destroy the world. The other gods sought to calm his fury, and in the ensuing struggle, Sati's corpse was accidentally cut into dozens of pieces. Her *yoni* — her female organ — fell here on Neelachal Parbat."

He led her to one of the smaller buildings, through a low arch and into a cave-like interior. The only light came from a few smoky lamps. Coming from the bright outdoors, Priscilla could see little at first, but she heard the burble of flowing water.

"We believe that this spring is her *yoni* — the holy sex of the great Mother. At certain times of the year, the waters run red, and then we know that the goddess is fertile. Some say that those who dare to bathe in the spring gain the gift of bestowing ecstasy. If you are a man, your penis will become like the bull's; if you are a woman, your sex will become so velvety and supple that mere entrance will bring your man to his crisis."

Priscilla's face grew hot with embarrassment. How could a near stranger speak to her of these things? Still, his words aroused her unbearably. He rubbed his thumb over the back of her hand, gentle and provocative, and she imagined him stroking the folds of flesh curled between her thighs. She stood beside him, gazing into the sacred spring, powerless to take back her hand or to protest this unseemly intimacy in this heathen sanctuary.

He lifted her chin and gazed into her eyes. "You are as lovely as a goddess, Priscilla." His mouth claimed her, his tongue more insolent than his fingers had been. One arm slid around her waist and pulled her body against his. She melted into him, grateful that she no longer had to resist her own desires.

Through the fine wool of his tailored trousers, she felt the hardness that testified to his own need. Panic and lust fought within her. *I am a married woman*, she wanted to cry out, but his lips played upon hers and stopped her voice. His hands roamed freely over her body, massaging her buttocks, cupping her breasts, fingering the tight nubs of flesh that poked so obviously through the fabric of her blouse. He strayed to the damp crease between her thighs. She moaned into his spice-flavoured mouth, urging him on to more brazen explorations. He began to unfasten the first of the buttons that closed her skirt.

All at once, thunder cracked around them. Lightning flashed outside the arched door, momentarily blinding her. She smelled sulfur and charred wood.

Anil broke the kiss, looking around them, "Oh dear. It sounds as though the rain I predicted has arrived." Another fierce peal of thunder echoed through the stone buildings.

Priscilla cringed. "I think that perhaps we should head back. Come."

Priscilla was simultaneously disappointed and relieved. She smoothed her skirt and ran her fingers through her curls, then followed Anil out into the courtyard. The rain had not yet begun, but the sky was a roiling mass of black clouds. Another lightning bolt lanced across the horizon, turning the clouds a livid purple.

Maybe the gods had intervened, to save her from herself. Or maybe they were angry at her faithlessness.

Anil hailed one of the carters huddled under a bamboo roof. "If we're lucky, we can make it down the hill before the heavens open." He held her tight during the bumpy ride back to the Bentley. The driver had wisely raised the convertible top. The two of them tumbled into the back seat and slammed the door just as the downpour started.

Buckets, sheets, torrents of rain assailed the car as it crept back along the road they had come. Huge drops battered the fabric roof, loud as gunshots. The windows were obscured dense, lead-coloured curtains. Darkness descended, though it was barely three in the afternoon. The driver switched on the headlights, but the pale yellow beams did little to show the highway ahead. Priscilla prayed that livestock or other vehicles stayed out of their path, for there was no way that they would ever be able to see any obstacles in this storm.

She leaned against Anil, seeking comfort. He hugged her to his body and she lay her cheek against his chest, listening to the strong, even rhythm of his heart. There was something about this man, some power he had to both rouse and calm the spirit. Her hand fell into his lap and she discovered that he was still erect. She cupped his bulk in her hand, stroking it gently. Anil murmured something in his own language and pressed his lips to her hair.

They sat thus, entwined, poised on the plateau of desire, through the whole achingly long drive back to the plantation.

Chapter Five

It took nearly four hours for the auto to creep back to the plantation. Full night had fallen by the time they arrived. The rain had slackened, but it was still heavy enough to drench them, despite their umbrellas, on the climb up the path.

Jon must be terribly worried, thought Priscilla. She imagined him pacing back and forth on the veranda, peering into the night for any sign of them. Guilt weighed on her spirit, though she knew she was not responsible for the weather or the delay. Her intense reactions to Anil did not alter her deep love for her husband.

She had not, technically, been unfaithful. Still, she was honest enough to admit to herself that, if the storm had not interrupted, she would have gladly surrendered herself to Anil. In public, in a sacred space, she would have been willing—no, eager—to allow the seductive native access to her body. Her sex ached, remembering his intimate touch. She looked up at him, but she could not read his expression in the dark. Did he still want her? Would he try again?

Priscilla tried to compose herself, to think only of Jon and his concern. As the house came into view, she stopped short in surprise.

Normally at this time, Lalida would have lit the kerosene lamps and golden light would be spilling out from the windows onto the path. But the bungalow was completely dark, and silent too, no sounds of clattering dishes from the kitchen, no scratchy jazz coming from Jon's gramophone.

"Jon? Jonathan?" Priscilla voice signalled her alarm as she and Anil climbed to the porch. The door was half open, definitely a bad sign. "Lalida?" Had they been attacked and abducted by some of bandits that occasionally roamed the hills? But there was no sign of any struggle or violence.

She clutched at Anil's soggy coat. "What could have happened? Where are they?"

"Where are the lamps?" Before she could answer, he located a lantern and a box of lucifers on the mantel. In a moment he had it lit. They looked around the parlour, seeking clues.

Priscilla saw it first. The note was scrawled on a scrap torn from a ledger, and fastened to the dining room door frame with a nail.

"Landslide at the village. Gone to help." The writing was barely legible, but she recognised Jon's hand.

A landslide! Priscilla recalled the heaps of mud and rock piled by the road on the way to Gauhati. "We must go to them," Anil insisted, reading over her shoulder. "A landslide can bury a whole town, or sweep it away." He searched her face. "Do you have shovels or picks? And buckets, buckets would be useful."

"In the utility shed, behind the house." Anil was already on his way out the door.

Jon had taken most of the tools, but they found a short spade and a mattock. They grabbed them and scrambled up the slippery path toward the village, rain still washing over them in dense squalls. As they approached the site of the village, home to the plantation workers and their families, shouts filled the air. Lanterns flickered in the wet, black night.

Priscilla had visited the village several times, bringing sweets for the children and English soap for their mothers. She hardly recognised the scene of devastation before her now. There was no sign of the wooden huts that sheltered the workers. She saw only a vast sea of mud, with splintered planks and beams jutting out at odd angles. Half naked men dug frantically in the muck, looking like an army of demons in the shifting lantern-light. Children hung onto their mothers, wailing or watching the rescue efforts silent and wide-eyed. An elderly woman, tattered sari clinging to her wizened body, crouched under a tree half-crushed by a huge boulder.

Priscilla saw Jon near the far perimeter, wielding a shovel and yelling orders to the other men. She stumbled across the ex-village, the treacherous mud sucking at her feet, and threw herself into his arms.

"Darling! I was so worried." she cried. "Are you all right?"

Jonathan held her so tight she could scarcely breathe. His chest was bare and streaked with dirt. His blond hair was black with rain and soil. "Priscilla! Thank God! I'm so glad to see you!"

"How bad is it?"

"Bad—nearly all the houses were destroyed—but it could have been much worse. Most of the villagers were up at the shrine when the hillside gave way. We think that there are only a few people buried. We're trying to find them before it's too late."

"Let me help. I can dig, too." She held up her spade. Jonathan looked at her for a moment, appraising her strength, then nodded. "Take the north east quadrant. Be careful—you don't want to slice into someone that you're trying to rescue."

"What about me? Where do you want me?" Anil had come up behind them during their embrace.

"Anil! Wonderful! Can you organise the men working in the south west? I'm not sure that they understand everything that I've been telling them."

"Certainly, I'll do what I can." Anil strode off toward the group that Jon had indicated.

Priscilla waded over to the area Jon had assigned to her. The Indian men eyed her curiously as she dug her spade into the saturated dirt. The mud resisted, sticky and heavy as cement, but she refused to be discouraged. She raised one spade-full, then another, scanning her expanding excavation each time for any sign of a body.

Her shovel hit some buried wood. The impact sent a jarring shock back through her shoulders. She thought that the thump sounded hollow. Priscilla dug in again, listening more carefully. Definitely hollow.

All at once, she heard a muffled cry, a human voice. "Jon! Over here, I think there's a partly collapsed house here, and someone's inside. Alive!"

The men swarmed over to where she was digging. "Careful now," Jon cautioned. Don't disturb the timbers or the whole place might collapse." He showed them how to lift off the soil in layers, standing away from the hole so that their weight would not affect the precariously balanced ruins underneath. It took half an hour, but finally they pulled an old man out of the ground, crushed and bleeding but conscious.

A shout rang out from the other side of the mud field. Anil's group had located another body. Priscilla went over to lend her spade to the efforts. Digging side by side with her husband and the Indian lawyer, she worked steadily to strip away nearly two feet of dirt. Underneath, they found the mangled corpse of a woman cradling an infant. The woman was beyond help. The baby, though, let out a lusty wail as the fresh air filled its lungs.

Priscilla bent down and took the naked child in her arms. It was covered with scratches and abrasions, but miraculously unharmed otherwise. A boy, perhaps six months old. He looked up at her with chocolate coloured eyes and cooed, waving his chubby limbs.

Tears streamed down Priscilla's cheeks, mingling with the raindrops.

* * * *

Finally, after hours of work, it was over. All the missing villagers were accounted for. Two of them were dead. Three, including the infant, had survived. The dark, sinewy men leaned on their shovels, drained, surveying the muddy wasteland where their homes had stood. The women huddled with their children under the remaining trees, seeking shelter from the showers that still watered the earth.

Priscilla sat on the ground near the village gate, shivering and clutching the baby to her breast. Water dripped from her sodden hair into her eyes. Her hands were black with mud and purple with blisters. Her blouse was torn at the shoulder, and soaked, though the baby snuggling against her did not seem to mind.

Anil crouched down next to her and put his arm around her shoulders. She was too exhausted to worry about her husband's reaction.

Jonathan stood on top of the boulder. He looked tired, but he stood tall, his voice ringing out over the devastated site. "My friends! I know that you have lost your homes, lost everything that you owned. But we will build new homes. We will choose a safe site, on flat land far from the hills, to keep this terrible thing from happening again."

The people turned dull, uncomprehending eyes to him. "Anil, can you translate for me? I don't think that they understand." The Indian rose and took a place next to Jon. He repeated Jon's words in Assamee. The villagers nodded.

"For now, you are welcome to sleep in the plantation house. It will be crowded, but you'll have a roof over your heads. Tomorrow, when the rain stops, we will decide where to build our new village."

The villagers muttered among themselves as Anil translated. An elderly man stood and addressed Anil, speaking for several minutes as the lawyer listened closely.

"They do not want to come to the house. They thank you for your generosity, and for your pledge to help them rebuild, but for tonight, they prefer to stay here, where their families have lived and died for generations."

"At least let them send the women, the children... The exposure is dangerous. And there is always the risk of another slide."

Anil consulted with the elder. "They understand, but this is their choice. They ask that you forgive what may seem like ingratitude."

Jon shrugged, unwilling to waste his dwindling energy on further argument. "Very well. If they change their minds, the house will be open to them. Let's get back there ourselves, before we collapse."

He reached out his hand to help Priscilla rise. Still holding the baby, she struggled to her feet. Jon smiled at her and wiped a smudge of dirt from her cheek. He did not speak, but took her arm to lead her back along the path to the bungalow.

She could hardly walk. Every muscle ached. Her blistered palms stung and the bruise on her knee, where she had hit herself with the spade, hurt more with every step. As she limped along, leaning on her husband's strong arm, feeling his warmth seep into her and drive away the chill, she was happier than she had been in a long time.

Chapter Six

Lalida reached the bungalow before them and lit the lamps. She took the babe from Priscilla's arms, firmly rejecting her protests. "I'll take him to my room and give him some milk, Madam. You need to bathe and rest. Tomorrow we will try to find his family." She bustled away with the sleeping child, leaving Priscilla, Jon, and Anil alone.

They stood facing each other in the parlour, a triangle of muddy, dishevelled bodies. Now that the emergency was over, no one knew what to say. An awkward silence filled the spaces between them. Tension crackled in the humid air.

Priscilla looked from one man to the other. Jon's hair was matted with dirt. There was blood smeared across his naked chest, but thankfully, she did not see any wound. Anil's fine suit was torn in two places, with the pale lining gaping out of the gashes. He was barefoot, the sucking mud having swallowed his shoes. A dark bruise swelled above his right eye.

She knew that she looked no better. Her filthy hair stuck to her forehead in damp strings. Her clammy skirt clung to her thighs. Her blouse was in tatters, the seams split from her exertion. Her lace camisole, now a muddy brown, was clearly visible.

They were tired, battered and bruised. But they were alive, when not everyone had been so fortunate.

Inexplicably, her heart soared. These two courageous, compassionate men—they had saved lives tonight. She felt blessed by their presence, full of joy, power and love—for both of them.

She walked over to Jon, pulled his face to hers, and kissed him, open mouthed. He was tentative at first, but in a moment he became eager, pulling her to his chest and mashing his lips against hers. He smelled of earth, iron, and sweat, masculine, intoxicating. Priscilla's nipples became hard little pebbles that set up exquisite vibrations each time they brushed his flesh. He reached behind her, grabbing her buttocks and forcing her pelvis against his. The hard bulk of his erection prodded the mound at the juncture of her thighs. Her sex, already damp, gushed in response. Boldly, she reached down to fondle his cock through his trousers. Her quick squeeze made him gasp.

Before he could completely recover, Priscilla moved away from him to Anil. The native's dark eyes followed her every gesture. The hint of a smile played across his full lips. He met her kiss halfway, sinking his tongue deep into her mouth while massaging her breasts. Priscilla feathered a quick caress across his swollen groin before breaking the embrace.

She took Jon's hand in her right, Anil's in her left, and led them toward the bedroom. "Come," she beckoned them . "I think that we all need a bath."

The bathroom was simple, Asian-style, a tiled area with a drain rather than a tub. Lalida had left an ample supply of hot water, filling every bucket and ewer in the house. Cold water came directly from the rain-fed cistern on the roof.

Quickly, before she could think too much about what she was doing, Priscilla stripped off her clothes and kicked them into a corner. She grabbed one of the pitchers of hot water and poured it over her head. Dirt sluiced out of her hair in muddy rivulets and swirled down the drain. The warmth soothed her aching muscles but made her scratches and blisters sting. She picked up a bar of her precious English lavender soap and began smoothing the suds over her breasts and belly. She lingered over the task, savouring the silkiness of her own skin under her fingertips.

The two men watched her, transfixed. Jon's mouth hung open as if he didn't believe what he was seeing, but at the same time his trousers were distended by a huge erection. Anil's lips were parted, his tongue-tip playing unconsciously at the corners. She could see that he was hungry to taste her. For long moments, though, neither man moved.

Her soapy hands slipped easily into the cleft between her thighs. It seemed so natural, to slide her slippery fingers along her folds and stroke the juicy bud of flesh that set her trembling. She had done this so many times; she knew instinctively the path to her own pleasure. No one had ever watched her, of course. Instead of inhibiting her, though, her audience stirred her to new peaks of excitement.

No longer was her self-pleasuring lonely and sterile. Now she was sharing it with the man—the men—that she loved and desired. As she climbed higher, she could see her own arousal reflected in their faces. Neither moved to expose his cock, not yet, but she knew that would come soon.

She rubbed harder, plunging three fingers into her depths while vigorously thumbing her clit. With her other hand, she pinched her soapy nipples, sending sharp bolts of sensation straight to her sex. She moaned, closer every instant to her final release. With her eyes closed, she could still feel their lustful gaze, hear their harsh breathing.

All at once, Jon groaned. Priscilla's eyes flew open. He had unbuttoned his trousers. His cock jutted out, pale as ivory, the helmet purple with blood. He gripped his length with both hands, jerking away desperately. A grimace distorted his sweet mouth; he seemed almost to be in pain.

He worked his cock faster and harder, his eyes never leaving her soapy form. She picked up his rhythm, her fingers probing and twisting, her thumb mashing her clit against her pubic bone. She was close, and so was he. She squatted, opening her thighs wide and burying both hands in the sloppy, soapy cavern between them. Jon groaned again at the sight of her lewd posture.

They were locked in a race toward completion, each urging the other on. Priscilla tottered on the brink, humping her hands, watching her husband ravage his beautiful blood-engorged cock. Energy whipped back and forth between them, circling, strengthening. Nothing existed but their two bodies, straining toward ecstasy.

A half-strangled cry from Anil drew their attention. He had freed his cock as well. He stroked the thick rod of tawny flesh gently, far from the desperation of climax, or so it seemed. Yet as they watched, his cock contracted, pulsed and sprayed viscous ribbons of cum all over his delicate brown fingers.

The sight was simultaneously beautiful and obscene. Priscilla ground herself against her hands, hurling her body into an orgasm that tore through her like a hurricane. Even as she quivered in the retreating gusts of pleasure, she heard Jon yell and knew that he was spewing his seed across the floor.

The next thing she knew, Jon was beside her, helping her to stand. He clutched her soapy form to his now-naked body and sealed her lips with his. Joy ballooned in her chest. It had been so long since she'd felt his decisive mouth or tasted his familiar flavour. She rubbed her breasts against him, smearing herself with his dirt. His rigid nipples poked at her chest. Below, she could feel his cock stiffening again, nudging into the gap between her thighs.

She opened her legs and tilted her pelvis toward him, inviting his entry. Then, all at once, a torrent of warm water poured down on their heads. They broke their kiss, sputtering in the surprise flood. Before they could respond, another bucketful drenched them.

"Anil!" Priscilla turned to find that the native was behind them. He too had shed his clothes. As she watched, he raised a pitcher and poured its contents over his own head.

The shower slicked his dark locks against his skull, emphasising the fine planes of his countenance. Rivulets coursed over his muscled shoulders and down his hairless chest. His skin looked oiled, cinnamon-hued and buttery smooth. Only in his groin did hair grow, in wild black tangles completely different from the golden fur at the base of Jonathan's cock.

Priscilla's palms itched with the need to caress that silky, dark skin, to mould Anil's flat breasts and flick her thumbs across his chocolate-hued nipples. She saw herself kneeling in the puddle at his feet, swallowing his majestic penis. The urge to turn image into reality was overwhelming. Did she dare to act on her desire?

She glanced back at Jon. He too seemed transfixed by the sight of Anil's glorious nakedness. His cock was fully erect once again. It twitched slightly, in rhythm perhaps with his racing pulse. His hands were clenched at his sides, but as Priscilla watched, he relaxed and began stroking himself. His cock swelled further. She willed him to look away from Anil and meet her gaze, with its unspoken question. He must have felt her thoughts. Their eyes locked, and for a moment Priscilla felt the old connection that they'd had at first, the sense that everything was understood. He nodded slightly, a half-smile playing on his lips.

She beamed her gratitude back at him, then turned back to Anil's body. Lowering herself to the tiled floor, she grasped the Indian's cock at the root and stroked it gently. The taut skin sheathing his hardness felt like silk. The bulb was scarcely wider than the shaft and peaked rather than round, like a blunted arrowhead. His foreskin puckered below it. Droplets clung to the tip, perhaps from the shower, perhaps his own secretions. Priscilla's mouth watered at the sight.

She bent closer and pursed her lips around the bulb, tonguing the slit, sampling his moisture. The taste made her crave more. She opened wide and engulfed him, sucking him deep into her mouth. Anil hummed with pleasure. He laid a light hand on her damp curls, guiding but not forcing her as she slid her mouth along his length. He hardly thrust at all, though the increasing tension in his flesh made it clear that his excitement was peaking. Reaching between his legs, she cupped the velvety sacs hanging there, thrilled to feel them tighten as she brought him closer to the edge.

Her own body was on fire. Her nipples were points of flame, and her clit was a glowing ember that the wetness in her sex could not quench. Juices trickled down her splayed thighs onto the floor. Anil's hands were on her shoulders now, kneading her flesh as she sucked rhythmically on his. He was nowhere near her sex, yet his touch sent hot shivers through her. She saw herself, skewered by the steely cock sliding in and out of her mouth, and the image nearly sent her into her own climax. She sucked more strongly, nipping at the bulb each time she reached the apex. The native groaned, moments away from coming.

"Pru!" Jon's voice was low and hoarse with lust, close to her ear. "Don't let him spend. Don't waste him. Let's get to the bedroom." Confused and dizzy with lust, Priscilla released Anil's cock and turned to her husband. Jon raised her to her feet and swept her into his arms.

Jon hadn't carried her since the night of their wedding. Priscilla threw her arms around his neck, glorying in the sensation of his naked body against hers. The strength he had gained in the tea fields was obvious; he lifted her with ease. She would have been happy to stay in his arms forever, but in a moment he had laid her upon the bed. He stood beside her, his eyes burning into her. She felt his fever raging.

Anil watched her from the other side of the bed. But no one touched her.

Her clit throbbed. Her cunt ached, hungry for one of the two magnificent cocks that bobbed on either side of her. She spread her thighs, shamelessly displaying the glistening folds of her swollen sex.

"Please," she begged . "Please, someone…"

Jon nodded to the Indian . "Guests first, Anil."

Anil answered not in words but in action. He climbed onto the coverlet and knelt between her legs. He bent and nuzzled her wet cleft, lapping up her juices, setting her whole body trembling. He did not play with her for long, though. He sensed her desperation. Positioning his cock at her entrance, he slowly pushed into her depths.

Priscilla could feel every inch of his taut flesh as it slid across her slippery inner walls. The whole length of him rubbed over her clit, kindling sparks that arced through her. She ground her pelvis against him to increase the pressure, the bead at her centre ready to explode. For long moments, he did not move, giving her time to appreciate all the sensations — the wonderful fullness where she had been empty for so long, the spasms in her clit whenever his cockflesh brushed over it, the pulsing in his shaft, so strong that she was sure it was voluntary and not merely the surge of his blood.

The pleasure grew, ramified, spreading from her sex to all her limbs. Her nipples throbbed, echoing the pulse in her clit. She was dying for someone to touch them. Even as that thought crystallised, she felt a hot mouth fasten wetly on one nipple. She moaned in gratitude as Jon pulled lightly on the rubbery nodule. Each suck, each brush of his agile tongue, made her sex clench around the cock filling it. Each time, the bulk inside her seemed to swell, stretching her wider. Priscilla edged closer to climax, driven by the simple presence of Anil's cock inside her and Jon's mouth outside.

Finally, Anil began to thrust. His strokes were still slow, measured, drawing out each sensation, focusing her attention on each nuance of pleasure. Meanwhile, Jon fastened his lips on her other nipple, while massaging the first breast with gentle fingers. She wound her fingers into his hair, urging him on, wanting his teeth now instead of his tongue. He sensed her need, and gave her what she craved, pinching her breast, biting then soothing the sudden pain with hot saliva.

The pleasure grew, inexorable, intensity building to the point where Priscilla was helpless to do anything but moan and shake under the onslaught. Gradually, Anil quickened his pace, as well as his force. Each penetration went deeper. Each left her less time to recover before she was impaled again.

There was no slope to climb. There was no barrier to breach. Without will, without thought, without effort, Priscilla slipped from indescribable pleasure into total ecstasy. Her body simply evaporated. There was nothing but light, wave after wave, washing over her—peace and joy, transcendent and overwhelming. And shimmering in the distance, lapped by the same waves, she sensed two other beacons that she knew were Jon and Anil.

She opened her eyes to find Anil's handsome face hovering over her. His smile warmed her, rekindling her recently sated desire. The Indian dipped down to brush his lips across hers before rising back on his haunches. His still-rampant cock slipped out of Priscilla's drenched sex.

The sudden emptiness was almost unbearable . "No! Please...!" she began. But her pleading was cut short by her husband's passionate kiss.

His mouth still locked to hers, Jonathan straddled her. She arched her back, rubbing her soaked curls against his hardness. He did not tease her. With one jerk of his hips, he sunk his cock into her depths. Her well-lubricated flesh offered no resistance. Priscilla moaned in joy as he began to move. Each thrust woke echoes of her recent climax and drew her inexorably towards a new one.

Jon was fierce, almost desperate, as he speared her again and again. After Anil's languid fucking, this was what Priscilla craved. *Harder, deeper.* She wanted him to split her open with his cock. *Take me, take all of me. My husband, my lover.* In his smouldering eyes, she saw that he sensed or guessed her desires. He slammed his cock into her sex with a force that shook her to the core.

Suddenly he groaned. His rhythm faltered. "Anil...?" In the flickering lantern-light, Priscilla glimpsed the graceful form of the native, standing behind her husband at the foot of the bed. Jon gave another cry, writhing above her. His cock made delicious spirals inside her. Eddies of pleasure swirled in her sex.

All at once, he yelled and rammed his cock deeper. He began to thrust again, but with a wild, irregular beat that left her breathless and confused. What was happening? Jon's head was thrown back, his back arched, his face a mask of tortured ecstasy. Behind him, Anil moved back and forth, with a measured pace much slower than Jon's frantic strokes. It was too dim for Priscilla to read the Indian's face, but she could clearly see his dark fingers, clutching at the pale flesh of her husband's hips.

No! It can't be...! Priscilla knew that her Jon, her masterful, masculine Jonathan, couldn't possibly be a sodomite. Yet there was no other explanation for the way he jerked and spasmed inside her, for the whimpers that escaped his clenched mouth on each of Anil's forward strokes. The damnedly seductive native had his cock embedded in Jon's arse and was fucking him, even as Jon was fucking her.

The lustful image was far beyond her most obscene daydreams. She couldn't help herself. She saw Jon's splayed white buttocks, held apart by dusky hands. She envisioned how Anil's smooth brown rod would stretch her husband's rear hole as it disappeared into his body. Jon had never taken her anally, but her own rear twitched and trembled as she imagined the sensations of being pierced in that most secret and shameful of places, of being opened and filled beyond bearing by Jon's unyielding hardness. Or by Anil's.

The pictures that her mind conjured swept her body away. She convulsed under Jon's weight, twisting and shaking as orgasm shook her. Through the fog of pleasure, she heard Jon's howl and felt the heat of his spend flooding over her tissues. The luscious sensation triggered another climax, liquid and seething, coursing through her body like molten gold. Finally, Anil called out in some foreign tongue as he came, his last thrusts forcing Jon's still rigid penis back into her depths.

* * * *

The reek of kerosene brought Priscilla back to her senses. The lamp on the bedside table was burning low. She shifted the weight of Jon's body off to the side. He did not wake. She leaned over to turn off the lantern valve, and velvet night closed around her.

Gradually her eyes adjusted. There was a huddled shape on the carpet next to the bed.

"Anil?" she whispered. The shape stirred. "Come up onto the bed with us."

Almost silent, the Indian rose and stretched out beside her, opposite from Jon's sleeping form. His aura of sandalwood enfolded her. His sticky cock brushed against her thigh, kindling a brief flare of desire that she was too tired to acknowledge.

On the other side of her, Jon stretched and murmured in his sleep. "Pru..." She turned to him and wrapped one arm around him. He snuggled against her breasts. Behind her she felt Anil turning and moulding his body to hers.

Exhausted, overwhelmed, awed, she sank back into sleep.

Chapter Seven

Priscilla woke to the hiss of the rain pelting the bushes outside her window. She was alone amid tangled sheets, surrounded by the scents of musk, sandalwood and semen.

She remembered. She blushed. Still, she felt so satisfied and content that she could muster very little shame. She stretched and her sore muscles protested, but it seemed that no amount of pain could dilute her joy.

Where was Jon? Where was Anil? She was suddenly eager to see her lovers. As she belted her dressing gown around her waist, she marvelled at how little embarrassment she felt. Indeed, her most noticeable emotion was her steadily rising desire.

She found Jon on the veranda, drinking tea and gazing out at the silvery hills. "Pru, darling!" He enfolded her in his arms and kissed her. She could feel his heart beating through the thin fabric of her wrap. His mouth had a faint taste of anise.

He wore an open-necked white shirt and dark trousers. His feet were bare. He looked young, healthy, relaxed and incredibly virile.

"Where is Anil?" Priscilla asked, then immediately realised her error. What if Jon was jealous? What if he thought that she cared more for the exotic native lawyer than she did for her own husband?

Jonathan, however, merely smiled. "He left early this morning. He thought that we might appreciate having some time alone."

Priscilla felt a stab of loss. Her dismay must have showed on her face, because Jon laughed. "Don't worry. He told me that he'd come back soon."

Now Priscilla felt a bit jealous. Had Jon and Anil been together, before the Indian had departed? Without her? "Did you have a chance to talk to him? About—last night?"

Jon sat down and poured her a cup of tea. He waited until she had settled in her chair before continuing. "A bit. Anil helped me to understand. To accept. He told me some surprising things about my father..."

Priscilla felt her brow knot into a frown. His father? All at once it was Jonathan who looked worried. "I know that last night must have been something of a shock for you. I hope that it won't change anything between us—our marriage, I mean. I still love you—I want you—more than ever. I'm not queer, you know. Anil is just—well, special."

Priscilla reached across the table to take his hand . "He certainly is. But I do think that things have changed."

"Don't, please! Don't tell me that you want to divorce me!"

"Divorce? Hardly!" Deliberately, she let her muslin gown slip open, giving him a glimpse of her breasts. Jon raised his hand, as if to reach for her, but dropped it as the door squeaked behind them. Priscilla did not move.

Lalida held the baby they had rescued. The boy had been bathed and diapered, and seemed highly content with himself. He babbled and shook his pudgy fists at Priscilla.

"Oh! Let me have him for a moment!" The child settled into her arms as if he belonged there. "Have you any news about his family, Lalida?"

"His mother just arrived from the south, for the picking season. So he has no relatives in the our village. They have sent word to her home village. We will know soon if anyone claims him." Lalida took the baby back and rocked him. "Poor thing. Most families have more than enough mouths to feed."

The servant stopped on her way back into the house . "More tea, Madam?"

"No, thank you, Lalida. We're fine."

"Why don't you take some food up to the village?" Jon added. "The mud covered most of the gardens. The people must be hungry. We've got plenty of rice and vegetables. Bring them a few of our chickens, too."

"Yes, Sir. I will do that. I'm sure that they will be grateful." Lalida disappeared, taking the child with her.

Priscilla and Jon sat silent, each searching the other's face.

"Jon, do you think — if there's no one else…?"

"The child?" She nodded. "Maybe. We'll see. We need to think about what would be best for him. It would be hard for a dark-skinned child like him, back in England."

"Here in India, on the other hand…" Excited, Priscilla leaned forward. Her robe gapped open, baring her tightening nipples to Jon's eager gaze.

"Yes. You're quite right." Jon pushed his chair away from the table and brushed the crumbs off his lap. "After the harvest, we might think about whether we really want to sell this place after all."

"The harvest? Are you going out to the fields?" All Priscilla's joy drained away.

"Hardly." Her husband picked her up and cradled her. A tidal wave of delight crashed over her.

Jon fondled her exposed breast. His touch rekindled her fever. She felt it burning in his flesh, too. "I'm taking you off to bed. Unless, of course, you object?"

He carried her into the bungalow, not needing an answer.

About the Authors

Lacey Thorn

Lacey Thorn spends her days in small town Indiana the proud mother of three. When she is not busy with one of them she can be found typing away on her computer keyboard or burying her nose in a good book. Like every woman she knows just how chaotic life can be and how appealing that great escape can look.

So toss aside the stress and tension of the never ending to do list. For now sit back, relax, and enjoy the ride with Lacey. It's your world...unlaced.

Brynn Paulin

When it comes to books and movies, Brynn Paulin has one rule: there must be a happy ending. After that one requirement, anything else goes. And it just might in any of her books.

Brynn lives in Michigan with her husband and two children, who love her despite her occasional threats to smite them. They humour her and let her think she's a goddess...as long as she provides homemade chocolate chip cookies on a regular basis. Brynn is president of her local chapter of Romance Writers of America and also hosts a weekly writing critique group. She's conducted workshops at several writers' conferences around the country as she enjoys mentoring and meeting new people.

According to Brynn, her writing success can be attributed to 70's music, her local road construction crews, a trusty notebook, and of course, her husband (and willing research subject), AKA Mr. Inspiration.

Ashley Ladd

Ashley Ladd lives in South Florida with her husband, five children, and beloved pets. She loves the water, animals (especially cats), and playing on the computer.

She's been told she has a wicked sense of humour and often incorporates humour and adventure into her books. She also adores very spicy romance, which she weaves into her stories.

Dakota Rebel

Dakota lives in Detroit Michigan because she loves the city at night and the shopping during the day. She loves David Bowie and vampire movies, The Beatles and Dolly Parton.
She is partial to pixie sticks and cannot stand nuts...in her food. She will always believe that pizza is the perfect food. She is as much in love with her partner as she is with herself. And she will be the first to tell you how incredibly witty she is.
She doesn't believe in lipstick but won't leave the house without eyeliner. She still won't admit whether or not she really believes that vampires exist. And if you let her, she can convince you she doesn't know how to ride a bicycle.

Desiree Holt

I always wanted adventure and change in my life, and I certainly got it. I grew up in Maine, a beautiful place to live, then lived in the Midwest and Florida. Now I make my home in the Hill Country of Texas, truly God's chosen place on earth. My husband, David, is a sixth generation Texan, tracing his roots here back to the time when Texas was a Republic, so retiring here was a dream we finally fulfilled.

I've had a lot of firsts in my life – first female sports report on The Michigan Daily at the University of Michigan; first woman to own a rock and roll agency in Detroit, the home of Motown; first woman president of the Pasco (Florida) Economic Development Council.

I graduated from the University of Michigan with a double major in English and History, and a minor in economics, and went on to have at least four careers. When my children were small, I satisfied my need for writing by working for weekly newspapers. I had a wild and wacky time managing rock and roll bands. I joined the insanity of retail with a string of shoe stores. I worked in fundraising, public affairs and community relations. But writing fiction was always my dream. I had a lot of stops and starts, but it wasn't until we retired that I could devote myself to it full time.

My wonderful husband, David, encourages me and supports me in my dream. Our children are all grown and on their own, and are my biggest fans.

When I'm not writing I'm an avid reader – anything and everything – and watching football, especially my beloved Michigan Wolverines. David and I golf and target shoot, and of course enjoy life in the gorgeous Texas Hill Country, where most of my stories are based.

Lisabet Sarai

I became addicted to words at an early age. I began reading when I was four. I wrote my first story at five years old and my first poem at seven. Since then, I've written plays, tutorials, marketing brochures, software specifications, self-help books, press releases, a five-hundred page dissertation, and of course, erotica. I'm the author of four erotic novels and two short story collections. I also edited the ground breaking anthology SACRED EXCHANGE, which explores the spiritual aspects of BDSM relationships, and the massive collection CREAM: THE BEST OF THE EROTIC READERS AND WRITERS ASSOCIATION. My short stories have appeared in more than two dozen print collections edited by erotica luminaries such as M. Christian, Maxim Jakubowski, Mitzi Szereto, Rachel Kramer Bussel, and Alison Tyler. In my so-called spare time, I also review books and films for the Erotica Readers and Writers Association and Erotica Revealed, and feature as a Celebrity Author at Custom Erotica Source.

My lifelong interests in sex and the written word became serenditipitously entwined nine years ago when I read my first Black Lace book by Portia da Costa. Her work inspired me to take my fantasies out of the closet (and the private email files) and expose them to the world. The rest, as they say, is history (although granted, no more than a minor footnote!)

I've always loved traveling; my husband seduced me in a Burmese restaurant by telling me tales of his foreign adventures. Since then I have visited every continent except Australia, although I still have a long travel wish list. Currently I live with him and our two exceptional felines in

Southeast Asia, where I pursue an alternative career that is completely unrelated to my creative writing.

The authors love to hear from readers. You can find their contact information, website details and author profile pages at http://www.total-e-bound.com

Total-e-Bound Publishing

www.total-e-bound.com

Take a look at our exciting range of literagasmic™
erotic romance titles and discover pure quality
at Total-E-Bound.

2336129